The Adventures of Lew and Charlie Vol. V

By Maurice Decker

Shadow Lake

First published October 1938

War Comes to Shadow Lake

First published September 1940

Danger at White Goose Bay

First published September 1941

ISBN 978-0-936622-41-5

Table of Contents:

INTRODUCTION:

Lew and Charlie—the ultimate outdoorsmen—hunted, trapped and fished their way from Arctic Alaska to the jungles of Central America and back again. Along the way they also solved mysteries, caught crooks, and rescued the occasional damsel in distress.

The stories ran for 35 years as a serial in *FUR-FISH-GAME* magazine, beginning in 1926. Each novella-length adventure was broken into monthly chapters with cliff-hanger endings. The final chapter of the final story appeared in December 1961.

To mark the magazine's 60th anniversary in 1985, one of the stories was republished in its entirety. As the story was coming to a close, a new generation of readers who had become hooked on Lew and Charlie flooded the office with letters asking for more. Another of the original serials was republished in its entirety the following year. Then another and another. The magazine's readers are still hanging on every word.

None of the stories had been available in book format before 2012, when the first three were collected in *The Adventures of Lew and Charlie*. Volume II took up where the first volume left off, and then came Volume III, Volume IV and now Vol. V.

The original magazine stories have been edited for this book, but all of the adventure remains.

Shadow Lake

Chapter 1 – We're Smarter than Daniel Boone

Charlie was staring soberly at a yellow telegram when Lew pushed through the door of their hotel room, carrying a package almost as big as himself. Charlie thrust the wire in his pocket.

"What did you do?" he asked. "Buy the store out?"

"What do you mean?" Lew demanded.

"Well, you left an hour ago to get a pair of socks."

"Socks can wait," Lew declared. "I got something better. I passed a railway auction, where they sell off the unclaimed baggage folks check but never come back and get. Everything is sold as is; you can't even open the packages. You take a chance, like a grab bag. I got this box for only $7.85. It's big enough to be worth a hundred."

Charlie got up and lifted the package. "Not very heavy for its size," he said dubiously.

"That's why I think it's valuable," Lew grinned. "If it were old books or junk like that, it would be heavy."

"Here," Charlie said, offering his pocket knife. "Open it up."

Lew cut the jute ropes, loosened the heavy kraft paper wrapping and exposed six smaller boxes neatly stacked. He jerked the cover from one and stared inside. "I'll be darned. It's a parachute!"

He opened the other boxes. "They're all chutes, six of 'em."

"That's a bargain, all right," Charlie said slowly. "If we only had a plane … suppose you could run back to the auction and buy one?"

"They're brand new," Lew declared.

Charlie did not reply, and after a minute of silence, Lew glanced over, saw the serious lines in his companion's face. "What's the matter? You aren't mad at me for buying this junk, are you?"

Charlie forced a grin of his own. "Of course not. I'd have taken a chance myself. This telegram came while you were out. Read it."

Lew glanced at the signature. It was from Frazier, the Canadian they had left in charge of their store at the northern trading post Hazzard House. The wire was brief, almost as brusque as the sender:

Building and entire stock destroyed by fire.

"Short and sweet," Lew said. "Just ten words. Well, I guess we're in no hurry to get home now. We might as well have stayed in Montana and shot some more coyotes."

Charlie nodded in silence.

"You aren't going to take this hard, are you, old-timer?"

"You don't have to worry about me," Charlie smiled. "But we must line something up quickly. Fall is almost here."

"Let's go trapping," Lew spoke promptly. "Buck the winter wind. Feel the hard, dry snow stinging our faces. Smell the pine woods and hear a mink stream splashing over its bed. Besides, we need to make some money, enough to keep us and leave a grub-stake for next spring. We don't know anything better than we know trapping."

He kicked at one of the boxes. "I certainly wish I hadn't wasted my dough on this junk."

"Stop that," Charlie ordered. "You never got a better bargain. We could sell them for a profit—but we won't. Ever since this wire came I knew you would want to start again up in the North Country. But it's so late I was afraid we couldn't make it this winter. Now we can."

"What do you mean?"

Charlie unfolded a map. "Look here. You remember this Wolf River country we talked about two years ago?"

"Sure. We figured it would be lousy with fur but hard to reach."

"That's where your bargain comes in," Charlie said, excitement rising in his voice. "It would take four weeks if we went in on foot. Even more if we used canoes because the river is so crooked and we would fight current every mile. But if we hire a plane to drop us there, we can make it in six hours. We'll have plenty of time to build a cabin, prospect our lines and get ready for winter. What do you say?"

*   *   *

As Charlie expected, the railroad junction boasted a flying service. True, there was only one plane, with patched wings and oil-stained fuselage. But its motor was ticking away with a steady, reassuring tone.

"We want to hire that plane," Charlie told the young fellow in flying togs who sat on the edge of the pine desk.

"Where you want to go?" he countered.

Charlie spread out his map and pinned it to the desk with a forefinger placed directly on the headwaters of Wolf River.

The pilot glanced at the map. "You're crazy. No man can get a plane down in that wilderness, and there isn't a lake big enough to set my crate on even if it had pontoons."

"Who said anything about landing?" Charlie retorted. "I'm asking you how much it will cost to spot your plane over this point."

"Eighty bucks. But it won't do any good. I can't land."

"Here's your money," Charlie said, counting out $10 bills on the desk. "Have your plane warmed up and ready at eight tomorrow morning. And you won't have to land. We're bailing out in chutes.

"Okay. Keep your outfit down to a total of 500 pounds. I won't fly a pound more. And it's your funeral if you get hung up in a tree."

"Ouch," Lew said as they left the office. "Five hundred pounds for traps, grub and everything else for a long winter in the North."

"We'll take nothing but necessities," Charlie assured him. "We'll live on game and make many of the things a trapper usually buys and packs in. Remember, Daniel Boone explored Kentucky with just a rifle, an axe, and a bag of salt. We're just as smart, aren't we?"

"We've been around more," Lew said with characteristic modesty. "I'll bet we're smarter than Daniel Boone!"

"The trouble with a lot of trappers today," Charlie was warming to the subject, "is they don't know how to pioneer. Think of the old Indian scouts and buffalo hunters. Any of them could make you a pair of pants with a camp axe and a couple of flour sacks."

"Maybe," Lew admitted. "But flour sacks for pants sounds sort of breezy at ten below zero."

"We won't go that far," Charlie grinned. "But there are lots of things we can make. Let's go to that big general store and see how many essentials we can get inside that 500-pound limit."

As they walked along, Charlie warmed to his topic. "First is a pair of guns that are versatile enough to cover all kinds of game."

"How about muzzleloaders?" Lew asked. "You want to pioneer, and that's what Dan Boone used. A muzzleloader shoots shot at birds, slugs at game. All we have to pack is powder, lead and caps."

"Black powder is weak compared to smokeless," Charlie objected. "How about one of those new single-shot combinations, a gun with changeable barrels, one rifle, one shotgun?"

"Okay," Lew agreed. "How about a .25-20 barrel? Then the ammunition for both barrels will be light and compact."

Charlie frowned. "I'm not sold on a .25 rifle barrel. To kill a deer we might need two, even three shells. There's no savings in that. Why not shoot the deer with one .30-30 and have it over?"

"I suppose, then, you want the twelve-bore shotgun barrel?"

"No. Twenty gauge is enough there. A 20-gauge shell loaded with a full ounce of shot can drop any small game, and we won't take long shots. I think 100 rounds of .30-30 and 200 rounds of 20 gauge will last a winter. The lot will weigh less than 40 pounds. Not bad at all for a season's hunting."

They found the exact guns and ammo they wanted at a well-equipped outfitter's store. Then they selected 70 pounds of assorted steel traps and two dozen cable snares. "I wish we could take twice as much steel," Charlie said. "But we can't, so we'll make deadfalls."

They bought two axes, one a light belt model, the other a 3-1/2-pound chopper head without the handle. "We can make a handle and save that much weight," Charlie said.

They already had knives, pocket and skinning, compasses and waterproof match boxes. But clothes wear quickly on a trapline, and food goes fast when a trapper's appetite is stimulated by cold and hard labor. Fortunately, the store did a heavy outfitting business and had an assortment of sturdy clothes. The final list of provisions included:
200 pounds flour
60 pounds sugar
25 pounds salt
5 pounds tea
5 pounds powdered eggs
5 pounds powdered milk
3 pounds mixed dehydrated vegetables
3 pounds dehydrated onions
2 pounds lemon juice crystals

"No baking powder?" Lew asked.

"We'll use sourdough. Counting on a six-month stay, that's enough flour to give us a little over one pound a day. We'll make it do by eating a heavy meat diet, and we'll use the powdered milk and eggs sparingly. We may run short on sugar, but we can live without that.

"Those dehydrated onions and mixed vegetables equal at least 70 pounds of fresh goods, and none of the vitamins are lost in the drying. Lemon crystals are just pure lemon juice reduced to powder, and sometimes you must have something sour to balance a meat diet. It will taste fine on boiled fish, which may be a regular dish."

"Sounds like a lot of salt," Lew said.

"It isn't all for eating. We'll also need it to tan skins and furs."

The selection of clothing they finally decided would suffice consisted of four suits of heavy wool underwear, two wool shirts, two pairs of mackinaw pants, 10 pairs of socks and two pairs of moccasin boots. "Makes a pretty small bundle," Lew said ruefully. "We'll have to keep busy with needle and thread. How about blankets?"

"No room for that," Charlie replied. "We'll arrive before cold weather and have time to tan rabbit skins for blankets and caps."

They bought two rigged fishing lines, extra hooks and a gill net. They also picked up thread and needles in several sizes, an aluminum cooking kit, powdered alum, linseed oil, a file, an awl, a light spade, assorted tacks, nails and rivets, small coils of copper and steel wire, soft cotton rope, razor blades, a 26-inch handsaw, a box of smoke-salt, paraffin, and a dozen boxes of safety matches.

Lew eyed the safety matches carefully. "I don't like those."

"Neither do I, but they're small and light. We will build most fires with flint and steel. That's what this file is for, to use as the steel as well as to edge the axes. For emergencies, we'll bring a few regular matches, melt paraffin and pour it over them so they never get wet. The wax will make them burn twice as long with a hotter flame. "

They purchased four squares of waterproof canvas to wrap the bundles. "We could land a mile apart," Charlie said, "and this canvas will protect the stuff until we find it."

One of the store's platform scales was used to divide the goods into four piles of equal weight, and the total ran a little over the 500-pound limit set by the pilot. Lew proposed an easy solution to this. "We'll stuff our pockets with the small things. That bird man never said a word about how much we could weigh."

A taxi dropped them at the airport at seven o'clock. Lew had a rotund aspect, wearing double garments with all pockets bulging.

The pilot checked the baggage on his own scale. The total was 2 pounds under the maximum. He eyed Lew's swollen form with a scowl as he helped them rope a chute to each bundle. Then he showed them how to strap the devices to their own bodies.

"What about the make of chute — is it a good one?" Lew asked.

The pilot shrugged and said, "They're all okay, if they open." Then he went outside to help his mechanic pour fuel and oil into the tanks of the plane.

"Encouraging fellow," Lew said. "If I ever need cheering up, I know where to apply."

They loaded the plane, the pilot climbed in and adjusted helmet and goggles. "You know how to pull a ripcord?" he asked.

"Sure," Lew said. "You count ten after you jump, then jerk her."

"You don't have to wait that long. But how about the chutes on the bundles. Who's going to pull those?"

They stared at him in blank surprise.

The pilot grinned at their forlorn looks. "We push them out the door, balance them on the edge, jerk the cord and let the wind pull them clear. You can do the same, climb out on the wing and let the chute lift you off. It's easier than jumping."

The pilot signaled the mechanic, who spun the prop. The motor fired, and Lew glanced across the tiny field, the serious nature of their expedition finally sinking in. Before them lay an unknown land and harsh winter weather. Hardship, even dangers would fill their days. Charlie also harbored sudden misgiving as he recalled the meager outfit in the plane behind them. Then the pilot gunned the motor, and the plane lurched down the field and lifted into the air. Wheeling about in a wide circle, the pilot headed straight towards the fleecy clouds that filled the northwest sky.

The hours passed swiftly. It was 15 minutes before 2 o'clock when the pilot cut the throttle and began a circling descent. Thin lines of silver marked many small streams. The timber was dark green.

The pilot leveled off, and swinging about in a slow, lazy circle, pointed below. "This is it," he shouted over his shoulder.

Charlie leaned out to get a clearer view and saw a larger patch of bright color almost underneath that marked either a small lake or a very wide river. "That isn't on the map," he thought. "If we had known, we could have hired a plane with pontoons and landed."

"Can you drop a little lower?" Lew called. The pilot shook his head. "You got to have this much altitude to use a chute."

They shoved one bundle partway through the little door, and Charlie jerked the cord. The chute billowed out in white folds then swiftly jerked the package away. The pilot banked, sweeping his plane's tail away from the floating cargo. They pushed out the others in quick succession as the pilot continued his lazy, sweeping circle.

Then they glanced at each other, and with a quick move, Lew shoved past his companion, stepped carefully out on a wing, and leaning slightly backwards yelled, "Happy landing!"

Then he jerked the cord.

Chapter 2 – A Lady Gets Socked

Lew had but a brief second to wait before his chute filled and jerked him smartly from the plane. Then he flung his arms and legs wide trying to regain his balance as he swayed dizzily back and forth like the pendulum under a giant clock. His weight straightened out the ropes, and he started to drop straight down.

He looked up for the plane and saw a white cloud puff out from a wing with a dark object dangling below. Charlie had bailed out successfully. The plane banked, turned and swept by. The pilot leaned out, waved a hand, and a minute later was only a speck on the horizon.

"Okay so far," Lew thought. "All I got to do now is land without breaking a leg or my neck."

He watched the ground rise rapidly. All of the outfit bundles had disappeared save one, and he watched that sink into a clump of trees taller than the surrounding forest. Lew realized he was hovering over this same tall timber, and he began pulling at the ropes that bound him to the chute to see if he could change his course.

He discovered that spilling air from one side of the chute drifted him laterally, and he kept on working the cords until he was past the tall timber. His efforts had increased his drop speed alarmingly. A branch ripped at his boot. A stiff bough raked painfully across a cheek. Then he hit the ground with a force that sent him sprawling.

He scrambled up, unfastened his chute and shouted. An answer came from a stand of thick cedar. Charlie had also missed the big trees but was badly snarled up in the cedars. Lew plunged in and hacked away with his belt knife until Charlie was free.

Charlie pointed to a small creek and said, "That must run into the lake we saw from above, and we will want to build camp near the lake. After we collect the outfit here, we will start packing it down the creek until we find a good place to set up camp."

The bundles were widely scattered throughout the forest, but the big white chutes made splendid markers, and they located all four in less than an hour. It took another hour to climb up and hack away the limbs that held two loads in treetops. Fortunately, the hand axe was in the first bundle they opened.

"Come on. We haven't a minute to lose before dark," Charlie

warned, and they started down the little creek, each packing a bundle over a shoulder. When they started to catch sight of the lake a quarter-mile away, the ground grew stony with outcrops of rock. The ground was fairly covered with loose stones of various sizes, and Charlie began picking up smaller chunks and discarding them after close scrutiny. Finally, he shoved a stone about as big as his fist into a pocket, saying it would serve as the flint to start their fire that night.

Some 400 feet from the lake a large moss-grown boulder blocked the path. Charlie dumped his load on the ground, eyes flashing with satisfaction. The boulder was as big as a house, and the side farthest from the lake had broken off straight up and down.

"Here is a made-to-order cabin site," Charlie exclaimed. "The flat side of rock is almost perpendicular, and we can build the rest right against it. That will save cutting logs for that end, and what's better, we'll have a fireproof stone wall for the fireplace and chimney."

In other ways, too, it was the perfect location for a wilderness cabin. The little creek ran less than 40 feet away, providing water. Across its bank they could see a fairly big area of standing dead timber, killed by some forest blight. That meant easy firewood, particularly when heavy snow covered all of the downed wood. The ground about the big boulder was well-drained, and on its north and west there were thickets of cedar to break the wind.

"Take the small axe, Lew, and cut sixteen of those straight cedars while I bring the rest of the outfit."

They had decided upon a tepee for shelter until the cabin was finished. A tepee would be secure in wind and easy to build with the materials at hand. Lew cut and trimmed out the poles, and when Charlie had packed in the last load, they lashed three of the cedars together at the top to form a tripod. They stood the remaining poles against this tripod, spreading the butts out in a circle. Then they draped parachute cloth at the very peak. Lew, standing on his companion's shoulders, could just reach that high. In less than an hour they had a circular tent some 14 feet across ready for occupancy.

The waterproof canvas in which the outfit was wrapped made a splendid floor, and they piled the bags of food on it. Three ropes were tied to the peak and staked out as guys to hold the tent against any wind that might arise in the woods.

Lew took a piece of rope and followed the creek down to the lake, seeking material for their beds. The lake was narrow and long, its far end not visible from where he stood. The banks were heavily timbered and sent deep shadows far out over the mirror-smooth surface.

He found marshy ground covered with tall, brown grass. It was sufficiently dry to serve as bedding, and he cut a big bundle. After roping it tightly, he packed it back to camp.

With handsaw and small axe, Charlie had already cut four logs and staked them to enclose a space five by seven feet. They filled this with the grass. With shelter and beds ready for the night, they assembled the two guns with the shotgun barrels and set off to hunt.

Charlie went only a short distance, reluctant to leave their supplies unguarded. A bear or just a swarm of field mice could cause serious damage to sugar and flour. He flushed two grouse and shot one, passing on the longer shot. He carried the bird back, and while he dressed it, he heard Lew's gun fire three times.

Using the found stone as a flint, he kindled a fire, catching the faint sparks on a pile of shredded birch bark.

Lew appeared with three grouse. "The woods are full of them," he stated. "So we won't go hungry for a while."

They slung a pot over the fire to make tea and fried the grouse in their own fat. When mosquitoes appeared, Charlie carried some coals on the shovel into the tepee and started a small smudge fire. When the interior was smoky enough, he scraped out the fire and closed the door flap. "That smoke will hang up in the upper half of the tent most of the night and keep them out," he said.

Then he started a sourdough pot, mixing a quart of flour with enough water to make a creamy batter. He added two tablespoons of sugar and some of the lemon crystals to hasten the action. Lew cut a sound stick from the dead wood across the creek and sat beside the fire whittling a crude but efficient handle for the big axe. Lacking blankets, they laid their coats beside the bed in case the night turned cool.

They slept soundly until a loon out on the lake awoke them half an hour before sunrise. There was just enough light to work by, and Charlie rekindled the fire from coals to brew coffee and cook the remaining grouse. They finished breakfast by the time the sun had cleared the rim of the lake.

"We haven't any kind of stove," Charlie began, "so we must build a stone fireplace that will cook and heat. There are rocks along the creek that contain lime. We'll burn them and make real lime for mortar that will hold the stones fast."

First, they built a circular stone wall 4 feet across and 4 feet high. Inside this, they piled alternate layers of dry wood and smaller lime rocks until the heap was 6 feet tall. They lit the pile through a hole left at the bottom of the rock wall, and when it was burning strongly, they piled sod over the entire heap to slow the burning.

At 10 o'clock, Lew left Charlie tending this lime kiln. He cut four 8-foot logs of buoyant spruce, roped them into a crude raft and poled out onto the lake. He set their gill net in deep-enough water and poled back. Not willing to trust fishing luck for dinner, he went into the woods and shot two more grouse.

At noon he thrust his head inside the tepee, but then jerked back with a wrinkled nose. Charlie laughed. "That's the sourdough fermenting. Just wait until tomorrow."

After eating, Lew asked, "Ready for cabin logs?"

Charlie nodded. "Cut all you want. But go easy with the axe. If something happens to it before we get enough cabin logs cut, we'll freeze to death this winter."

While Lew chopped, Charlie smoothed out the ground where the cabin would stand, sorted out square stones for the fireplace and chimney, and cut four big wedges of dry, dead timber. He hardened the timber points in the fire, and when Lew turned out a log with straight grain, Charlie scored its upper end and drove these wedges in with the hatchet, splitting off slabs to use as door and window frames.

He switched off with Lew regularly, and the man swinging the axe worked at top speed to keep that tool steadily busy.

When night approached, Lew went out on his raft and pulled two jackfish from the net. Then they both stripped off and plunged into the lake for a swim. The cool water soaked the soreness from their muscles, and they came out refreshed and clean.

Lew stepped on something hard in the water, and reaching down, pulled up a long, slender object. "Looks like pipe," he told Charlie.

"That's a gun barrel," Charlie exclaimed. "A musket barrel, about 70 caliber. I wonder how many years that has lain in the lake?"

"I don't know," Lew replied, "but I do know this piece of iron is going to prove mighty useful."

"Yes, it will," Charlie agreed. "I've been wondering how we might manage to bore holes in wood without an auger. Now we can just heat this old barrel and burn them out. Then we can make better furniture, door hinges and also a solid maul. With a maul, I can really get places splitting out slabs."

The boiled fish tasted fine with salt and a little lemon juice.

"We've got to lay in a supply of bigger meat," Lew said. "Fish and small game taste fine but take too much time to gather."

Next morning, Charlie cut out a big, solid knot, burned a handle hole in one side and made his maul. By noon, they had enough material on the ground to finish the cabin walls. The logs were reasonably light and would lay up rapidly and notch easily. The fire in the lime kiln was still going. It would have to burn another 24 hours before opening.

They laid down the sill logs, notching them at the front corners. Then they hewed off the top of the front log to serve as a doorsill and spiked two upright slabs to act as a door frame. The rear ends of the side logs were butted against the rock, and an upright slab spiked to the ends of the wall logs held them plumb and secure. Cross joists would be set as ceiling, spanning from one wall to the other.

In the middle of the afternoon they heard a wolf yelp out in the forest. They turned facing the sound, surprised a wolf would come so near a noisy camp. Then a chorus of yelps broke out, and they heard the crashing of a large body forcing its way through undergrowth.

Lew quickly stripped the shotgun barrel off the forearm of his gun and mounted the .30-30 barrel. The noise was approaching rapidly, and he jumped across the creek to meet it head-on. He saw a flash of gray-brown, and a buck deer leaped into view. It stood panting.

There was a sharp, eager yelp, and a timber wolf flashed into view. Lew whipped up the rifle and shot it through the lungs. Then he shot the still-panting deer through the heart.

They skinned both animals quickly, cut the deer in quarters and hung the meat well up in a close-by tree to cool.

"The cabin will have to wait now," Charlie said. "It will take two days to cure this meat. We will tan the skins, too. Since it's so early in the season, the hair must come off so they can be made into leather."

He spread the skins in the creek, pinning them under with stones so they would soak until the hair loosened.

The following morning, Lew climbed the highest tree he could find. From its top, he peered about for 20 minutes.

Then he came back down and said, "We started this business backwards. We just assumed we were alone, but the first thing we should have done was check to see if any other trappers work the area. From that tree, I could have spotted the smoke if there was a breakfast fire within five miles. There wasn't, which means the area is likely un-inhabited. I propose, however, that we explore today, to make sure we don't have any close neighbors."

"Okay," Charlie agreed. "That is sensible. But we can't both leave camp and risk our supplies. You go. I'll stay and jerk venison."

After breakfast Lew wrapped four flapjacks and several pieces of fried deer liver in birch bark and shoved it in a pocket. Then he put the shotgun barrel back on the gun and took off at a brisk hike, skirting the east bank of the lake.

It was a glorious morning. Birds sang in the trees, and Lew found ample sign of furbearers including the tracks of mink, muskrat, coon, fox and weasel. He passed two otter slides and the trail of a lynx. His satisfaction grew as he failed to see any trace of old trap sets or any other trapping activity. "We landed in a paradise," he gloated. "I'll bet there isn't another human within a hundred miles."

And then his keen ears caught the sound of voices, someone speaking in the brush less than 50 yards away. Then a rifle fired with the sharp, whipping whine of high velocity. Someone screamed, and Lew began running.

"That was a woman!" he thought as he crashed through the elders into a sunlit clearing that held two figures. One was a woman, the other a taller man. Both were young and smartly dressed in sport suits, plaid shirts and leather-laced boots. The man's left hand clutched an elaborately engraved bolt-action rifle.

As Lew paused at the edge of the opening, the stranger lifted his right hand and struck the woman in the face. She screamed again. Hot anger filled Lew, and he jumped into the fray.

Chapter 3 – I Got Him Booked as a Snake!

Neither heard Lew until he was quite close, then they both spun about. The man, seeing Lew's angry scowl and clenched fist, flung up the rifle to guard his face. But Lew's blow landed on the side of his jaw, and the fellow went down like a jack pine blasted by lightning.

"My goodness!" the girl cried. "Where did you come from?"

"I heard you scream," Lew panted. "I didn't lose any time."

"No, I guess you didn't." Her blue eyes, wide with surprise, swept over him. Then she pulled a stick of gum out of a pocket, stripped off the paper without looking and shoved it in through well-painted lips.

"I don't know who you are, big boy, but won't DuBonner cuss!"

Lew's eyes were fixed on the red mark across her cheek.

"Did he hurt you?" Lew asked.

"Hurt me?" the girl repeated. "Yeah, a little. But that's why I'm drawing two hundred a week. To get socked and like it."

"Two hundred a week?" Lew echoed. She didn't seem at all grateful for his intervention.

Then a plump little man with a short, stiff mustache came running up. His face was flushed a deep purple, and his eyes rolled wildly as he waved short, pudgy arms about his head. He jumped into the air, and landing, dashed his hat on the ground.

"Imbecile!" he cried. "The scene, she is magnificent. Then you ruin all. *Mon Dieu*! You ruin Roman, too. You …"

The little man stopped, jaws still wagging silently. With a supreme effort he controlled his emotions. Then he sat down abruptly beside his hat, picked it up, started to fan his face. "*Parbleu!*" he said. "I must not forget my position, my responsibilities."

Then another man appeared at the edge of the tall trees, and when Lew noticed a big box standing beside him on a kind of tripod, the truth flashed upon him. Lew started backing away, filled only with a desire to get away from these people as speedily as he could.

But a cry halted him. The man he had punched had opened his eyes and struggled up on one elbow. The eyes were red with rage, and he swung the rifle and covered Lew with the muzzle.

Lew jumped to the right as the rifle fired. He heard the bullet sing by his ear, and all embarrassment vanished. He sprang forward and deftly kicked the gun out of the fellow's hands just as he was drawing back the bolt to reload.

"Stop it, Ran!" the girl cried. "He thought you were really hitting me. I don't suppose he ever saw a movie camera before."

Lew's embarrassment returned, and he didn't feel any more comfortable when the girl walked close and whispered, "Don't worry. I know you meant all right. If somebody like you happened around every time I got in a jam, I'd be wonderfully lucky."

Her eyes, her entire blonde beauty left him even more befuddled.

The man on the ground scrambled toward the rifle. But the plump little man reached it first and planted both feet on the barrel.

"Get off, DuBonner," the man screamed. Then rage constricted his vocal cords, and he started running in a circle like a mad dog.

The cameraman, a lanky fellow with high forehead and lean face walked up. "I shot a couple hundred feet of Roman taking the nose-dive," he drawled. "Maybe you can work it into the script, DuBonner."

That brought Roman up abruptly. He turned blazing eyes upon the speaker. "You insult me? Fire him, DuBonner. I won't work for a director who permits a cameraman to insult the star."

"Take it easy, Ran," the cameraman said calmly. "There isn't another cameraman within a thousand miles. This may be a 'B' picture, but someone still has to turn the crank."

"Why are you so excited over a sock to the jaw?" the girl asked peevishly. "You've already hit me four times this morning—twice as hard as you had to sell the scene."

But Ran Roman would not be mollified. He shot a murderous glance at Lew and strode off into the forest.

"I'm awfully sorry," Lew finally spoke again. "When I heard her scream and saw him hit her, I followed my first impulse. If I had seen the camera, I would have known what it was all about."

"Can't say I blame you," the cameraman replied. "We don't exactly look like a real movie outfit on location. There's only six of us, another actor and a cook back at camp. DuBonner is trying out some experimental ideas for scenic effect. He had a pilot fly us in here three days ago for shots he said he couldn't get in the studio."

"Where is your camp?" Lew asked.

"On the east side of the lake, about a mile. You here alone?"

"I got a partner," Lew replied.

"Living in a cabin?" DuBonner interrupted with sudden interest.

"No, in a tepee. But we're building a cabin we'll finish in three or four days. Why do you ask?"

"That's a lucky break, DuBonner," the cameraman cut in. Then to Lew, "You wouldn't object to us renting it for a couple of scenes?"

Lew didn't want any more to do with this bunch. But on the other hand, now that he had ruined their shoot, he didn't see how he could decently refuse. "Sure," he said. "And you don't have to pay a penny."

"It will be a real Northern trapper's cabin?" DuBonner asked. "Everything as genuine as the lake and the trees?"

"You needn't worry," Lew assured him. "Our cabin will be a lot more authentic than these rigs your actors are wearing."

"Say, what's wrong with these clothes?" the girl demanded. "I thought I looked pretty swell in them."

"You do," Lew admitted. "Your clothes are perfect. And that's the problem. Nobody living in a wilderness like this one could be so immaculate. Everything you have is too new, too clean. And this bit with him socking her—not up here."

"Oh, him socking her was just a build-up for the love scene," the cameraman replied. "After he hits her, she falls for him hard."

"Sure," Lew said. "Maybe in the movies. But just try it in real life." He was backing off slowly, more eager than ever to leave.

"We'll drop over in a few days and look at the cabin," DuBonner said. "All we need do is follow the bank of the lake?"

Lew nodded, turned, and began hiking briskly back home.

"Can you beat that?" he muttered. "We pick a place so wild and rough we have to bail out of a plane to get in. Then I find it populated by a gang making a movie. Next thing there'll be an excursion boat running up the lake and a school picnic on the beach."

When Lew arrived, Charlie was placing strips of venison on a rack of slim poles he had built 3 feet above a fire of black birch.

"It didn't take you long to explore," he said. "I didn't expect you back before nightfall."

"You will never guess what I've been doing," Lew said. "What would you say if I told you I was going to be in the movies?"

Then Lew recounted his morning. "I made a fool of myself. But any man would have done the same, and boy, did I sock that guy."

Charlie pondered Lew's story for almost a minute. Then he said, "It's funny DuBonner's pilot would know of this lake. Ours didn't. Our man missed; this can't be the place I marked on the map."

"Maybe," Lew admitted. "But I don't see how it makes much difference. I saw lots of fur sign and none of trappers. When that gang of actors scrams, we'll be fine. But I had to promise to let them use our cabin when it's finished. They want some scenes with a real North-woods trapper's home. So I suppose we better get busy. The sooner it is finished, the sooner they'll be gone."

Lew set his gun inside the tepee, picked up the axe and started notching logs. By nightfall, the cabin walls were built to eave height. They decided to begin work on the fireplace and chimney and let the roof wait until this masonry was completed. They opened the lime kiln and found the stones crumbled to coarse powder mixed with ashes. Wood ashes are often mixed with clay and salt to construct a fireplace in a woodsman's cabin. They covered the warm heap carefully with canvas to protect it from dew or any rain.

Next morning, Charlie located a bed of clean sand at the edge of the lake, and they carried many loads to the cabin. Charlie leveled a small place and enclosed it with four logs to serve as a mortar box. Into it, they poured sand, lime and water then mixed the mass thoroughly.

Lew began laying the foundation of the fireplace, making a solid footing of block-like stones sunk level with the ground. On top of this he built the fireplace walls, a full 12 inches thick since it would be easier to lay a wide wall than a narrow one. They wanted a fireplace big enough to burn 4-foot logs, to save chopping.

Charlie busied himself getting the necessary lintel stones to support the chimney over the front of the fireplace. Woodsmen often carry in steel bars for this, and Charlie considered the iron gun barrel they had found. Then he decided it would prove more useful in other ways.

He searched until he found a slab of rock 6 feet long, 3 feet wide and about 7 inches thick. Cut in two, it would make a pair of splendid lintel slabs, one placed on top of the other.

Charlie marked the center of the stone on both sides. Then, using the small chisel he had included in their outfit, he chipped the stone along each line. It was tedious work, but he persevered until each cut was an inch deep. Then he stopped, for the cuts were intended only to serve as guides for the stone to fracture along.

He managed to get the big slab up on smaller stones and then built a fire underneath it. With soft clay he constructed sides along the top indentation to make it into a little trough. After three hours the rock was heated through, and he poured cold water from the creek into the trough. There was a snap, and the rock broke cleanly.

When the fireplace proper was finished, they stopped work to allow the lime mortar time to harden. If they kept on building the chimney now, its weight would crack the green mortar below and loosen the stones it was supposed to hold in place.

Next morning they found the lime set hard enough to stand more weight and built 5 feet of chimney on top of the two lintel slabs.

While waiting for the chimney to harden, they worked on the roof, laying short rafter poles vertically to form an "A" frame. The rafters were covered with small poles nailed horizontally and very close together. Then they cut coarse, dead grass to cover the poles when the chimney was finished.

The jerked venison was dry, and they packed it in three bags sewed out of parachute cloth then hung it up in the tepee.

The following morning they finished the chimney. Laying up its three sides was easy as they had the flat, straight face of the big rock to work against. It was impossible to make things exactly perpendicular because the stones varied so in shape and size. But they had sorted their material carefully at the start, and by using larger stones at the bottom, were able to build a flue that tapered regularly its entire length.

As they worked, two men emerged from the timber. Lew saw them first and groaned.

"The little fat guy is DuBonner, the director," he told Charlie. "The other is the cameraman. He seemed a rather decent sort."

"Howdy," the cameraman hailed them in friendly tones. "We thought we'd look at the cabin. DuBonner is nearly satisfied with the shoot, save for those particular scenes."

Lew climbed down from the roof. "We'll be done day after tomorrow. Come back around noon and you can do your stuff."

DuBonner thanked them profusely as both men walked about, examining their work carefully. "It's a mighty nice job," the cameraman said. "Only trouble is, it looks so new."

"Like your actors' clothing," Lew grinned. "Well, I can't help that. Maybe a little mud smeared over the axe cuts will make the walls look weatherbeaten."

When they turned to go, the cameraman hesitated and then motioned Lew closer. "If I was you, I'd watch myself," he said in a low voice. "Roman, I got him booked as a snake, the kind that rattles in the grass." Then he turned and caught up with DuBonner out in the forest.

Chapter 4 – The Titanic Nerve!

Charlie and Lew completed the chimney by mid-afternoon and immediately started closing in the roof. So far, the weather had been ideal. But they knew late-summer rain might start any day, and they wanted the cabin roofed before this disagreeable period began. They covered the roof poles with a thick, even layer of grass. Then they worked up large quantities of clay, mixing it with water and some of the remaining lime and spreading it thick over the grass. The clay was tramped down and smoothed off with wooden paddles dipped in water.

It was hard, tedious work, and they had finished only one small corner when sunset halted their progress and sent them down to the edge of the lake for their regular evening swim.

"A clay roof isn't ideal," Charlie said as he floated lazily on his back. "They leak after heavy rain. And there's the dust dropping on your table and bed. But I've figured out a way to stop that. When we're through with the tepee, we'll tack the parachute cloth up on the inside of the roof rafters. That should catch the dust and drips of rainwater."

Next morning they finished putting on the clay. As they worked, they splashed water over the surface to slow the drying process and prevent the big cracks that appear in clay roofs allowed to dry too fast.

Two pieces of chute cloth were coated with linseed oil and tacked over the openings left in the cabin walls for windows. The oiled fabric was fairly transparent and admitted plenty of light. Later they would make shutters to close the openings against storms and critters.

Charlie chopped the hooves of the deer in chunks and put them in a pot with water and set it over a slow fire. After half a day's cooking, he set the pot in the creek to cool. The neats foot oil, which had cooked from the feet, came to the top of the water and hardened sufficiently to be skimmed off. "Nothing beats this stuff to soften and waterproof boots," he said. "It will also preserve our guns as well as any oil."

Charlie checked the hides in the bottom of the creek and found the hair had begun to slip. He hung them in the shade to partially dry. When still damp, he spread them over the top of a smooth log and scraped the hair away. Charlie had dulled the edge of their small axe with a file for this work. Care was still needed to avoid cutting the hide as the hair and the cheesy layer in which it grew were pushed away.

Charlie would have liked to soak the skins a day longer, but he feared they might spoil in the summer weather.

"We need containers," Charlie told Lew as they worked, one at each end of the log. "That movie bunch is likely living on canned goods. Why don't you go over there and pick up a dozen or two empty tins? They could come in pretty handy."

"I would rather wait until they clear out," Lew said. "Then I'll go look around. I don't want to see that bunch any more than I must."

When each hide was bare of hair, Charlie greased the flesh sides with deer fat and covered that with a layer of wood ash. Soap, he knew, was often used to make buckskin, and since soap was nothing more than lye and grease, he hoped this would work. The ash was sprinkled with water, the hides rolled up tightly and laid in a shady place.

Charlie glanced at the sinking sun. "We've got time for one more job, something I've been looking forward to. Let's start a fire in the cabin, to see if the fireplace draws the smoke."

Lew gathered dry kindling, and Charlie built a small blaze in the fireplace, watching anxiously as the smoke curled up and then ascended slowly but surely inside the flue. Charlie added green pine limbs as a further test, and the chimney worked to perfection.

"We did a swell job, if I say so myself!" Lew crowed.

Charlie grinned. Then his grin faded. Lew was cocking his head towards the door, listening.

First he heard a confused murmur of voices out in the forest and then the sound of many feet pushing through short brush. Presently, the entire six-person movie crew emerged from the trees.

"Good gosh," Lew cried. "What do they want now?"

DuBonner was leading the company. Besides Roman and the girl, he saw two men he did not know. At the rear marched the cameraman, straining under the ponderous machine.

DuBonner halted before the door, removed his hat with a flourish and spoke. "Pardon, Messieurs. I am sorry to have to disturb you, but it is a matter of much importance. Our camp, all three tents, they burn today. All is gone. All our food, even our clothes save these we wear. Thankfully, Striker saved the camera, and we have enough film to finish our work. For these small things, we give thanks.

"But we have no shelter and no food. So we come. We will pay for a place to sleep, for our meals. Pierre, my cook, will assist."

The little man bowed and rubbed his hands with a conciliatory smile, stepped a little closer and looked past them into the cabin.

"Our wants are few," he explained. "We require dinner, but it need not be elaborate. A soup, a meat, a vegetable perhaps two will suffice. Pierre knows exactly how my tea must be made. Perhaps you have cots in the tent that we will use?"

"We don't," Lew said bluntly. "And there won't be soup or vegetables. All we got is dried venison. There's a little flour, barely enough for one meal a day. We can give you that with tea, but nothing more."

Charlie shouldered past his companion. "It won't be as bad as you think," he said briskly. "Listen folks. Night is close, and we have to work fast to get you settled before dark. And you must help. Lew and I will put up another shelter since the tepee and cabin won't hold everybody. While we do that, you hustle down to the edge of the lake and pull dead grass for your beds. You'll be surprised how comfortable it is. If you get enough, you will sleep fine."

DuBonner sank on a short log. "You hear, *mes infants*? We must bear up. We have acted the parts of strong men in the woods before the camera. Let us now partake of their lot in reality." He mopped his face with a brightly colored silk handkerchief and then added, "Pierre, you will go with the rest and procure grass for my bed, too."

Pierre, a counterpart of his employer save he was even shorter and his face rounder and more red, bowed and waddled off towards the lake. The girl had already started. The actor Lew had not seen before followed. He was an unassuming sort of chap with bright, good-humored eyes. Striker leaned his camera against the cabin wall and sat down beside DuBonner.

"I'll go when I catch my breath," he said. "Old Betsy here is no featherweight." He nodded towards the camera.

Ran Roman scowled first at Charlie and then at Lew.

"Tell Pierre to fix me a bed, too," he snapped at DuBonner. Then he swaggered over to the cabin door, and glanced in. "Pretty crude," he sneered. "Tell Pierre to put my bed in here. I need rest."

Lew set the axe down and approached the actor, walking lightly on the balls of his feet. "Listen," he said slowly. "There's only one cabin, and only one lady. Does that add up, or have I got to explain?"

Roman flushed and took a step forward, fists clenched. Lew waited, smiling. Maybe it was the hard glitter in his eyes that stopped the actor dead in his tracks. "DuBonner," Roman cried sharply. "You arrange for my accommodations with this ... this person."

Then he sat sulkily beside the smoldering campfire.

Striker rose, stretched his arms and said, "Got a piece of rope I can bundle my bed in?"

Charlie handed him some cord. Then he and Lew began cutting cedars, and using one of the remaining parachutes, built a small covered shelter about 7 feet across. This would house three of the company; two more could sleep with them inside the tepee, leaving the cabin for the girl.

"Why, oh why did this happen to me?" Lew groaned.

Charlie could not help a grin. "I'm surprised at you, Lew. Don't you know hospitality is the inflexible rule of the woods?"

The others were straggling back from the lake, carrying loads of grass of varying sizes. Little Pierre was buried under a bundle that sagged over his shoulders. But his thick little legs marched manfully along, and he dumped the stuff before the tepee with a satisfied grunt.

Charlie made another decision. "DuBonner and Pierre are not so tall; they can find plenty of room in the tepee. You other three men will use the lean-to."

He helped them spread the grass smoothly and evenly while Lew hung their largest pot over the fire and filled it with dried venison. "I hope the mosquitoes eat that punk Roman," he thought as he worked.

The party had saved practically nothing from the fire. It appeared Roman was the only one who had been able to salvage anything. He happened to run back in time to discover the blaze, and he had carried out his make-up box, toilet case, and two spools of exposed film.

Lew decided he must visit the burned camp first thing in the morning, to see if there was anything to salvage.

The venison stew was tasty, for Lew had seasoned it with some of the dehydrated onions. Pierre and the actor whose name they learned was Kendall ate from the pot lids. Their two plates went to the girl whom the others called Olive and to DuBonner. Striker ate from the skillet, and Lew grudgingly gave Roman a bowl.

The only two cups were filled with tea and passed about until everyone had drunk. Charlie and Lew waited until the company finished, then they ate what was left of the stew and each had a cup of tea.

"We can't turn them loose on the flour," Lew groaned. "They'd eat the whole supply in a week. That reminds me, how long are we going to have them on our hands?"

"I'll find out," Charlie replied.

"We finish shooting in three, maybe four days," DuBonner said. "One week from today, the pilot he returns for us. "

Charlie kindled another fire in the cabin then smothered the blaze with green cedar. By locating the fire well out in front of the flue, he was able to fill the interior of the cabin with pungent smoke. "That will clear the mosquitoes," he told Olive, who had followed him inside.

"Thanks," she said, regarding the doorless opening in the cabin. "Got a gun I can borrow?" she asked suddenly. "I'd like one lying beside my bunk. Just in case a wolf turned up in the night."

"There are no wolves anywhere near camp," Charlie said.

"Maybe there wasn't before," She replied.

Charlie went to the tepee and brought her one of the combination guns with the shotgun barrel in place.

"Can you use this?" he asked.

She asked him to open and load the gun for her. Then she nodded. Charlie set the loaded weapon down beside her grass bed.

Roman joined them furtively, and Lew suspected he had been out in the woods doing something. Charlie had decided that flapjacks would be necessary in the morning, so he filled his sourdough can to the top with fresh flour and water, wincing at the gap left in the sack.

Sitting by the fire, DuBonner spoke with Striker about the work they would do tomorrow. The frequency of yawns increased until all arose as if on cue and went to their respective beds.

Lew quickly fell to sleep, but Charlie was more wakeful. DuBonner had offered to pay for what they ate, but he knew money would be of little use out here.

He must have fallen asleep then, for he remembered nothing more until he awoke with a start, sat up and glanced out through the tepee door. A dim figure was creeping towards the fire, and Charlie heard sounds of a stick scraping in the ashes. A faint glow sprang up, and Charlie lay back, thinking someone in the lean-to had been driven out by mosquitoes, and, unable to sleep, had stirred the fire back to life.

Charlie decided to join the person by the fire. But to his surprise when he crawled out of the tepee, the area about the fire was empty. Charlie walked over and sat down, anyway, wondering if the man he had seen could have gone down to the lake for a drink. Suddenly he was aware of whispers coming from the cabin. He remembered what Olive said when she had asked him for the gun.

Charlie tiptoed cautiously towards the cabin. He paused just outside the door to listen. The conversation inside was probably none of his business. But if there was something wrong …

Chapter 5 – Death is a Shadow

"Get out, you rat!" Olive whispered vehemently.

Charlie took a step forward but paused. Her words were not fearful, only angry.

"Don't be a fool," Roman answered. "You don't dare tell him."

"You can't prove it," she said.

"Oh, I can. And I will, if you don't act reasonably," he retorted.

A stick snapped on the opposite side of the cabin, a thin, sharp sound that resounded like a gun report in the still night. "Somebody's listening," Olive whispered. "Go—hurry!"

"All right," Roman replied. "But I won't wait past tomorrow."

Olive apparently was safe for now, so Charlie slipped back around the cabin, wondering if somebody had been listening on the other side. He walked down to the lean-to and peered inside. All of the beds were occupied. He returned to the tepee. Lew, DuBonner and Pierre were as he had left them, apparently sound asleep.

The meaning of what he had heard was plain enough. Roman was blackmailing the actress. Blackmail is always nasty business, and there was the possibility of another listener hearing the threat. Apparently, an undercurrent of intrigue was also sharing their camp.

Charlie lay awake another hour, convinced that trouble, perhaps danger, lurked in the offing. Finally, he fell asleep.

He and Lew awoke at their usual time, some 30 minutes before sunrise. Charlie kindled the fire while Lew checked the gill net. There were three fish, all small, and Lew decided he also must get a couple of grouse for their group breakfast. He went out into the dew-soaked woods with the shotgun barrel on the combo gun.

Olive was the first of the movie party to appear. She came yawning from the cabin. "What I wouldn't give for my bathing suit so I could take a morning swim," she said.

"Can you sew?" Charlie asked.

She grimaced. "I'm not so hot at it, but I could make out."

Charlie brought out a piece of chute cloth, their barber scissors, needles and thread. "See what you can do with this," he told her. "But go easy with the scissors. If anything happens to them, by next spring we'll look like Russian scientists wintering at the North Pole."

"Ran left his toilet kit in the cabin. I'll use his cuticle shears. He won't like it, but you wouldn't look as handsome with a beard."

She fingered the silk. "It's really sheer, isn't it? If I run short of lingerie, can I have some more?"

The rest of the crew began to emerge, tousled and somewhat disgruntled. When Roman joined the group about the fire, his temper was venomous. The mosquito bites across his face were swollen and red. He said he had barely slept the entire night.

Then he went into the cabin for his toilet kit but came rushing out seconds later with only a cake of soap in hand.

"Who used my soap?" he yelled. "It's still wet."

"I did," Olive answered in her slow, easy way. "But I used as little as I could, seeing it is the only soap we all have."

"You got a nerve, you ..." whatever he called the girl was spoken under his breath, so softly no one heard. Then he spoke loudly.

"Get this, woman. Keep your hands off my things."

He strode into the cabin and reappeared with a toilet case of richly ornamented leather. Then he went down to the creek. They heard him splashing about, and when he returned, he paused beside the fire, locked the case with a little key and carried it down to the lean-to.

"Better put some extra soda in the hot cakes," Striker grinned. "Ran's temper seems more sour than usual." The cameraman had watched Charlie's culinary work with obvious interest.

Lew returned with two grouse, and Pierre cleaned and fried the birds and then the fish in the same skillet to use what fat remained. Charlie also cooked a huge stack of flapjacks. Then the food melted away like snow before the soft Chinook winds of spring.

After breakfast, DuBonner was eager to begin shooting cabin scenes and urged Charlie to finish the door.

He and Lew cut four log slabs to the proper length and nailed them together with split-pole cleats. Then they cut a stout pole six inches longer than the door to serve as a hinge and nailed it along one edge. They heated the old gun barrel red-hot and bored a hole in the log above and one in the log below the doorway to serve as bearings for the pole hinge. The door slipped neatly into place, and when the pole ends were greased with deer fat, swung easily back and forth. It was held shut with a thong of green hide, fastened on the inside.

"I'll make a door bar after DuBonner finishes with his pictures," Charlie told Olive. "That will keep the wolves out—and the rats."

She glanced quickly at him, but Charlie walked on, face blank.

The director marshaled his company before the cabin. Charlie and Lew drew back to the edge of the timber out of the way and listened, their astonishment growing. No actor was satisfied with his position or script, and everybody questioned the direction given by DuBonner. They clamored for more favorable places, a different angle of face or light. Roman was bitter in his protests and also in his scorn of everything he was asked to do.

Only DuBonner and Striker remained calm. They conferred concerning the position of the camera, and DuBonner repeated his instructions patiently without yielding an inch.

The actor Kendall was the villain, strangely made up out of the single cosmetic box. His good-humored face took on cruel lines with the addition of grease paint and a mustache. But, even then, Lew declared confidentially, "He's twice as likable as that snake Roman."

Finally, Lew said, "I can't take any more of this. I'm going hunting." He started for his gun, and then remembering a resolve formed last night, he borrowed one of DuBonner's pens. When the director declined to part with any of the leaves of his notebook, Lew stripped off some squares of birch bark and wrote the same message on each. The message explained the destroyed movie camp and stated their exact present location. Then Lew disappeared into the timber.

Charlie decided to relieve the shortage of dishes. He cut short sections of log and split them into slabs which were then hollowed out as well as he could with axe and hatchet.

As he worked, he recalled stories of the old Great Lakes voyageurs who paddled mammoth freight canoes along the wilderness waterways. These men lived for days at a time on pemmican boiled in water thickened into soup with nothing but flour. The gruel was ladled out on bare rocks, and the paddlers scooped it into their mouths with their hands. "Just like pigs," Charlie muttered. "And the way this outfit acts, eating from a stone would be plenty good enough for them, too."

This thought comforted him as he viewed the crude results of his labor to make wooden platters. Lew, he knew, would bring back empty tin cans from the burned camp, and these would serve as tea cups.

Lew did return at noon with a small load of empty cans. He also brought a miscellaneous assortment of iron strips and straps wrenched from the frames of the flame-twisted cots.

Pierre was adapting nicely to the limited facilities. When Charlie brought back a nice catch of whitefish, Pierre made a lemon sauce that lifted the boiled meat to an ecstasy of flavor. Even Roman, appetite sharpened by the morning work, ate without grumbling—at first.

Then he held out his cup with a command for Pierre to fill it with more tea. Lew glanced up and said, "Set your cup on the ground when he pours. That stuff is hot."

Roman turned his back on Lew and snapped at Pierre, who stood hesitating, teakettle in hand. Pierre tilted the pot and slopped tea in the cup. The boiling heat passed through the light metal instantly, and with a howl, Roman dropped the cup to the ground. Then he stepped forward and swung a fist at the cook's head.

The Frenchman easily ducked the blow, sprang nimbly back and snatched up the sheath knife he had used to clean the fish. He spouted ferocious French, taunting the actor to come a step closer.

But Roman turned out to be a rank coward, as most bullies are. He stood, glancing around for a weapon that would outweigh Pierre's knife. Lew stepped between them, saying, "No fighting in camp."

Then, eying Roman with undisguised disgust, he added, "Didn't I tell you to set the cup down? If you should happen to fall in the lake and drown, nobody is going to feel sorry—except for the fish."

Roman glared at Lew with a murderous look. The enjoyment of the fine fish was ruined for everyone, and the crew prepared to depart into the timber to film a scene. Pierre went to take a nap in the tepee. Before they left, Roman walked over to Olive and whispered in her ear. The girl flushed, bit her lip and walked away without replying.

There was plenty of work about camp to keep Lew and Charlie busy. First, they unrolled the wolf and deer hides, found them growing stiff and ready for a second application of wood ash and water.

The wolf hide carried a heavy load of fat, so they trimmed off several pounds, melted it over the fire, skimmed it well, and when the grease was partly cool they added a small quantity of the concentrated lye brought in for this express purpose. When the mix was almost cold, Charlie poured it into small tins that acted like molds. Later, they tested the wolf soap with lake water. It made a fair lather and removed the layers of soot and grime that had thickened over their hands.

When the crew returned in late afternoon, Charlie gave Olive one of the tins. She smelled it dubiously then went down to the lake to wash. She came back with a clean if reddened complexion.

"What is this stuff, carbolic acid?" she demanded.

Charlie grinned. "I know it isn't what you're used to, but it's the best I can do, and certainly better than none."

"I'm not complaining," she added hastily. "But I only got one face, and I'd like to keep it a few years longer." Charlie looked at her with frank approval. Despite the challenges, Olive managed to remain neat and clean. Her honey blond hair was carefully pinned back under the sport hat, and her clothing looked fresh.

But the men were looking seedy. Roman had grudgingly permitted the other actor to use his razor, only because this was necessary so they could keep on filming. But that was all he consented to loan from his toilet case. How, Charlie wondered, was this girl doing it?

She brought the half-finished bathing suit from the cabin and sat down beside the fire to sew. DuBonner walked over to Charlie. "This lake is so beautiful. How do you name it, M'sieur?"

"We call it Shadow Lake because all day it is covered with shadows from the timber," he replied.

"That's a nice name," Olive said. "Just as pretty as the lake itself. I could stay here forever. It is so quiet and peaceful."

"You mean it was quiet and peaceful," Lew muttered, looking across the fire at Roman who had returned from his wash.

"DuBonner," the actor called. "I want something to eat besides half-cooked wild meat. My stomach can't stand any more of it."

The director spread his hands helplessly. "*Nom de Dieu*," he exclaimed. "We must make the best of things. What would we eat if these splendid friends had not invited us to share their hospitality?"

The sun set early, clouded over by a big, dark bank that crept up over the horizon. The wind increased, and fearing they were in for a storm, Charlie drove the tepee stakes down a little deeper and arranged a canvas curtain to partially screen the open front of the lean-to.

The rain began about midnight and only lasted half an hour. Shortly after it ceased, DuBonner awoke with moans of pain. His hands were wrapped tight about his middle. "Cramps," he half-sobbed when Charlie sat up in bed. "Hot water, please. Hurry."

"Here," Lew said, handing a small bundle to Pierre. "Make him some tea. I stripped this bark from a sassafras tree yesterday. I'll bet it's the farthest north specimen in existence."

Charlie brought water from the creek while Lew kindled a tiny fire in the center of the tent. DuBonner drank the hot liquid and thanked them profusely. His stomach frequently played tricks like this, he explained. Charlie noted now in the dim light of the fire that the man's hair was wet. "You go out in the rain?" he asked.

DuBonner nodded. "I was afraid I would vomit," he replied.

Charlie and Lew missed their usual awakening time by some 20 minutes. The sun was nearly visible when they walked out of the tepee.

Yesterday had been a strenuous day for the movie folks, and all slept later than usual. Charlie and Lew cleaned up camp then sat down to wait for the others. The air was washed fresh and sweet by the night's rain, the treetops alive with singing birds. It was nearly 8 o'clock when the actors appeared.

Charlie helped Pierre prepare breakfast.

They were all seated around the fire before anyone noticed that Roman was nowhere in sight. Pierre banged a spoon on the bottom of a pot; then DuBonner called the missing man's name.

There was no response.

DuBonner looked at Striker, who said, "His bed was empty when we got up. We thought he beat us to breakfast."

"He has his moods," the director replied. "It is the actor's temperament. He will return when he is hungry."

"I'm afraid so," Lew muttered.

But Roman had not appeared by the time they finished eating, and a frown of worry gathered on DuBonner's face. The company sat idle, waiting. No work was possible without the missing man, since he was the star and appeared in all of the final scenes.

Lew went to the lake, untied his log raft and poled out to check the net. He was hoping for a heavy catch after the rain.

The net was set about 30 yards from shore, inside the curtain of long shadows cast by the timbered bank. Lew poled up close to the three wooden floats that supported the net and peered down into the water. The shadows this morning seemed deeper, and a mass of deep black puzzled him. Lew grabbed one of the floats and began to lift.

It was Ran Roman, his hands and feet entrapped in the meshes of the net, broken cords testifying to his futile struggles to extricate himself before he drowned.

Chapter 6 – Murder Stalks the Camp

Lew's first thought was to get the body back to shore as quickly as possible and try resuscitation. But when he gripped an arm and felt its wooden rigidity, he knew there was no hope. Lew knew, too, there was little chance he could separate the body from the tangled net, so he pulled it all in so he could drag all back to land.

He folded the ends of the net together, stood on top of it and began poling back. As he pushed the raft and its dragging burden, he thought of the words he had spoken to the unfortunate actor:

If you fall in the lake and never get out, nobody will feel sorry— except for the fish.

"I talk too much," Lew told himself bitterly. Roman had grasped at every opportunity to make himself unpleasant. Yet death is a great leveler, and now Lew felt only remorse for his unkind words.

After the raft slid up on shore, Lew dragged Roman's body out on top of the structure. Then he hesitated, wondering how he should break the news to the others. Olive saved him from that decision, for at that moment she appeared, tin of homemade soap in hand, a bundle of thin lingerie in the other. She smiled at Lew. Then her eyes dropped to the raft, saw the grisly burden and she stepped backwards with a piercing scream. The soap and suit both fell from her hands.

The girl's face was white, and she swayed so unsteadily on her feet Lew stepped toward, fearing she would fall. But she motioned him back. "I'm all right," she whispered.

Striker called out, "What's the matter?"

Lew shouted back, "Come here. All of you."

Charlie and Striker reached the shore first.

"My god!" the cameraman declared.

Charlie's bronzed face went white.

"Where did you find Roman's body?" he asked Lew.

"Tangled up in the gill net."

DuBonner wrung his hands and sank to his knees. "*Mon Dieu*," he moaned. "It is awful." Then he sprang up and seized Lew's arm. "Do something, M'sieur. Life may not be gone."

Lew shook his head soberly. "It's too late. Many hours too late. I would have begun if I thought there was the barest chance."

"How?" Kendall asked. "Ran was a dandy swimmer."

Lew shrugged. "The best swimmers are the ones that usually drown. They take a chance. I suppose Roman went for a swim early this morning. He's dressed that way, you see, just his undershirt and shorts, no shoes or socks. He may have had a cramp about the time he ran into the nets, started grabbing at the cords to try to hold himself up, got tangled and sank. That's what I guess happened."

Charlie reached down and pulled up on an arm. "He's been dead longer than that. This happened in the night."

Kendall's colorless lips were drawn tightly together; he showed every indication of a man about to be violently sick.

"What can we do?" DuBonner said. "Without Roman, the picture cannot be finished."

"Devil take the picture," Striker cut in. "The question is, what are we going to do about this?" He pointed to the body.

"Of course," DuBonner agreed and then looked at Charlie. "We must notify the coroner—at once. Why do you wait? Oh. There is no doctor, no coroner. We can do nothing until our airship returns."

"And that," Striker said, "is five days off. We got to decide what to do now. We can't wait that long."

"Let's carry him back to camp," Charlie suggested. "If the plane is on time, you can take the body back with you. If it is late, we may have to bury him here."

"Shall we carry him in the net?" Lew asked.

"Yes," Charlie said. "No, wait. Don't do that. Get one of the pieces of canvas from the tepee floor." Charlie disengaged the body from the net, rolled the latter up carefully and stood holding it under his arm.

When Lew returned with the canvas, the crew laid their dead comrade on top, and with a man gripping each corner, carried him back to camp. They laid the dead man on his bed in the lean-to. Then the party gathered in silence about the fire. Olive was looking especially bad, shining eyes circled with dark streaks that made them look even larger. Her mouth worked constantly as if inner thoughts were trying to break through her lips. DuBonner had the flushed countenance Charlie was inclined to couple with a bad heart. Even the stoic Striker fingered a light meter nervously, turning it over and over in his hands.

Charlie saw they must be given something to occupy their minds. "Since you can't make pictures," he suggested, "how about helping us finish the cabin? I want to put down a floor and move our food inside. That will make room for two more beds in the tepee."

Striker and Kendall jumped to their feet. "Sure," they said, "we'll be happy to help."

Charlie had decided a clay floor would be more easily maintained than one of split logs. Such wood floors can never be hewed smooth or laid tight with a woodsman's tools. A well-tamped clay floor is firm, easily swept with a shaved hickory broom, and it affords no hiding place for vermin. By adding some lime to the clay, Charlie hoped to harden the surface, making it less inclined to wear into dust.

He started the men carrying clay up from the creek and dumping it in the mixing box. After covering this with a thin layer of lime, it was all mixed with the light spade while more water was slowly added.

Striker proved a tireless worker, Kendall was willing but not so handy. Pierre stuck to his cooking fire and utensils. DuBonner fluttered about in a pitiful attempt to be useful, actually impeding any progress. Olive carried the water.

Seeing that there were already enough hands on deck, Lew went hunting. Not far from camp, he flushed a big gray rabbit, raised the shotgun but then lowered it, loathe to waste one of their precious shotshells on any animal that, due to the warm weather, might prove unfit to eat. Instead, he returned to camp and got out four of their smallest traps. Then he went back out in the woods and placed the traps along the dim trails that crisscrossed in every direction.

"Now I won't have to shoot so many birds," he thought.

The floor was progressing nicely when he returned. Charlie had made a tamper from a section of log with a sapling handle, and he beat the stuff down until it was firm, flat and hard. Then he smoothed the top with a wet paddle. The entire floor was finished by noon.

After they had eaten, Lew said, "How about mending the gill net? It shouldn't be idle even a part of the day. We need the food."

"We brought two rigged fish lines," Charlie replied. "They could be working, too. Are there any fishermen in the crowd?"

DuBonner looked up and said happily, "I have fished." Pierre offered to accompany him, and Charlie cut them a couple of slender poles, rigged them and sent the pair down to the lake. "Look under rocks and logs for worms and bugs to use as bait," he advised Pierre.

Charlie unrolled the gill net, stared at it for several seconds, then began to mend the meshes. But he had not worked longer than two minutes when he stopped, rolled the net back up and carried it into the tepee. Lew watched this with some surprise. "I can hardly blame him, though," he thought. "I'm not anxious to handle the thing myself."

Then he said aloud, "Shall I go gunning for more birds?"

"No. Let's wait and see how the anglers do. That first box of shells is almost gone. We only brought eight. At this rate, they won't last to Christmas, and they must last until spring."

Striker and Kendall were eager to resume work. So Charlie helped them build a table close to the open fire with rough benches along either side. The construction was simple. Four stakes supported crossbars which in turn were covered with slabs split out of the centers of 8-foot logs. The table was permanent, so they built another different version that could be moved inside the cabin.

Then they nailed a rack of poles against one wall to serve as shelves and drove rows of pegs into the log joints well up towards the eaves to use for hanging things. Crude as the fittings were, they made the little building home-like and cozy. They began to move the supplies from the teepee. Lew set the bags and packages outside; the others lugged them across to the cabin. The bags were stacked neatly on a platform of short logs, thick enough to raise the bottom sacks off the floor dampness.

Charlie told Striker and Kendall to move their beds to the tepee. "Or," he added, "you can cut grass to make new ones, if you prefer."

All day everyone had carefully avoided the lean-to.

Passing the burned-out lime kiln Charlie saw the small pile of lime left, and that reminded him they would probably need more lime during the winter to repair cracks or breaks in the fireplace and chimney. So he got two of the largest tins Lew had salvaged from the burned camp, cleaned and dried them and packed them full of lime from the bottom of the pile. He set the cans on a little pole shelf nailed to the peak of the cabin. He decided, too, that he should gather a quantity of clay and a few stones of assorted sizes for fireplace repair as required.

DuBonner and Pierre came back from the lake and laid two strings of fish before the fire. "The fishing, she is magnificent," the director said. "We have not done so badly, yes?"

Pierre was in the cabin when Charlie entered, standing by the food sacks. "M'sieur," he began, "if I could have ever so small a quantity of flour and just a fragment of powdered egg, I could fry the fish in a batter. They will be divine."

"All right," Charlie grinned. "But make it stretch, Pierre. That one small stack of provisions has to last us the entire winter."

When dinner was served, Charlie found that his generosity had been rewarded. The fish, while not exactly divine, were delicious. And what was better, they were so different in taste everyone ate eagerly and did not seem to notice the lack of variety in the meal.

They had eaten somewhat earlier than usual, and sunlight still flooded the clearing about camp. Charlie rose, face grim for one who had just finished a fine meal, and went into the tepee. When he emerged he carried the gill net. He walked up to the fire and said, "Will all of you come closer? It's about Roman, the way he died."

He glanced around at the faces arranged before him. Was the late afternoon light playing tricks, or had each countenance bleached whiter? Charlie scrutinized them in silence. Finally, he spoke, "I feel it is my duty to show you what I've discovered."

He laid the net on the table and motioned Lew to help spread it flat. "I want all of you to examine the broken places," he continued. "They occur only at the bottom of the net where Roman's feet were caught. The mesh, you see, is large enough to let his hands push through. That leaves the cords unbroken at the top, but something had to give way to admit his feet. Look at the broken strands, Lew."

Lew picked at the ends of the separated cords. Then he looked up, his face rock hard; his hand trembled just a little.

"You see?" Charlie asked, and Lew nodded.

Then Charlie motioned the others forward. One by one, obeying Charlie's pointing finger, they looked at the net and stepped back.

Charlie looked at each for a reaction. Olive broke first. At first she tried to stifle the pitiful cry that bubbled up out of her throat. She was not successful. "What are you trying to do? He's dead, isn't he? He drowned in the net, didn't he? Why must we look at this thing?"

Striker pulled a cigarette from his pocket and struck a match. "I take it you aren't satisfied that Roman swam out in the lake and got himself drowned. That's right, isn't it?"

Charlie nodded and simply said, "Roman was murdered."

Kendall spoke next, his voice oddly jerky. "What makes you say that? You better have a good reason."

"The cords weren't broken by Roman struggling," Striker spoke before Charlie could reply. "The ends are not frayed as they would be if they had been broken. They are cut clean—with a knife."

"Then somebody ..." Kendall began but stopped.

"Yes," Charlie said. "Somebody carried Roman out in the lake, pushed his hands through the net, cut places for his feet and then left him underwater. He was likely already dead when this happened, and that means one of you murdered him."

Chapter 7 – Charlie Sticks His Neck Out

Charlie expected a flare-up when he bluntly said one of the movie crew had murdered their fellow actor. But they seemed shocked into silence. He watched them closely. When Olive sank to the ground sobbing, Striker took a step toward her, stopped and instead turned to Charlie. "What do you mean, one of us?" he demanded.

"Why not you? Or your partner? He's the one who said nobody would be sorry if Roman fell in the lake and never got out. And that's exactly what happened, isn't it?"

"I didn't kill Roman," Charlie replied evenly, "and I know Lew didn't, either. We had no motive. Yes, Lew quarreled with Roman, even slugged him. But there's more to this than a sudden quarrel. Something that goes back farther than when we first saw you. One of you hated Roman or maybe feared him enough to kill him."

"I'm still listing you both as suspects," Striker insisted.

"Are you sure, *mon ami*, that this is murder?" DuBonner asked. "I admit the evidence of the net, but is that enough? Cords may part without fraying. Have you nothing else?"

"I think I have," Charlie said. "No one has examined the body. It isn't a pleasant business, but it's got to be done. Come, all of you."

They followed him into the lean-to. Charlie knelt beside the body. It was hard to do, and he hoped he could find what he hoped to find without a prolonged examination.

"Ah," he said, satisfied, "I thought so. Put your hand here, Du-Bonner. Right above the back of his neck. Feel that soft, spongy place? The skull is crushed. Roman was killed by a blow to the back of the head. He didn't drown in the net."

DuBonner drew his hand away quickly, nodded assent, and then stepped back into the line of seven men and one woman circled about the body. For a full minute the silence remained unbroken.

Striker spoke first. "Well, suppose you're right. Suppose Roman was killed by a blow to the head and then put in the net. What are you going to do about it?"

"Me?" Charlie answered. "Nothing. I'm not a policeman. It's up to you to report the crime. Roman was a part of your organization. Some member of it killed him. Seems to me it's the duty of those not guilty to work together to expose the one who is."

"Excuse me," Striker said. "But if Roman was knocked off, he only got what was coming to him. I'm no detective."

"What do you say, Kendall?" Charlie looked at the young actor.

"I think Striker is right. Better to just let it go. Roman drowned in a tragic swimming accident."

"This is quite interesting," Charlie said. "DuBonner?"

"They are right. I think it will save much trouble, much grief, if we simply say our companion drowned."

"I think differently," Charlie said. "I don't intend to be accused of this crime later on. There are harsh legal penalties for concealing a murder. You all seem to be willing to run that risk. But I'm not. This was cold-blooded murder."

"You won't get far trying to solve it," Striker told him.

"Maybe not. But I have no intention to sit back twiddling my thumbs and trying to make out it was an accident. I expect to discover who killed Roman before your plane returns to haul you home."

Charlie turned his back on them and marched down to the edge of the lake. Lew followed.

"You sure stuck your neck out that time," he said.

"I guess I did. But they're not willing, or maybe they're afraid, to know the truth. Regardless, none of them will turn a hand to discover the killer. We've got to do it ourselves."

Lew sighed. "Okay. But we need clues, something to work with. And you haven't a single one, have you?"

"Not yet. But I'm going to find some. I've already looked along the shoreline for footprints, marks that might explain how it happened. But everybody has tramped across the sand so many times, the tracks I do find tell me nothing."

"It won't be pleasant living and maybe sleeping in the same tent with a killer and not knowing who it is," Lew observed.

"Think it will get any more pleasant when we do find out?" Charlie demanded.

Lew shook his head soberly. "Since you elected yourself head sleuth," he said, "the murderer will want to put you out of the picture to save himself."

"I'm in no danger," Charlie replied. "Not until I dig out something important enough to make me worth a double murder charge."

"Just the same," Lew said. "I'll shift our beds so you sleep inside—with me between you and the rest."

They walked back to camp. The actors were still gathered around the fire, staring into the flames. Nobody had anything to say.

Next morning, Lew found two rabbits in the traps. He cleaned the animals and made a pleasant discovery. The plump meat was free of worms. He scraped the hides, stretching each over a supple limb bent in the shape of a horseshoe.

"We should tan these," he told Charlie when he got back to camp. "If we can make a big enough crock for hides and tanning solution."

After breakfast, Charlie puddled some clay and water together. He thought it would be fairly easy to make a crock if he could build some sort of a form to mold the wet stuff around.

He finally cut a big-enough piece of parachute cloth to sew a ring 16 inches wide and 20 inches deep. Then he cut a circular piece for the bottom to make the bag stand square at the seam and sewed it all together. When it was finished, he filled it full of damp sand and tied the top. Then he turned the bag upside down and spanked the bottom flat to make a mold that could be easily removed after the clay dried.

Charlie plastered the bottom of the upside down bag with two inches of wet clay. Then he plastered on thick sides and set it in the sun to dry. When fine cracks appeared, he plastered them shut with more wet clay. The next morning, he would cure the jar with low heat. At noon, he would build a small fire inside it to hasten the drying. Then a hotter fire, and Charlie hoped some of the sand content of the clay would melt and glaze the jar water-tight.

Knowing that Charlie could make the crock without him, Lew set out with one of the guns. After a half-hour tramp, he crossed a little creek into land he had not visited before. At some earlier time wildfire had levelled this timber. Charred logs lay on the ground, and a few black snags reared ugly tops above thick regrowth.

The place appeared impassable, and Lew was detouring around the tangle when he noticed some of the bushes were loaded with blue-berries. The sweet fruit was dead ripe, starting to dry on the stem. The idea came to pick a quantity to dry for winter use. Blueberry pie and shortcakes, Lew knew from experience, made a mean dish for a hard-working trapper.

He ate steadily for several minutes, appraising the quantity of fruit available. There appeared to be hundreds of bushels for the pick-ing. The burn extended for nearly a mile, ending in a bank of green timber where Lew figured a creek had stopped the fire.

He had about satisfied his hunger when a commotion drew his

eyes. The bushes were weaving back and forth, and when Lew heard a muffled grunt he brought his gun up, crouched and stole forward with extreme caution. A dark form reared up, and he found himself facing a half-grown black bear.

Lew wished he had put the .30-30 barrel on the combination gun. But he hadn't, and the bear was at point-blank range, so he fired a 20-gauge load directly into the animal's face. The bear dropped, and Lew was upon it instantly, clean slicing its throat with his sheath knife.

Lew eyed the young bear the way a butcher might appraise a side of beef. Here was meat in plenty, and because the bear was no more than half-grown, it would be tender and tasty. He field dressed the carcass, let it drain for 20 minutes, tied the four feet together, and slung it over his back.

The company at camp was more cheerful than it had been the night before. They hailed Lew with happy cries and congratulated him heartily upon his hunting skill.

Lew dumped the bear on the ground and beckoned Pierre. "Now, young fellow," he said. "I want to see what you can do with some fresh red meat. I'm partial to steaks, chops, and a roast of standing ribs."

Pierre rubbed his hands eagerly, anxious to demonstrate his considerable ability along those lines. He trimmed away layers of fat and immediately started frying them over the fire. Grease from a young bear is excellent for cooking and would provide something lacking from a lean meat diet that had consisted of mostly fish and grouse.

Lew decided to rub a quarter with salt and hang it in one of the trees shading camp. The rest would be jerked over the fire as soon as it had hung long enough to cool.

After finishing his pottery work, Charlie unrolled the deer and wolf hides and prepared to tan them into buckskin. First, he soaked them soft in the creek, rinsing off the ashes and grease. Breaking would be the final operation. The buckskin would not be softened with chemicals but with back-breaking labor.

"A breaking stake is our best bet," he told Lew. "And as we're short on nails, I'll cut off a stout sapling 30 inches above the ground, shave the top chisel-shaped, and we can pull the hide back and forth across that edge. With the butt still growing in the ground, it won't need any bracing."

After such a tree had been cut off and shaped, Charlie began with the wolf hide, drawing it back and forth, bearing down with most of his weight. Striker came over after he was nicely started and offered to finish. "You've bought yourself a job," Charlie grinned. "It will take about five hours to soften the fibers of each hide so they won't harden again after wetting."

"That's okay. I need something to do," Striker replied. Then he began working the hide with measured, unhurried movements.

For lunch, Pierre served slightly rare bear steak smoking hot. Between mouthfuls, Lew told everyone about the big patch of berries where he got the bear. Olive cried out in excitement. "I've missed fruit so much. I'm going over there right after lunch and pick gallons."

Kendall and DuBonner offered to accompany her, and they asked if he could supply empty pots for them all to pick.

They were acting cheerful, but Charlie realized the gaiety was forced. Behind the light words lurked a taut suspense that might break through any minute. He knew they all shared his belief Roman had been murdered, and while none would admit it, they knew the murderer was one of their own party.

One of the flour sacks had been so depleted the remaining contents could be tied up in a square of cloth, so Charlie emptied it and gave the sack to the berry pickers along with two kettles and all of the large tins Lew had salvaged from the burned-out camp.

When Striker went back to his breaking stake, he found the wolf hide so stiff it would not bend. It had dried as hard as wood while he ate lunch. Charlie dipped the skin in the creek then rolled it up in a tight bundle. "Skins must be dampened every half-hour or as often as you work them dry," he explained. "Work on the deer hide, now."

Pierre began rendering more bear grease, and during the intervals it required no attention, he scoured the coffeepot with sand and ashes. Pierre never volunteered for any other kind of work. But he never shrank from any kitchen task, no matter how tedious.

Charlie and Lew decided to get in some firewood. So much cooking had cleaned the campsite of the blocks left from building the cabin and had also depleted the nearby supply of "down and easy" fuel. Accordingly, they walked into the patch of dead timber across the creek and chopped down a dozen small trees. They trimmed the trunks, carefully piling up the dead branches for kindling.

The berry pickers returned in late afternoon with a flour sack full to the top, as was every utensil they had taken. "We can get you a ton of berries if you can use them," Kendall boasted. "We found a bee tree, too, a big old hollow stub with hundreds of bees buzzing in and out."

Pierre turned to Charlie, his face shining with eagerness.

"You must cut the honey tree, M'sieur. What I cannot do with honey for biscuits and cakes! Let us go at once."

"Wait," Charlie protested as the little Frenchman picked up the axe. "We haven't time tonight, and we must have a plan. The bees have to be smoked stupid or they will sting us to death."

"We will not need smoke," Pierre replied. "Bees do not sting me. I can work them with my bare hands."

Olive had gone to the cabin as soon as she returned, and now she beckoned Charlie to the edge of the timber. When he joined her, she gripped his arm so hard he winced.

"What's the matter?"

"The gun you gave me is gone. I looked all through the cabin and it isn't there."

"Don't get excited," Charlie said. "Lew went hunting this morning. Maybe he took it."

Charlie raised his voice. "Give me a hand, will you, Lew?"

They walked to the cabin together, and Charlie did not speak until they were inside. "You know I let Olive have one of our guns. She says it's gone. Did you take it hunting?"

"No. I used the one from the tepee."

"You've got to find it," Olive whispered fiercely when they stood motionless, thinking. "Can't you understand?" she demanded. "There may be another murder if you don't find that gun."

"You think the murderer took it?"

"I know … at least, I suppose he did. Who else would?"

"You were about to say you know he did," Charlie replied in a flat, even tone. "Maybe you saw him. Anyway, you suspect somebody. Now you need to tell us who."

Chapter 8 – She Wouldn't Talk

The theft of the gun had plainly frightened Olive. But now, when Charlie suggested she had seen the thief or at least suspected who it was, she closed lips that had been trembling and managed a laugh.

"Say, what is this, the third degree? I don't know who took the gun. I just found it gone."

"Go and search the tepee, Lew," Charlie said. Then, turning to the girl, he continued, "We are dealing with murder, and even if you're not sure of your suspicions, telling us might help prevent another death."

But Olive persisted that she knew nothing.

Lew returned shaking his head. "No luck. He has probably hidden it out in the timber. Was it loaded?"

"Yes," Olive replied.

"We must hide the rest of the ammunition," Charlie said. "He only has one shell, and we mustn't let him get any more. Keep quiet about this," he cautioned Olive before she left the cabin.

They wrapped all of the shells and cartridges except for six of each in waterproof canvas. They put the loose loads in their pockets and then carried the bundle through the woods to a very large tree. Lew climbed it and hung the ammunition in a crotch high in the top where it was invisible from below. They paused under the tree to talk in private.

"She's frightened, knows more than she told us," Charlie began. Maybe she isn't sure, but she has strong suspicions."

"If we knew who took the gun, we'd know who killed Roman, wouldn't we?" Lew commented.

"Maybe," Charlie replied slowly. "Maybe not. I haven't made much progress on that one. But I've lined up a pair of suspects."

"Who?" Lew demanded.

"DuBonner, for one. Remember when he got us up in the middle of the night with cramps? That was the night Roman got his. It had rained, and DuBonner's hair was wet. He had been outside in the rain. He told me he was afraid he would vomit in the tent, but that could have been a stall. He might have faked the cramps, too."

"I don't know about that," Lew said. "The man looked pretty sick to me. Well, who's the other?"

"Olive."

"No," Lew said incredulously.

"Yes," Charlie replied. "I found pretty good evidence she was down on the bank of the lake that night. Look at this."

He pulled a gum wrapper from his pocket.

"So far as I've seen," he continued, "she's the only one who has gum, and she's hoarding her last few sticks like a miser. I found this wrapper by the lake after we carried Roman up. I tested the printing on the back; the ink runs when wet, but these letters are sharp and clear. That means it was dropped after the rain. It was under a bush with enough leaves to keep off dew but not enough to turn rain. Olive was at the lake after it rained. And if she isn't guilty, she saw something that has given her a pretty good idea who is."

"Olive couldn't tow Roman out in the lake and tangle him in the net," Lew replied thoughtfully.

"Don't be so sure of that. Have you seen her since she finished that bathing suit? The girl swims like an otter. She's got plenty of muscle, too. She dug her fingers in my arm and it hurts yet."

Back at camp the flour sack full of berries caught Lew's eye. "We've got to do something with these," he said. "Dry them before they spoil."

Charlie solved the question of drying racks by making wide cloth trays with four notched sticks nailed at the corners for a frame. They made three of them then drove stakes to support them out where the sun would dry the fruit most of the day.

It was too late to begin the drying this day, but Lew decided the berries should be cleaned. There were a lot of hulls and stems mixed in. He cut more stakes and poles, went to the tepee and brought out their two wool coats. Shoving poles down the sleeves, he stretched the coats to form a flat platform, high at one end and low at the other. The slant was steep, and when he slowly poured berries on the cloth at the high end they ran down and fell into a pot at the low end. But the nap of the thick wool caught and held the lighter dirt, stems and hulls. Only clean berries bounced off into the container.

"That is clever," Olive said, watching.

"I call it being lazy," Lew replied. "Laziness is the fundamental force behind most clever ideas. You have a disagreeable or tedious job to finish. So, instead of starting on it the hard, slow way like some honest worker might, the lazy man figures out a shortcut. I always say it takes a lazy fellow to make a good woodsman. A guy who likes to work will kill himself in the woods."

It was nearly dusk, and they eagerly answered Pierre's hail for supper. But everyone was tired, and the time they sat about the fire after eating was short that night, and all were soon in their beds.

When Charlie needed to awake at a certain hour of the night, he could do it within a few minutes by simply making a strong determination before he went to sleep. Tonight, he set his "mental alarm" for midnight and awoke a few minutes before the hour. All of the occupants of the tepee, save Lew, were breathing regularly.

"I've been awake a couple of hours," Lew answered his whisper. "Nothing happened except Pierre went out for a few minutes."

"All right," Charlie said. "Go to sleep. I'll take over."

Lew rolled on his side and in a few minutes was sleeping soundly. Charlie lay on his back after that, ears and eyes tuned to catch the slightest sound or movement. The moon hung big and bright over the lake, and the interior of the white-cloth tent was light enough for him to see each sleeper. Pierre had no doubt answered nature's call, and Charlie dismissed that as expected with a middle-aged man. But if any of the others left the tepee for more than a few minutes, he would investigate.

Charlie did not know how long he lay awake, listening and watching, but it must have been a full three hours before he fell back asleep. He did not arouse until he heard Lew go out to kindle the fire.

Immediately after breakfast, the company prepared for the bee hunt. Charlie decided a sack of canvas would be the best honey holder available. He asked Olive to sew one and then set his green clay jar a few feet from the fire to hasten the curing. He wanted to remove the form, refill it with sand again and begin another crock.

Equipped with the canvas sack and several tins, the party headed into the timber. Lew was the designated axe man.

Charlie remained in camp to keep an eye on things there.

The bee tree was a stub some 30 feet high. Lew swung the axe into it, and the heavy iron head almost bounced back out of the seasoned wood. Several bees flew out, descended and buzzed about his head. Lew stepped back. "Maybe you can handle bees without getting stung, but I'm not so lucky. I'm going to build a smudge to keep them away while I chop."

A few minutes later, with smoke curling around his head, Lew plied the axe vigorously. Bees buzzed above him, and a steady hum grew louder inside the hollow tree. The stub fell so heavily the softer top split open exposing an interior lined with a massive comb. Pierre walked calmly in and began prying it out with his knife.

Bees swarmed him, lighting on his hands and face. But Pierre merely brushed them gently away and worked unharmed. He filled the canvas sack to its top, and there were still gallons of honey left. The only thing was to return to camp, empty the bag and make a second trip. The problem was carrying the sack so the comb would not be squeezed and broken. Lew suspended it with the four corners tied to a long pole. He and Striker slung the pole over their shoulders and walked briskly back, leaving word that the fire should be maintained to keep the bees off and prevent them moving any honey.

Back at camp, Charlie spread a clean piece of chute cloth on the ground and they dumped the honey on it. The comb was so solid very little of the liquid had leaked out.

Striker went back alone for the second load, and Lew helped Charlie begin molding another jar. They hoped the first would be firm enough to hold honey by nightfall.

The bee hunters returned just after 11 o'clock, the sack two-thirds full this time. Lew estimated they had 100 pounds of honey. Pierre fried bear steaks for lunch and served cups of berries with the honey poured over them for dessert. It was a delicious treat.

Charlie wanted to separate some of the comb to obtain the beeswax, and Pierre volunteered to do the work. He made a sort of grill by laying thin split sticks closely together over the top of a can. Picking up chunks of comb, he sliced off the ends of the cells with a sharp knife and laid them so the thick sweetness drained into the can. When draining ceased, he squeezed the comb in his hands to extract the remaining honey. Then he boiled the comb slowly with a little water, and, when molten, he poured this into cups to cool and mold into cakes.

The beeswax would seal any leaks in the tepee, of which there were several because of the flying campfire sparks. It would also make clothing watertight and stop small leaks in any utensil not used over heat. A thin coat of warm beeswax on the outside of a gun would prevent rust in the wettest weather.

Charlie coated the gun he kept in the tepee under his bed. Then he removed the laces from their boots and pulled them across a cake of wax, adding considerably to their wear life.

DuBonner and Pierre went to the lake to fish. Lew took his gun and three shotgun shells and started out to hunt for grouse. Olive sat outside the cabin sewing. Striker was inside rubbing wax on his camera to protect the metal parts from rust. Kendall went down to the lake to watch the fishermen.

When the first stone jar was dry enough to move, Charlie inverted it over a small heap of hot coals. Then he left, circling around inside the timber to the rear of the lean-to. All day he had been thinking about the missing gun and the logical places a thief might hide it. He decided the gun was either out in the woods or in the most unvisited spot in camp. He favored the latter. The thief took the gun because he might have to use it. A weapon hidden in the woods would be hard to reach in a hurry. It also must be wrapped to protect it, and Charlie had carefully checked their supply of both chute silk and canvas and found no pieces missing.

No, the gun must still be in camp—and what better place than the lean-to with a dead body inside? "That," Charlie thought, "is exactly where I would hide something I wanted no one else to find."

When he was sure no one was watching, he entered the lean-to. He glanced at the other grass beds. But the one under the body was most likely, and he found the gun immediately by merely shoving his hand in under the back edge. Charlie smoothed the grass and walked out. Then he circled back around through the woods to enter camp from a different direction.

An hour later, DuBonner and Pierre returned empty-handed. "We tried," the director explained. "But the fish, they do not bite."

"The lake is cursed," Pierre said. "No fish are caught where a man has died."

"How about that nice string you brought home yesterday, the same day it happened?" Charlie asked.

Pierre shook his head. "The curse had not had time to work."

Lew came in with one grouse. "Birds are getting scarce around camp," he said. Pierre looked up from the bear meat he was slicing.

"What did I tell you? The woods, too, are cursed."

"What's eating him?" Lew asked as he and Charlie walked over to the garbage pit at the edge of the woods to clean the grouse.

Charlie explained the curse, and then he added, "Found the gun."

"Where?" Lew demanded.

"In Roman's bed."

"Not bad. The thief is clever. Where did you put it?"

"I left it there."

Lew stared at him in disbelief.

"For a trap," Charlie added. "I want the thief to go there tonight and move it."

"You want him to kill someone else?"

"No danger of that. I removed the shell. But if I can scare the thief into moving it, we can watch the lean-to and catch him in the act."

"Then we'll know who killed Roman." Lew said.

"Maybe," Charlie replied.

That night after they had eaten, Charlie addressed the crew. "There's something I'm afraid we must do in the morning. We must move the lean-to farther from camp," Charlie said. "Otherwise ..." he shrugged, leaving the gruesome thought unspoken.

"Of course, M'sieur," DuBonner agreed quickly. "If you think it should be done, we will help."

Lew stood. "I bet the fish will bite on this kind of evening. Let's go fishing."

Charlie agreed quickly. They picked up the tackle and walked down to the lake.

"We'll fish for five or six minutes in case anybody follows," Lew said. "Then we'll cut back around through the woods and hide where we can watch the lean-to."

"I'm going alone," Charlie told him. "And I plan to wait inside. I'm not taking a chance of missing the man. He'll have to move the gun tonight to keep us from finding it tomorrow. You stay here, and if someone comes along, tell them I wanted to try my luck farther west, which will be true. That is the way I'm starting out."

Charlie was already winding the line about his pole, and he left before Lew could muster a protest.

It was almost dark when he slipped into the lean-to. He had picked up a stout club in the woods, and he hid the fishing pole under a bed. Then, club in hand, he crouched behind the strip of cloth that partly closed the door.

His wait was short. Without any warning sound, a dark figure blotted out the dim square of light. The figure entered swiftly, almost brushing against Charlie as it passed to kneel beside Roman's body.

Charlie stood up, raised the club and said quietly, "Come out to the door where I can see you."

Chapter 9 – I Know Who the Killer Is

When Charlie spoke the figure leaning over the dead man jumped. Charlie stepped back out through the door of the lean-to and stood outside. The figure had nowhere to run but still did not come forward, instead standing silently where the shadows were darkest.

"The gun is not loaded," Charlie continued. "I unloaded it today." Then he took another step back to gain room. The thief might swing the buttstock, and Charlie positioned his club to turn such a blow.

But the person inside mistook Charlie's club for the other gun and instead said quickly. "Don't shoot. I haven't done anything."

"You stole a gun," Charlie replied. "Now tell me why."

Kendall came out reluctantly, carefully set the gun down and said, "I don't suppose you'll believe me, but I was scared. That's the absolute truth. There's a killer in camp, and I wanted to be armed."

"A gun hidden there wouldn't help you," Charlie observed.

"I could take it with me, couldn't I? If I had to leave?"

"Why would you leave?" Charlie asked.

Kendall hesitated but then said bluntly, "I think either you or your partner killed Roman, and if things get bad, I intend to scram."

"You didn't like Roman," Charlie replied.

"Nobody did. But you don't kill a fellow just because you don't like him. If you did, there wouldn't be anyone left in Hollywood. "

"True enough," Charlie admitted. "Still, this looks bad for you. Stealing the gun is exactly what a murderer would do, so he could kill anyone who might learn his identity."

"Look," Kendall said earnestly. "I was a fool to take the gun. But I didn't kill Roman. I never even met him until a month ago when I started working for DuBonner."

"Alright," Charlie said, picking up the gun and settling it under his arm. "You know, Kendall, I'm only trying to work this business out. But no one's giving me anything much to go on. I thought I had something when the gun was taken. Is there anything you know, anything at all that might help me?"

"No," the actor said thoughtfully. "I can't think of a thing."

"What about the night Roman was killed? Did you see or hear

anyone leave the lean-to?"

Kendall shook his head. "I sleep like a log. But here's an idea that might help. Roman kept a diary. I saw him writing in it several times at our other camp before we burned out."

"There isn't much chance he wrote down the name of the man who killed him," Charlie said. "But I'll consider it. Thanks."

Kendall turned and walked up to the fire. Charlie went back inside and got the fishing pole. He began to detour towards the lake, but at the edge of the trees Lew's voice stopped him.

"You let him off pretty easy."

"What else could I do?" Charlie asked. "His explanation might be true. Anyway, I want him to believe I thought it was."

"That tip on the diary. We'll follow that up?" Lew asked.

"You bet. That might be our first big break, although I tried not to seem keen on it. I suspect that journal may tell us the first thing we need to know—the motive for the crime."

"Yeah, Roman was the sort of guy who'd keep a diary and fill it with stuff other men would be ashamed of. I wonder where it is?"

"The likely place is inside his toilet case. We'll look just as soon as we circle back to the lake and return to camp from that direction. And, say, did you catch any fish?"

"No time. I was only about 50 feet behind you. I was afraid you might need a hand with the gun thief."

When they arrived back at camp Olive got up from beside the fire and came to meet them. She handed Charlie a square of cloth. "It's a pillowcase. I'll make another tomorrow and you can stuff them with grouse feathers. You've already thrown away enough of them to make a small feather tick."

"We won't anymore," Charlie promised. "This is a swell idea."

Lew went to the tree where the broken gill net hung and carried it to the fire. Then he sat in the circle of light and began to splice the broken strands. Olive was sitting to one side, DuBonner the other, and they drew away when they saw what he held over his knees.

"Can't help it, folks," Lew said simply. "We have to catch fish to eat, and this is the surest way."

Charlie lit a birch bark torch, went into the cabin and got Roman's case, an expensive leather box trimmed with golden hardware. He had searched through the dead man's clothing when he visited the lean-to and already had the key. He opened the case.

It was filled with small bottles of cut glass and silver. There was hair tonic, hair color, hair oil and liquid shampoo. He noted a container of mascara, shaving lotion, skin tonics, and cold creams. There were tools and preparations for all kinds of manicuring. Charlie pulled out a stopper, grimaced at the heavy musk odor.

The diary was on the bottom, a thin volume with gold-edged leaves and a slick leather cover. Charlie took it and closed the case. He didn't lock it. There were so many useful things here it seemed a pity not to use them. He decided he would tell Olive to take what she wanted, first, and then pass the rest on to the others.

He shoved the diary inside his shirt and went outside. Lew had already mended the net. "I'll place it first thing tomorrow," he said.

Just seeing the thing cast a depressed mood over the group, and they again left for their beds before the fire died down. Charlie and Lew lingered for a while, and then Charlie doused the coals with water. It was approaching the season for high winds, and they dared not risk any chance of wildfire spreading through the timber. A forest fire would drive fur and game beyond their reach, might even burn them out as the movie camp had been burned.

"Did you get it?" Lew whispered.

Charlie nodded.

"When you went to the cabin," Lew continued, "Kendall said casually he supposed you were looking for Roman's diary. And he added you thought it might contain some clue to his murder."

"That boy talks too much." Charlie's said, his voice grim. He had counted on surprising them with any discovery made in the book. Surprises, he knew, often shocked men and women to betray facts they might otherwise be able to keep concealed.

"I'll go down to the lake at sunrise tomorrow and read it through," Charlie said. "How many heard Kendall?"

"Everybody. They were all still at the fire."

Charlie pushed their beds a little closer that night and lay both guns between them. He wrapped the diary in the coat that served for his pillow, confident it could not be taken from under his head without awakening him. With both guns in their possession, Charlie considered the safety situation much improved, and he made no attempt to stay awake but slept soundly until sunrise.

In the morning his hand went first to the coat, then to the edge of his bed. Book and guns were there. He put the book inside his shirt and went outside. He kindled the fire with flint and steel, catching the tiny spark on a shred of birch bark.

Lew appeared next. The morning was cool and foggy and they sat close to the fire until the sun topped the tall spruce on the east side of the lake. Lew picked up the gill net and started for the raft. Charlie followed. There was enough daylight to read, and he sat on the shore, back against a tree. He thumbed the book open and turned directly to the day the party arrived in the woods by plane.

The daily notations varied from a few lines to an entire page, sometimes two. Most of it was complaints or criticisms of DuBonner's directing and the acting of his companions.

The words betrayed a vainglorious, arrogant and conceited egotist. He expressed supreme belief in his attraction for women and intolerance for anyone who disagreed with him on any matter. Charlie puzzled slowly through several pages. The dead man's writing was queerly slanted with letters squeezed closely together.

Then he found the first mention of Olive. "I won't let that dame give me the runaround any longer," Roman had written. "I'll tell her husband. Didn't I hand her a jolt when I told her I knew …"

The blow came without any warning. Charlie slumped over, senses reeling amid dazzling streaks of light.

His first thought as he regained consciousness was he had fallen or been thrown into the lake, for his face was wet and his eyes blinded with more water. He rubbed them and managed to see Lew standing over him, dripping hat raised to douse him again.

Charlie gasped, "The book."

"Gone," Lew said. "Why didn't I have enough sense to stay with you? We might have known the murderer would make a try for the diary. I saw nothing. I was bending over the water, fixing the last float. When I turned around and looked this way you were already leaning over, head on your knees. I knew that wasn't right and almost tore the old raft apart getting back, but he was gone. Were you able to find anything out at all?" Lew added as Charlie stood up on his feet.

"Not much. I had just got started where Roman was writing about Olive. I told you he was blackmailing her, and I learned she is married but keeping it secret. Her husband might even be one of the men here. In that case, he is probably the one we want. Likely, Roman named him someplace. I was just turning a page when I got hit."

"We better hurry back to camp and see who is awake."

"Sure. That's an idea. The fellow who struck me can't crawl back into bed without being noticed."

But when they reached the clearing, every one of the party was up and moving about. "Shall we question them?" Lew asked.

"Wouldn't do a bit of good. This gang hangs together like bats in a cave. If they knew something that would help us, they'd never tell."

Lew realized the truth of this. Still, he went over to Pierre and asked casually, "Who got up first this morning?"

Pierre hesitated a second. "I don't exactly recall, M'sieur. I think we all came out at about the same time."

"Anybody leave camp?"

"I think all have been away. Myself, I go to the creek for water. On my way back I meet Mademoiselle with soap in her hand. She is going to wash. M'sieur Striker obliges me by bringing an armful of wood. Everybody has been to the creek, I think. Why do you ask? Is something wrong?"

"Nothing serious," Lew replied.

After breakfast, Lew announced, "Do you know what day this is? Well, it's Sunday, a day for rest, and I'm taking advantage of that. We've been working like beavers ever since we got here. Today, I'm taking things easy, and I hope you all do the same."

No one objected to the proposal.

DuBonner decided that fishing in the warm sunshine would be the most pleasant form of relaxation, and he took the poles and went to the lake. Pierre followed as soon as his cooking utensils were scoured bright and hanging on the pole rack Charlie had nailed above the camp table. Olive sat down to sew more pillowcases, claiming that relaxed her better than doing nothing at all. Striker and Kendall decided they would walk over to the berry patch. The first lot of berries was drying nicely on the cloth-bottomed trays, and there was room for more.

Charlie walked out into the timber with a gun.

Lew stretched out in front of the cabin for a nap. But he could only lie there an hour. The inactivity made him restless. First he rolled about, and then he got up and filed both axes. He hunted along the creek bed, found a flat stone and ground it smooth against a harder rock. It made a fair whetstone, and he gave the axe blade edges a keenness that he proclaimed would, "shave the hair off your chin."

Then he unpacked the remaining traps and adjusted their pans so each released under just the right pressure. He took one of the empty tins, filled it with water, added hemlock bark and boiled the traps two at a time to color them and remove any grease or oil. The hemlock did not produce a dark dye, but it dulled the bright metal.

He used the big axe to chop off a block of spruce and then the small axe to split it into thin strips. He whittled these into trigger releases for deadfalls. Once he discovered the correct size for each part, he cut more blocks of spruce, split them and hung the pieces in the cabin to dry. With a scarcity of steel a great many deadfalls would be needed for their winter trapline.

At noon Olive came to Charlie and asked if it would be all right for her to use some of Ran's things in the case. "I need them so badly."

Charlie scrutinized her carefully. "You aren't doing so bad without them," he said. Her face glowed with the soft pink color acquired only by healthful outdoor living. "But sure," he added, "go ahead and use the stuff. I think the case is unlocked."

He followed her into the cabin. She took the case down, opened it out on the table. Charlie got a surprise that brought him swiftly forward. Lying on top was the missing diary.

"That's Ran's diary, isn't it?" Olive asked quickly.

"Yes, and I want it. You can have the rest."

Charlie went outside. Catching Lew's eye, he motioned with his head and walked off into the woods. Lew followed, and when they were out of sight of the camp, Charlie pulled out the book.

"Where did you get that?"

"It was back in Roman's case."

He was already turning the pages. "I thought so. Three, four, five pages have been torn out. I wonder why he went to the trouble since he could have just burned the whole thing."

"Looks goofy, alright," Lew agreed. "Maybe he wanted to rib us a little. You know murderers are supposed to do that. Every killer makes a slip, maybe this is his."

"I think you got something there," Charlie said slowly, "about the murderer making a slip, anyway. I got a lot of thinking to do. Go back and leave me alone to do it."

"Think you're safe?"

"No danger with those pages gone. The murderer has lost all interest in the book. But if I can revive that interest ..."

Charlie did not return to camp until dinner time, approaching with something so determined in his stride they all watched. This observation, Lew noticed, quickly into a watchful sort of wariness.

DuBonner spoke first. "You have discovered something about this unhappy affair of Roman?"

"Yes," Charlie replied confidently. "I know who killed him."

Chapter 10 – Dead Fingers Pointing

Charlie wished he had been able to watch each face when he announced he knew who had killed Roman. But he could only shift his eyes twice in that fleeting moment of initial surprise. He heard Olive's gasp, saw Kendall's face drain of color, DuBonner's full lips tremble. Then all struggled to control their features.

"How did you discover this, M'sieur?" DuBonner asked.

"I didn't," Charlie replied. "The killer gave himself away. They say every murderer makes at least one slip. This one slipped badly. He has revealed his identity in such a way there can't be any doubt. It will be as easy to name him as reading the name on a page of print."

Charlie paused to frown at Lew, who was struggling to his feet, mouth gaping. Lew took the hint and sank back down, trying to capture a calmer look. He didn't carry it off very well.

When Charlie took the diary from a pocket, Lew saw it was now covered with a piece of parachute silk. Charlie unwrapped the cloth with obvious care to keep the cloth between his fingers and the book.

"This," he began, "is Roman's diary. You all knew he kept one, probably saw him writing in it. Yesterday, I got a tip it might contain something of value, perhaps telling why Roman was killed. I found the book in his toilet case around dusk last night."

Charlie paused, rubbing the swollen place on his head. It still throbbed with a dull ache. "This morning," he continued, "I took the book to the lake and started to read. Someone stole up behind me, hit me over the head with a club and took the book. That proves conclusively that it does or at least did contain important information. The killer knew he must do this to avoid discovery. So, he tore out the betraying pages and, I suppose, burned them. But that was when he signed his own death warrant. He should have burned the entire book."

Kendall spoke quickly. "But why? If he destroyed the pages that incriminated him, what was his fatal mistake?"

"His error came when he put the book back in Roman's case. I had expected an attempt would be made to take the diary, but I hadn't dared to hope it would be found again. Lew, bring me a cup of flour."

When Lew returned with flour from the cabin, Charlie held the book up so all could see it plainly.

"Knowing only the murderer would steal the diary, I laid a trap. I cleaned the book, cover and pages, wiping them with a damp cloth. That removed the fingerprints of all who might have handled it before. Then I wiped the covers and some inside pages with warm linseed oil, leaving as thin a film as I could. I avoided touching the book with my own hands. If there are fingerprints on the oiled cover or pages, they belong to whoever took the diary, and only the murderer had enough motive to risk attacking me in broad daylight to do that."

Charlie thought he heard somebody gasp, but he was not sure. "Fingerprints," he went on, "are conclusive evidence recognized by every court. Give me the flour, Lew."

He held the book slightly tilted and dusted the flour over the cover. Most of it stuck, and when the leather was evenly coated, Charlie titled the book a little more and began tapping the upper edge with a finger. The flour sifted off until bare leather began appearing. Charlie tapped a little harder, tilted the book a little more, and slowly but surely two distinct smudges resolved into a pair of fingerprints, every line and whorl clearly defined.

"There you are," Charlie said. "The fingerprints of the person who stole this book and also murdered Roman." He glanced around at their faces. All contained amazement, apprehension, perhaps, but none displayed the slightest skepticism or disbelief.

Pierre said, "What now, M'sieur? Take our fingerprints?"

"That isn't necessary," Charlie replied. "And I'm not trained to do it, anyway. All I need do is preserve these and send them back with the pilot when your plane lands, together with a signed statement of how I got them. The authorities will do the rest."

"How can you be sure the prints will stay readable until then?" Kendall asked dubiously.

"They don't have to," Charlie replied. "Striker will take a close-up photo, and I will carefully guard the book itself. Then, there will be no chance for the killer to wriggle out."

Striker immediately went in the cabin and came out lugging his heavy camera. He spread the tripod, pulled out the lens and motioned Charlie out in the sunlight. Striker focused the lens, moved the camera closer until he was less than two feet from the book.

"All right," he warned. "Hold steady." The big camera ground away for several seconds then went silent. Striker folded the tripod. "All finished," he said and started back towards the cabin.

"Wait," Charlie spoke sharply. Striker halted, glanced back surprised. "I want that film. Take it out."

DuBonner ran forward. "No," he cried. "You cannot. You will ruin scenes we have worked so hard to make. They are on that film."

"Devil take your scenes," Charlie said. "Don't you care that a man's been murdered? Do you want to be an accessory after the fact?"

"Of course not," DuBonner faltered.

"Then shut up," Charlie said. "Besides, the film won't be harmed. Your precious scenes will be developed along with the fingerprints. You don't suppose the authorities won't handle evidence in a murder case with the greatest care, do you? In the meantime, I'll be responsible for it until the pilot arrives. Now take it out of the camera, Striker, and seal it up in the metal box you use for exposures."

"Yes, do as he says," DuBonner added. "He is right. One of us is a murderer. I will not sleep again until I am safe in my own home."

Charlie followed Striker into the cabin. Lew lounged in the doorway, outwardly indifferent, inwardly alert. Striker put the exposed film in a thin, round box, sealed the box and handed it to Charlie.

They went outside. By then the others had drawn apart, were watching each other with puzzled eyes. Apparently, the truth had finally hit home. They were seeing things stripped of all evasion. No one could dodge the responsibility of this affair.

"I'm going to hide this box out in the woods," Charlie said. "I want all of you to remain here until I return. Lew, see that they do. Anybody who slips away to follow me will assuredly be the guilty person."

Then he disappeared among the trees. Forty minutes later, he returned from the opposite direction. He called Lew to the edge of the camp and spoke in a low tone. Then he addressed the others.

"My partner now knows where the film is hidden, so it won't do any good to put me out of the way."

"M'sieur!" DuBonner cried. "Are we all butchers?"

"I don't know," Charlie said. "I was addressing the one who butchered Roman. But you know the saying, if the shoe fits, put it on."

DuBonner flushed, and Charlie continued, "The diary in my pocket is not so all-important now. Still, I want to give it every care. I will hide it here in camp, someplace we can keep an eye on most of the time." He glanced at the sun. "Suppose we start cooking supper."

Pierre jumped up. "I am sorry, M'sieur. I forget the time. I will hurry now."

"I'll see if we got any fish," Lew offered and started for the lake. Charlie followed. He had decided they should stick close together for mutual protection. He knew he had put Lew in danger along with himself. If something happened to both of them before the plane arrived, it would not be difficult to find and burn the diary, and the film would remain lost in the woods.

When they were out of hearing of camp, Lew spoke with admiration. "Where did you learn that fingerprint stuff? I didn't know you went to all that trouble cleaning and oiling the diary."

"I didn't," Charlie said.

"You didn't?" Lew asked incredulously. "Then how did those fingerprints get on the cover?"

"I put them there myself. After the book was recovered."

"I'll be darned," Lew said. "You're running a bluff."

"It's all I've got," Charlie admitted. "Only the murderer doesn't know it. He thinks the prints are genuine. Even if he's not sure, he's got to do something that puts us out of the picture so the film won't be found and then destroy the diary. Altogether a rather daunting job."

"So what do we do now?" Lew asked.

"We wait," Charlie said cheerfully. "We've got to catch him trying to kill us or destroy the diary. My guess is he'll try the latter first."

"I wish I shared your confidence there," Lew sighed. "Aren't we running more risk than the game is worth?"

"No," Charlie said soberly. "We can't fail. If we do, we, too, will always be under a cloud of suspicion."

"I guess you're right."

"I know I am, and there isn't any other way to handle this. The killer must be found before he leaves this camp. So far, it's been a near-perfect crime. Not a clue to point conclusively to anyone. Olive dropped a gum wrapper; DuBonner was out in the rain that night. We caught Kendall after he stole the gun. All interesting, perhaps suspicious, but they prove nothing."

They had reached the lake and Lew was untying the raft.

"Where will you hide the diary?" he asked

"I'm working on that. It must be someplace safe yet where the killer thinks he can steal it without getting caught."

"You work on that while I check the net."

Lew returned with three fish.

"Got it doped out?" he asked.

"Sure. Come on and listen."

The fire was burning briskly when they got back to camp. Pierre was boiling meat, had a pot of water heating for tea, and was sliding a whitish substance carefully into the frying pan.

"What's that?" Lew asked.

Pierre beamed. "A surprise, M'sieur. Saved for Sunday dinner. It is mushrooms, the special kind that grow on logs and stumps."

"I hope nobody gets surprised after they eat them," Lew replied.

Pierre drew his plump figure erect. "M'sieur," he protested, "for thirty years I have cooked mushrooms. I have never made a mistake."

"Those kind are okay," Charlie said after inspecting the pan. "No poison varieties look like that."

Charlie drew the diary from his pocket and laid it on the table. All eyes immediately riveted on it.

"I want all of you to see that the two fingerprints are still here. Now I'll wrap it up again to preserve them. Then I'll put the package in the safest place I know, in the peak of the tepee where we sleep."

He noted the differing degrees of surprise before continuing. "There are seven people here, six innocent, one guilty. It is the duty of the six to safeguard this book from the one. It is not only your duty, it is in your own interest to make sure justice prevails. The only way the innocent can clear themselves of suspicion is to expose the guilty.

"If you see anyone slip into the tepee, yell the name as loud as you can. Nobody must enter alone; you must always go in pairs. And one person is never to be left alone in camp. You understand?"

"*Sacre Dieu!*" DuBonner cried. "Must you hang the book where we sleep? Why not put it in the woods with the film?"

"Because only two of us know where the film is hidden," Charlie replied, "and something might happen to us. But now you all know about the diary. Any survivors must see it reaches the proper authorities. That's a responsibility you cannot dodge."

Charlie turned to Lew. "Help me hang it up."

The entire company followed them into the tepee. Even Pierre set his skillet off the flame and trudged along behind.

Charlie bent over and Lew scrambled onto his back. Then Charlie gradually straightened, and Lew climbed until he stood on his companion's shoulders. Then he tied the book to a tepee pole, at one side of the open peak where rain could not reach it.

"There's only one more thing I want to say," Charlie began after lowering Lew back to the ground. "Some of you have suspected Lew or myself of killing Roman. I hope the efforts we've made to solve this crime have changed that."

The mushrooms proved delicious. Pierre had dusted the slices with flour and fried them in hot bear fat. He stood over the fire cooking pan after pan before the group appetite was satisfied.

"Listen," Lew said, "I hear wild geese." As if that had been a signal, a perfect clamor floated down from the sky. "There must be hundreds of them," Lew said. "You know what that means? A cold wave has hit north of here and driven these fellows south."

He stood and stared up into the dark sky, but the daylight was too faded to reveal the long wedge-shaped lines he knew were flying past in the cold, thin air.

Later, Lew accosted Charlie close to the tepee door and said, "I want to know more about those fingerprints on the book. You said you put them there. Whose prints are they? Yours?"

"Hardly. Think I would run a risk like that? No, I had to use a print that would incriminate no one, least of all myself."

"You didn't ..."

Charlie nodded. "Yes, I carefully pressed Roman's own fingers against the oiled book cover. Seems appropriate, doesn't it? The dead man's fingers will point to his murderer."

Chapter 11 – The Expose

"You are smooth," Lew admitted when Charlie told him the fingerprints on the cover of the diary were those of its dead owner. "The murderer will froth like a cat with rabies when he learns this. Think he's going to pull something tonight?"

"No," Charlie said. "This fingerprint stunt has been a surprise. He needs time to dope out a way to handle it. But tomorrow night we must be alert. That will be his last chance before the plane returns."

After the evening meal they discovered another use for the beeswax they had molded into cakes. After eating a full cup of honey, DuBonner complained of a piercing toothache. Charlie looked in his mouth and saw a molar with a gaping cavity in one side, packed full of honey. Charlie dug the honey out with a splinter. Then he had DuBonner rinse his mouth repeatedly with warm water to cleanse the place while he prepared a "filling."

Charlie knew the exposure of nerve ends in a tooth's pulp is what causes pain. So he scraped some of the nap from a clean wool shirt, put it in a teaspoon with beeswax and heated it over the fire. He packed the resulting mix of fluff and wax into the cavity to seal it.

DuBonner complained bitterly as the warm plug was applied. Then the pain eased, and he congratulated Charlie on his skill in emergency dentistry.

As Charlie had predicted, the night passed quietly. After breakfast, he announced, "While we're working with the clay (he had asked Olive to sew another cloth form so he could make two jars at once) there's another project I want your help with. Who will help build a clay oven on the ground outside the cabin? Then we can have roasted bear meat and baked fish, besides a place to finish drying the berries."

Although they would not be there long to enjoy the benefits of the project, everyone volunteered. Lew took the axe to chop a large number of small, straight sticks. Charlie went to the clay bed to loosen up shovelfuls and mix them with water to form a plastic mass.

Twenty feet outside the cabin, he built a 5-inch floor of this clay. Upon this, Lew built a form from the sticks he had cut. He drove four stakes into the floor and piled the slender sticks between them to make a square-cornered bundle 2 feet long, 18 inches high and wide. Then he cut a round block 6 inches thick and 18 long. This he greased so clay would not stick to it and set it on top of the form at the rear to make a chimney hole. The entire form was then covered with green leaves to prevent soft clay working down around the sticks.

Then they plastered an inch of clay all over the form and around the smoke hole block. An opening was left at the front for fuel and utensil access. Then they continued packing more clay over the form until it was a full 2 feet thick. That much material was necessary to hold the heat and also give it strength to resist crumbling.

An hour after the oven was finished, they twisted the smoke hole plug out and saved it to close the opening while food was being baked. A day later, they would pull out the form sticks one at a time starting at the bottom of the pile. The third day, a small fire would be started inside, and the fourth day, a much larger fire built. After that, they could bake whatever they wanted. The four corner stakes would burn out as the oven was heated.

Pierre followed these details with interest. "I regret, M'sieur, that I will not be here to test such an ingenious affair."

"The operation is very simple," Lew told him. "When we want to bake or roast, we build a fire inside the oven. By leaving the door and the smoke hole open, there's enough draft to get up plenty of heat. We keep the fire going a few hours. Then we rake out most of the coals and ashes but push them up against the outside walls. This makes room for a pot or pan, which must be set on four small stones so heat circulates around the sides and bottom, too. The food must be covered, and you want a little water in the dish with meat.

"We block the door with sod, push the smoke hole plug in place and seal both with mud. Then we forget about it for five or six hours. Less time, of course, for bread and biscuits. I wish the oven was finished now. It makes me hungry just telling you how we use it."

At noon, DuBonner sighed as he piled his plate again with boiled meat. "I would give much for a single pickle."

DuBonner's remark gave Charlie an idea. He wondered if he could make vinegar from the berries. He mashed some, added water and a very little sugar and set the mixture out to ferment.

Lew watched him dubiously. "You may think you are making vinegar, but I'd call it wine," he said.

"I didn't add enough sugar for that," Charlie replied. "When it gets sour, I'll strain the pulp out. Next time you go near DuBonner's burned-out camp look for glass jars. I bet he brought in plenty of pickles, and a few of those jars will hold our vinegar nicely."

Charlie expected something to happen that night. It was the murderer's last chance to recover the diary should the plane return on time. He planned to remain awake most of the night, but he did not anticipate trouble early in the evening. None of the six men in the tepee had gone to sleep when loud screams from the cabin brought them all running outside. Lew reached the cabin first. "What is it?" he cried.

Olive stood in the doorway.

"Something crawled over my face. I know it was a snake. You must find it. I'll never be able to sleep if you don't."

Lew lit a torch and stepped inside. Kendall came in with a second torch. They went over the cabin carefully, moving the furniture out to look behind. The other men stood at the doorway.

When the screams began Charlie started out with the others. But he had gone more slowly and halfway to the cabin, he turned around and circled back to the tepee. This, he thought, must be the moment. Even if Olive was truly frightened, the murderer would seize the opportunity to steal the diary. Charlie crouched outside the tepee. He knew he wouldn't be waiting long if the murderer intended to act.

Quick footsteps approached, and a figure darted in through the door. Three violent tugs caused the tepee to sway. He heard cloth rip, and then the tepee grew still.

The man came out, running towards the fire. There had been no wind, and Charlie had purposely neglected drowning the coals with water. He followed slowly. When the man reached the fire, he used a stick to rake some coals bare. Then he flung the book upon them. It blazed up, and the man jumped back, startled at being so plainly outlined by the light.

He almost bumped into Charlie, who said, "Makes a nice fire, doesn't it?"

The other whirled and swung a fist that swept by his face. Charlie seized it with both hands. The man lost his balance, would have tumbled into the fire if it had not been for Charlie's iron grip.

He swung up his other fist, and Charlie released one hand to easily block it. Then he stepped in, tripped his assailant and flung him heavily to the ground. The man was springing up when Charlie pushed him back with an open hand.

"Stop or I'll have to knock you cold," he warned. "It's no use, Striker. I've been thinking it was you."

Striker relaxed, and Charlie stepped back, watching him. The cameraman lay on the ground panting, then he got up slowly and forced a grin.

"You win," he said. "Only you don't. You haven't got a thing on me. The book is burned; it can never be used as evidence."

"What's going on here?" Lew demanded as he ran up and planted himself beside Charlie.

"Striker burned the diary," Charlie said.

The others were close behind Lew.

"Mon Dieu," DuBonner cried. "So it was you?"

"That snake business must have been a stall," Lew growled. "You ought to be ashamed of yourself," he scolded Olive. Then he tried to rake the ashes of the burned book out of the coals.

"Never mind," Charlie said. "It is no use now." Then he turned to Striker. "You might as well tell us why you killed Roman. We know you did it."

"I'm not talking," Striker said, his confidence returning. "They can't hang a man because he burned a book."

"I think they can," Charlie replied.

"We don't need the book," Kendall agreed. "We have the film."

Striker laughed at that.

"I'm not counting on the film," Charlie said. "I know it is blank where Striker said he photographed the fingerprints."

"Blank?" Lew echoed.

"Sure. He left the cap on the lens. That was the moment I knew for sure he killed Roman. I had my doubts when he agreed so quickly to shoot the prints. No excuses about bad light, wrong kind of lens or film for close-ups. He just went to work. Only he left the lens cover on so light wouldn't pass through.

"That would have been easily explained as a nervous oversight, if anyone had noticed besides myself. With no exposures made, all he had to do was destroy the diary. That was the idea, wasn't it, Striker?"

"I told you I'm not saying anything," Striker laughed.

"You don't have to," Charlie said. "It isn't necessary. You don't know it yet, but I've been two moves ahead of you all along."

Striker laughed again, perhaps not as confidently this time.

Lew had been piling more kindling on the fire, and the space about was brilliantly lit. Charlie faced Olive. "You screamed because he asked you to?"

Olive refused to meet his eye.

"So, you two are married, aren't you?" Charlie continued. "That explains what has puzzled me. I suppose you kept the marriage secret on account of her screen career."

"No, that wasn't the reason," Striker spoke up. "We had separated, once. Then we met again when I started working for DuBonner. She wasn't so sure she wanted to come back to me. So I agreed to keep quiet until she made up her mind."

Charlie still watched Olive. "You've been playing with fire, and you've laid yourself open to suspicion as an accessory to murder."

"Leave her out of this," Striker snapped. "She doesn't know anything. It isn't criminal to scream when a snake crawls across your face, is it? You haven't got a thing on her—or me."

DuBonner wagged his head sadly. "I fear he is right, M'sieur. You seem to have bungled. If you had hidden the book with the film as I suggested, you would still have evidence. Now you have nothing."

"Think so?" Charlie asked. His voice was calm. Not a trace of disappointment or regret on his face.

"Didn't I say I was always two jumps ahead of you, Striker?" Charlie said. "Tonight you did just what I wanted you to do. I had to put the book in a place where you could get to it and burn it. Then I could be sure. You came through splendidly, convicted yourself beyond any doubt."

"You're bluffing," Striker replied. "What can you prove?"

"Listen closely," Charlie said, addressing the others. "All of you know Striker burned the book. You will all swear in court he did that?"

Olive spoke up, "I won't."

"You won't be asked. A wife can't testify against her husband. Besides, there's enough proof without you. If the book wasn't burned, if the fingerprints were undamaged, then my case would be tight."

"Sure," Striker admitted. "Only that's a pretty big 'if' to hurdle."

"Not so big," Charlie told him. "Not so big—for here's the book, good as new." He pulled a bundle from his shirt.

Unwrapping it, he said, "Stand over here beside me, Lew. Don't let anyone come close." Charlie held it up and showed them the two fingerprints, outlined with flour as distinctly as before.

"Is this magic?" DuBonner cried. "We saw the ashes in the fire."

Striker was silent, his features frozen hard.

"Not magic, just forethought." Charlie continued. "You have all heard of the fakers who sell soap at county fairs? They wrap a dollar bill up with each cake and sell the package for a quarter. You think you're making 75 cents, only when you undo the soap there isn't any dollar bill. That's what happened to the book. You thought you saw me wrap it up the second time and hang it in the tepee. But I switched packages. I used a dummy, mostly bark, and put the real one in my shirt. Striker burned the dummy."

Tense silence enveloped the circle. Lew was staring at his companion with keen admiration. "How that boy can bluff," he thought. "He knows those fingerprints aren't worth last summer's bird nest. But he's got me standing here with a club to guard them, and Striker is going to crack. I can see it coming."

Then, Striker did crack.

"All right!" he admitted. "I killed him. Of course I did. He wasn't fit to live. But it wasn't murder. He jumped on me when I went down to the lake and found him threatening Olive. We fought. She will tell you that. She saw us before she ran back to the cabin. I called to her, told her not to arouse the rest. I was on the bottom, getting pounded pretty badly, so I reached down, got hold of a rock and let him have it.

"There isn't a court in the world that will convict me for that. Not when Olive tells the kind of threats he made." Striker sat down on the ground. His face was streaming sweat but his voice grew calm.

"I'm sorry it had to happen here. You all have been pretty decent to me. There's nothing for you to worry about. I won't hurt anybody. Nobody is in danger. I'll tell exactly how it happened, too, when we return. I'm glad I did it, I'm not sorry. He wasn't fit to live."

"I guess that ends it," Charlie said. "We better get some sleep."

"Sleep?" DuBonner cried. "I sit beside the fire until morning. I could never sleep with a murderer."

"Why so fussy, now?" Charlie asked. "You've been doing it right along and it never bothered you before. Striker, I'm half-sorry I had to do this. But I didn't want to be suspected of murder myself."

Even now, Charlie could not repress a feeling of pity, even admiration for the man. He had killed Roman, a snake blackmailing his wife. It was truly nasty business, but he felt Olive was entitled to the protection of her husband.

Striker stood, stretched his arms high. "If we're going to sit here all night, how about some bigger wood to hold the fire?" He threw on several chunks. "I'm glad this is over. You don't know what a relief it is. The quicker that plane gets here, the better I'll feel."

Lew's keen ears caught the drone of powerful gasoline motors shortly after sunrise.

"She's coming," was all he said. Then the sound became loud

enough for the others to hear, too.

"There it is," Kendall cried, pointing to a silver bird-shaped object high in the sky. He ran excitedly across the little clearing.

"He won't stay long, after he reads my notice," Lew said.

"We might as well get our few belongings ready," DuBonner said. "I have kept a secret, M'sieur," he added, turning to Charlie.

"My pilot, he had instructions to bring several hundred pounds of food in case we were not finished with our picture. It is all yours, M'sieur, for as we depart your hospitality, I gladly pay my bill. We have caused you much trouble, much work. Shall I add twenty dollars a day for the time we have lived with you?"

Charlie expressed himself entirely satisfied with that payment. But as he watched the director count out the money, he thought, "Funny stuff, money. I couldn't buy a slice of bacon with a hundred dollar bill up here."

Lew watched the actors preparing to leave with much satisfaction. "What a relief it will be when they're gone," he told Charlie.

"We can stop this detective business and get back to work. There's plenty we have to do before cold weather settles in. I'm tired of trapping a murderer. I'm ready to start trapping fur!"

The End

War Comes to Shadow Lake

Chapter 1 – Footprints from Nowhere

It was quite dark when Charlie left the shore of Shadow Lake and started through the trees separating it and the cabin. He was glad the path was so familiar he could walk it blindfolded. Crossing the little cleared space where they had cooked and eaten in the fair weather of a summer now past, Charlie paused before the split-log door of the cabin and slipped the canvas pack from his shoulders.

His nostrils caught a new odor in the night air. Mingled with the clean breath of pine and the pungent aroma of burning wood was the richer smell of cooking food. It brought a glow of anticipation to his eyes. Charlie opened the door, picked up his pack and shoved it in ahead of his weary legs. An impatient howl greeted him.

"Hurry, can't you?" Lew demanded. "You're letting in the cold."

Charlie shoved the door shut, turned and scanned the scene before him. The cheerful cabin glowed with firelight that flowed out of a wide-throated fireplace. Directly before the fire sat the folding bathtub made of rubber cloth and aluminum tubing that Helm had given them when he and his party of hunters left Shadow Lake.

Steam poured up from the big fabric container, and Lew's head was just visible over a side wall. All around Lew, pale blue suds billowed, and it smelled like a hothouse of hyacinths. The odor almost covered the delicious smells steaming out from beneath the lid of a cast iron Dutch oven setting beside the fire.

"Stew me for a prune," Charlie declared. "What are you doing?"

Lew grinned. "Haven't you ever heard of a bubble bath?"

"I've heard of bubble dancers," Charlie replied.

"A bubble bath," Lew explained, "is tops for relaxing sore muscles. And anybody who worked as hard as I did today deserves one."

Charlie unloaded his rifle and stood it in a corner.

"Where did you get that, that bubble stuff?"

"Don't you remember? Helm cleaned out his wife's toilet case when they left. Said he couldn't be bothered with so much junk, though I guess his real reason was being mad at her for trying to kill him. Anyway, he left a package of bath salts. Smells great, don't it?"

"Like a convention of pantywaists," Charlie replied. "What's in the Dutch oven?"

"I lined the bottom with sliced bacon," Lew began. "Then I put three pounds of deer meat on top of that. I added water, just a little, and let it slow-cook about six hours, to keep the flavor in. Then, a little while ago, I dumped in some dried onions and some of the mushrooms we dried last fall. Last, I made a thin sauce of flour and water and poured that over top. Want to help me name it?"

"No, but I'll help you eat it." Charlie lifted the lid and took a look. Satisfied, he sat down on one of the log benches and pulled off his boots. Lew stepped out of the tub and dried himself before the fire.

After he had dressed and carried the bath water outside, he made tea, and while it steeped, he moistened a pan of cold biscuits and propped them slanting before the blaze. Charlie slowly rubbed his bare feet together. They ached to the bone from his long tramp. "Did I hear something about you working hard today?" he asked.

Lew nodded as he filled two plates. The meat was so tender the slices broke and fell back into the rich gravy when he tried to lift them on a fork. "I chopped enough logs to build the fur shed. They're all piled and sorted for length. Each is rough-barked and notched. They'll go together with very little fitting."

"That's swell," Charlie said. "What with the weather getting colder, it won't be long before we need to store furs." He broke four biscuits and stirred the pieces into the gravy on his plate.

"How did the surveying go?" Lew asked.

"I worked an hour later than I should, but I wanted to clean the matter up." Charlie took a notebook from his pocket and opened it beside his plate. "I figure the south loop of our trapline is 32 miles, and there are at least one hundred and thirty good places to set traps."

Charlie and Lew never set a long line without first scouting in all directions and then working out connecting trails that include the very best spots to trap. Charlie had just finished such a survey of the land south and east of their cabin. As he walked, he made notes recording distances, compass headings, and locations for sets. Now, only a short time would be needed to put out a long line.

In addition to saving time, the organization increases efficiency.

They had been able to bring only a small number of steel traps into the northern wilderness and needed to obtain maximum results with each.

After Charlie finished eating, he went to a wall cupboard and brought back a pad of cross-ruled paper, tore off four sheets and used flour and water to paste them into a large square. This provided enough space to lay out a map of the 32-mile line using a scale of 2 inches to the mile. The rule lines created 10 squares for each mile of ground.

Charlie employed the timber cruiser's way of estimating distance by counting 2,000 paces to the mile. This made scale mapping comparatively easy and surprisingly accurate. With such a map. One man could lay down a hundred traps, give his notes to his companion, and be assured the other could run the line and not miss a set.

A hard-lead pencil is best for marking maps. Soft lead smudges and ink runs. But a hard pencil point creases the paper, and those lines may be followed even if the lead is worn away.

Charlie worked for an hour on the map, until his eyes started to smart from the strain. Finally, he pushed the work away.

Lew set out the bathtub again, filled it two-thirds full and added a liberal quantity of salts. Charlie undressed and lay back in the warm water with a sigh. He began talking to Lew about the halfway shelter they expected to build tomorrow.

It would be stocked with candles, kindling, dry birch bark, a flint and steel as well as a few matches that had been dipped in melted wax. They bent the top of each match tin with a straight fold to protect the contents but allow anyone to spring the edge open with fingers stiff from the cold. Every precaution was taken to ensure the ease and speed of building a fire. The shelter would be well marked on the map and on the trail. Also, they planned to blaze short trails out in all directions, like the spokes of a wheel. Then, if they missed the path in a blinding storm, there still would be a chance of cutting a short line and following it in.

They left the next morning before sunrise. It would take a day and a half to build the shelter, a rough table and bench. So they planned to spend three days on the work and round-trip journey.

Supplies included both axes, the shovel, nails, two duck-feather sleeping robes, flour, 20 pounds of venison, tea, sugar, dried blueberries, combination guns, and a kit of cooking tools.

Charlie figured that by cutting diagonally across the oblong trapline, they could reach the halfway point walking 17 miles. That should take five-and-a-half hours, and they would use this as a check against the accuracy of Charlie's notes.

They reached the location 15 minutes short of the calculated time, and Charlie suspected Lew had walked faster than his usual gait.

The site was a timbered slope down to a small bog. The shelter would have an open front so it could be heated with an outside fire, and by using the hill as a rear wall, there were only two sides to build. Charlie laid out the design with the rear somewhat wider than the front. "I've often wondered if a jug-shaped shelter would hold heat better than one with straight sides," he said. "This is a chance to find out."

They cut away the hill with shovels, piling the dirt close by to bank around the log sides and to cover the roof. They were both expert axe men, and the walls were more than half-finished when night fell. They built a big fire before the unfinished structure and went to sleep hoping it would not snow before morning. The night stayed clear, and the temperature dropped sharply.

By noon, the sides were complete and the roof covered with neatly halved logs. Weeks before, they had gathered every empty tin from the site of DuBonner's burned-out movie crew camp. They had also saved each empty tin from Helm's cumbersome stores.

The tins had been split open and flattened into sheets, and each time Charlie had surveyed the line, he had carried a load of them here. Now there were enough to cover the joints between the roof logs. After these little tin sheets were nailed down, they heaped dirt over everything. Then they stocked the birch bark and kindling, piled a rick of firewood along an outside wall. The bog would furnish water, cloudy but pure. When the bog froze, they would melt snow for water.

Lew wanted to start home, but Charlie was curious to see how the shelter would heat. He insisted they spend another night, and to his satisfaction, the structure heated very well, warmed by the blaze outdoors. Charlie got up once to add fuel, not because it was necessary but because he wanted to test his skill in waking up at a selected hour. This is very important when sleeping in an open shelter. Men, especially exhausted men, have been known to sleep into a frozen coma and perish when the fire died with no one aroused to rekindle it.

Charlie glanced at his watch and saw he had missed midnight by only eight minutes, which was rather good. When he went outside the air was filled with large flakes, the first snow of the season. He watched it settle with pleasure.

Next morning, two inches of snow blanketed the ground and plumed each tree, bush and stalk of dead summer grass. Lew placed a piece of dry bark before the fire and stood upon it in his socks while warming his boots in the heat. He took a little cylinder of birch bark from his pocket, removed a stopper, and rubbed a mixture of deer fat and beeswax over the seams of the foot gear. He looked at the soles.

"Getting thin, Charlie," he observed. "I'll be running barefoot if we don't get to work on some moccasins."

They packed up after breakfast and started home. They were always a little anxious when they left the cabin unguarded. Theft was not the worry. They never locked the door when gone. A needy traveler was always welcome to enter the shelter and eat the food inside. But there was a remote possibility of the wrong visitor. A man who might destroy or more likely carelessly handle fire. A burn-out of the cabin would be a serious blow, perhaps a fatal one in bitter weather.

Lew started out whistling cheerfully to show his companion he was not worried, or at least not much. He glanced over the snow, unmarked save for an occasional rabbit track and the tiny trails of mice. "There isn't another human within a hundred miles," he declared.

The trail climbed a moderate slope, which because of stony soil and a northerly exposure was almost devoid of timber. Lew had quickened his stride to take advantage of the open walking.

Then he halted so abruptly Charlie bumped into him. The deeper snow 10 yards ahead held fresh boot prints.

"What the devil does this mean?" Lew asked.

"Means you spoke too soon about nobody being within a hundred miles," Charlie replied.

They detoured a little so as not to tramp up the marks. Each was clearly outlined. The boots were smaller than what they wore, with a deeper imprint at the heel. They followed this strange trail for about 70 feet. Then the tracks vanished, just ceased to be.

Lew rubbed his chin. "Who the deuce did this?" he asked.

"Not who, Lew," Charlie replied. "But how? Where did they go? And where did they come from back there at the other end?"

"Good gosh!" Lew exclaimed looking around. "It's uncanny. I never took any stock in ghosts before. But this could change my mind. No human being could do this."

Chapter 2 – A Face at the Window

Baffled, Charlie and Lew stood gazing at the short trail of footprints. "You're right," Charlie said slowly. "A man can't materialize, leave a few tracks and then disappear without leaving a trace."

"I'm going to circle around and see if I can cut any more tracks," Lew said. "Maybe snow blew across the open ground and filled up the missing part of the trail."

Charlie picked up a handful of the soft snow and compressed it between his fingers. "Snow this wet?" he said. "I don't think so."

The search for more tracks proved futile.

"The little man who wasn't here," Charlie mused and then began to whistle the popular tune.

"How about another circle farther out?" Lew asked.

"What for?" Charlie replied. "I have a hunch we ought to hurry back to the cabin instead." The thought that all might not be right at Shadow Lake was growing more persistent each minute.

"You're right," Lew agreed, starting off in a shuffling half-run that would cover the distance with surprising speed.

Charlie only grunted.

The nearer they came to the cabin, the more familiar the path became. Consequently, their pace quickened even more, and Lew was trotting smartly when an hour later he pointed ahead and cried out, "I see the top of the chimney. At least that much is okay."

The building itself then appeared, and a glance around showed the smooth carpet of surrounding snow unmarked by tracks. They pushed the door open and entered. All was as they had left it.

"It had me worried," Lew confessed. "And the more I thought about what could have happened, the worse it seemed."

"Sure," Charlie agreed. "That's always the way with worry."

After a closer look around revealed all in order, Charlie said, "You know, I think we should finish the fur shed today. It isn't noon yet, and you have all the logs notched. Come on. Let's get to work."

The shed would be 8 feet on a side, built against the west side of the cabin to eliminate the need for one of the walls. Furthermore, the shed wouldn't have an outside door. Entrance would be from inside the cabin only, gained by cutting a small door through the cabin wall.

"I'm not counting on fur thieves up here," Lew had remarked, "but if they come, they'll have to break into the cabin and wake us up before they can get in the shed."

A fur shed without outside doors or windows presented ventilation problems. But they left small spaces along the eaves where the roof joined the sides, openings too small for porcupines. They could hardly be closed against mice, and ever since the first cool days had driven mice closer to the cabin, they had been trapping them and already had caught several dozen. Two kinds of improvised mouse traps were used. One was a clay jar filled two-thirds with water. A stick furnished a ramp from the floor up to the lip of the jar, and inside on the water floated a wooden chip baited with toasted meat.

Mice that climbed the stick and jumped on the chip invariably tipped over and drowned.

The second trap was simply a catsup bottle coated with grease and shoved neck first into a crevice of the wall where it extended horizontally out above another jar of water. Drawn by the smell of the grease, mice climbed out on the bottle, lost their footing, and fell off to drown in the jar beneath.

In any case, mice would prove more aggravating than destructive. Real losses, however, might occur should a wolverine or other marauder enter. The roof was the vulnerable spot, and they planned to make this so heavy and strong even a wolverine couldn't rip it loose.

As expected, three walls went up quickly. Most of the logs already were in place when Lew stopped to cook a late lunch. Charlie stayed on the job until his companion called him in to eat.

Lew also had chopped 10-foot logs and split them for roof timbers so stiff it was not necessary to use rafters or braces. The half-logs were simply hewed until the edges fit. This roof would be flat but slanting down from the cabin. In ordinary construction, this might leave a triangular opening between the top of the log wall and the roof, an opening that must be filled with shorter timbers tediously hewed to fit.

Instead, Lew placed all of the side wall logs with the thicker ends against the cabin. This gradually created a slant, which increased in pitch as each log was added. By the time the final log was placed at the top of the wall, the roof lay flush along the top log. Such construction may not present the best appearance, but it is stronger, tighter, and easier to complete.

The split roof timbers were covered with two layers of bark pried from good-sized trees in the fall. These bark sheets had been soaked in the lake until supple and then dried flat under heavy stones. They went rapidly in place, layers staggered so joints and any defects in the bark did not coincide. Knowing that trees die when rings of bark are removed, they had stripped only a few big trees close to the cabin, marking these for winter firewood.

To protect the bark, it was covered evenly with flat stones. Then moist clay was tamped in the cracks between the stones. This made the roof somewhat watertight and also prevented fire from sparks sifting down from the chimney onto the bark. The finished roof was solid against water, fire and marauders.

The floor was just dirt pounded hard with a log tamper. This offered another potential weak point, but after the ground froze solid, they doubted any animal would dig down deep enough to burrow beneath the bottom log. When really cold weather arrived, they would pour water on the ground outside to provide a sheeting of solid ice.

There was an hour of daylight left when they climbed down from the roof of the finished shed. They stood surveying their work, finding it entirely satisfactory. Then they started chopping firewood. Usually the day's supply was cut after breakfast. No matter what hour they started, they invariably worked up a surplus to store for winter. This surplus was piled in a long rick close to the cabin wall farthest from the fireplace. This would surely be appreciated later, should winter weather confine them to the cabin.

"Another thing about having wood on hand," Lew commented, "is nobody must go out before breakfast. When you wake up to a foot of wet snow, axe work before eating doesn't click."

Charlie carried in the last armful of wood for the night and dumped it on the floor beside the fireplace. Lew opened a sack of flour and mixed a double batch of biscuits. Just before pinching them into shape, he stirred two cups of dried blueberries into the dough. The supply of fruit they had dried last summer was holding up well.

Lew put slices of venison in a skillet, added suet and a little water, covered the pan and started it slowly bubbling over coals raked out of a deep bed. Charlie carried in water from the creek and made tea. Then he took two candles off a shelf and lighted them from the fire's blaze. After dinner, Lew went outside and took down four long, slim strips of wood from underneath the roof edge.

"The snow reminded me we'll wake up some morning to find three feet of it," he said. "Then we'll have to have snowshoes. I'm going to work these frames down now."

The strips had been split from 6-inch birch saplings without knots or other flaws. Each was about 1-1/2 inches square and had been taken from close to the outside, away from the soft heart wood. Lew whetted his knife keen and started shaving a strip thinner, working with the grain and being especially careful in the center where the frame would be bent almost double to form the toe of the snowshoe.

Charlie joined in. They had shaved and whittled in silence for some 40 minutes when Lew got up and walked softly to the door. He pushed it open, glanced outside, shut it and then came back to his seat in front of the fire. Charlie saw he was frowning.

"Hear something?" Charlie asked quietly, aware that Lew's ears were so keen he often heard things others did not.

"Somebody walking outside," Lew said. "Could have been a critter, but I doubt it."

Charlie gazed thoughtfully into the fire, thinking of the mysterious footprints they had discovered that morning. He wondered if they were going to solve that mystery now.

Lew seemed to acquire a case of nerves as the minutes dragged by. Finally, after sitting perfectly still for five minutes, he went outside and Charlie heard him come around the corner of the cabin and stop before a window of oiled cloth. When he came back in, he said, "I found tracks in the snow underneath the window."

Charlie reached in the corner, picked up his rifle and slipped a shell in the chamber. Then he laid the weapon close to his feet.

They worked in silence for another quarter-hour. Lew raising his head to listen at times, and when he did, Charlie stopped working with his fingers not far from the gun. But each time, Lew relaxed and began cutting again. Finally, he let his knife fall to the floor. When Charlie leaned over to get it, Lew leaned over, too, and whispered, "He's at the window. I saw the firelight shine off his eyes."

Charlie was ready to pick up the gun. But before he could, Lew addressed the situation in his own inimitable way. He looked casually at the window and said, "If you're through looking us over, why don't you come on in and get warm?"

They heard a sharply indrawn gasp. Then silence. Finally, footsteps no longer stealthy crunched through the snow towards the door. Charlie stood, holding the loaded gun in his hands.

Fingers fumbled at the thong latch that hung outside. The bar rasped up from its wood sockets, and the door opened slowly. The moonlit sky illuminated a figure heavily bundled in fur.

Chapter 3 – A Ship in the Night

Lew spoke first to the fur-wrapped figure in the doorway. "Are you coming in? I'm getting cold from the draft."

"I don't know," a woman replied.

The voice brought Lew to his feet. "I'll be a ringtail razopotamus!" he exclaimed.

She advanced two steps towards him, but cautiously left the door open behind. "More trouble," Lew muttered under his breath.

The quick ears of their visitor heard. She whirled around and started for the door. "I won't trouble you," she cried. "I thought woodsmen were hospitable, even kind. I see I'm mistaken."

"Stop," Charlie ordered.

She paused, compelled by the quiet force in his voice.

"Lew didn't mean to be unkind. He was just surprised. Five-hundred-dollar mink coats don't often walk into our cabin, you know."

"This isn't a five-hundred-dollar coat," she retorted, and Charlie thought he could detect a sob in her voice. "It cost three thousand."

That brought Lew to his feet. "Charlie," he exclaimed, "we're sitting on the wrong end of this fur game."

"What are you talking about?" she demanded. Then, before Lew could answer, she spoke almost hysterically, "Don't think for one minute that because I'm a girl I can't take care of myself. Don't come one step closer." Her hand plunged into a pocket of the coat and came out holding a short revolver. It gleamed in the firelight.

Lew sat down. "I was only going to shut the door," he said. "It's still open, you know."

"Put that gun away," Charlie said. "Nobody is going to hurt you."

"You better not. I am not afraid."

"Yes, you are afraid," Charlie replied. "You're scared half to death. Your hand shakes so if you tried to shoot you'd probably hit one of your own feet. Now come up to the fire where you can get warm."

"And," Lew added, "Please shut that door. Or let me walk by you so I can. I don't mind chopping firewood, but not enough to heat the whole outdoors. There's too much of it to heat."

He detoured slowly past her, pulled the door shut, and dropped the bar in place. Returning, he dragged another bench up to the opposite side of the fire. "Sit down," he said kindly. "I'm not inhospitable to strangers, really I'm not. I just don't like visitors standing outside my window spying on me. It doesn't look friendly."

"I was afraid to come in," she admitted, laying her coat on the bed. "I didn't know what kind of men you were."

"Well, you still don't know much about us," Lew grinned. "But I can tell you this. My worst fault is laziness. I hate to get up earlier than four in the morning, and I simply will not spend more than 16 hours a day chopping wood." Lew was speaking lightly, to give the girl time to recover. He saw the effort she was making to steady herself, saw the trembling of her lips. Charlie calmly stirred the fire.

After a minute, she said, "You must be wondering what brought me to this wilderness. I don't know where to start."

"I'll bet you're hungry," Lew said.

She started. "I had forgotten. Actually, I'm starved. I haven't eaten a meal since night before last."

That made Lew jump. "Good gosh!" he cried. "That was two days ago. It's a wonder you're still alive. You can start with some of these blueberry muffins. It won't take me five minutes to warm the venison and gravy, and I'll make fresh tea. Take your time figuring out the things you want to tell us, and where to begin."

"You're ... you're being awfully good to me," she said. "I have walked ever since morning, and this is the only cabin I saw. I simply couldn't walk any more, but still, I was afraid you ..."

"Might be something worse," Lew finished for her.

The girl removed a brown turban hat matching her coat, unfastened talon galoshes and slipped them from her walking oxfords. When she stood up to lay the hat beside her coat, they saw she was dressed in ski pants and a tight-fitting jacket. Her hair gleamed like burnished copper. Glancing up from the table, Lew was suddenly aware of what a drab place the cabin had been before she arrived. Then he scowled and hastily put the thought out of his mind. He sent a guilty look towards Charlie, wondering if his companion had been watching him.

But Charlie was gazing thoughtfully into the flames, the strong lines of his face composed and calm.

"Come on," Lew said. "Dinner's ready."

She ate eagerly, wolfing down six biscuits and then all of the venison. She drank two cups of tea, and Lew was beginning to wonder what else he had in the cabin that could be quickly prepared when she said, "That was the best meal I've had in months."

Pacing nervously before the fire, she began her story.

"I suppose you want to know how I happened to come here alone and half-scared to death, as you said a little while ago. You were right. I thought about trying to go on without stopping."

"It's a good thing you didn't," Charlie said gravely. "So far as we know, there isn't another cabin within a hundred miles."

"That can't be!" she cried, fear again filling her eyes.

"Where do you think you are?" Charlie asked quietly.

"Not far from Ottawa, or at least someplace on a line connecting Ottawa and Winnipeg."

"You're many hundreds of miles north of that," Charlie said.

"I don't understand," she said. "We left Winnipeg Tuesday."

Charlie took out his pocket calendar and checked the days. He never went into the wilderness without a calendar that showed the time of sunrise and sunset. These last figures were useful in case a watch went wrong or simply stopped. Knowing the approximate time of sunrise, a timepiece may be reset with fair accuracy.

"That was Tuesday," he said. "Today is Thursday."

She frowned, hands twisting nervously. After a minute, Lew started to fidget on his bench. She glanced up, saw his impatience and smiled. "I'm sorry. I promised to tell you all about it, didn't I?"

Lew nodded. "I can't deny I'm curious. Swell-looking girls in expensive furs don't walk into our trapping camp every day."

"I'm Sally Bern. Tuesday night, I went aboard my father's dirigible airship to accompany him on a trip from Winnipeg to Ottawa."

"A dirigible?" Charlie asked.

"Yes. My father is Colonel Bern, the scientist and explorer. This was a trip to test his latest invention. I don't suppose you know much about what is called a topographic map?"

"We have used enough to know a lot of them are bunk," Lew said dryly. "We usually go ahead and make a map of our own."

"I'm glad you understand that. Dad discovered so many differences between the maps and the country they were supposed to represent he finally decided to invent a way to record land with mechanical precision. So, he invented the Bern aerial topographic camera."

"Sounds interesting," Charlie encouraged her.

"It is more than interesting, it's remarkable," she said with pride. "On a clear day, our camera photographs a strip of ground two miles wide from an elevation of 4,000 feet. We tried to use an airplane, but the plane was too fast for clear photos. So Dad ordered the dirigible, and we began testing last week. At the slower speed, the camera can accurately record 50 square miles of ground each hour. That is more than a surveying crew could finish in a month. The camera exposes a continuous strip of film eight inches wide. Because of special lenses, this film accurately reflects the elevation of the land; every hill and valley measured more accurately than it could be with field instruments."

"I suppose quite a lot has to be done with the film before it can be read like a map?" Charlie asked.

"Of course," Sally said. "The method is Dad's secret, but I will say it depends upon the shading of the tones in the photo. When films are developed, they are enlarged ten times. Then a trained operator wearing special glasses reads it and transfers the data to a map."

"You know a lot about map making," Lew said with a grin.

"I've heard Dad go over it so often," she replied modestly.

"How about water courses and timbered areas? Do they show up on the film?" Charlie asked.

"Certainly. Timber can be plotted out to the acre, and what's more, the film shows the height of the trees. Rivers and lakes are all accurately located. Once the key to interpreting these things is learned, the images may be read very quickly."

"OK," Lew said. "We got the camera business. But it doesn't explain how you happened to drop in for supper."

"Dad planned a test trip that would last two weeks. He intended to fly up near the Arctic Circle, to test the camera in frozen wilderness. But first we were going to Ottawa to pick up two of the Geological Survey men to give them a demonstration. No one believes it will work as well as Dad knows it will.

"We planned to leave Winnipeg at midnight. The camera was installed, and Dad was at home packing the film. I got tired of waiting, so I went out to the airport alone and boarded the ship. I was tired and went to bed. When I woke, I was alone. Dad was nowhere in sight.

"The dirigible has two cabins connected by a narrow walk. Dad and I use the forward cabin; the crew of two sleep in the rear where the engines are located. When I didn't see Dad, I called the rear cabin on the speaking tube. Max, the lens expert, told me Dad was doing some fine adjustments on the camera and wouldn't be finished until noon.

"It was windy and cold. I didn't want to walk back to the other cabin. Then Max came in with hot coffee. He told me Dad would be along in a few minutes to eat breakfast with me. I drank a cup, and that was the last thing I clearly remember until I awoke sometime in the night. My head hurt and I could hardly move my eyes.

"I must have dozed off again soon after that. I remember waking again when it was daylight. But then I slept again, and when I finally got strength enough to climb out of the berth it was night. The coffee, of course, had been drugged."

"Why?" Charlie asked.

"That's what I can't explain. There isn't any logical reason."

"Drugged coffee would have put you to sleep for a few hours," Charlie told her. "Apparently, you were given something more afterwards. Are there any sore places on your arm?"

"Why, yes. My arm still aches," she said, flexing it slowly.

"The last time I woke the ship was moving slowly, and I could hardly hear the engines. I felt better. So I got up to look out. It was night, but I could see we were not more than a hundred feet off the ground, and I could see it was covered with snow.

"When the craft grazed the tops of some trees, I went to the door and looked towards the other cabin. Max was leaning out over the catwalk. He didn't see me, but I saw he held a rope in his hands that was hanging down. The rope started to jerk, and then the other member of the crew, Andre, come up hand over hand. Max pulled the rope up and they both went into the cabin."

Charlie nodded. "So that solves the disappearing trail of footprints. Andre made the mysterious tracks in the snow. He took a few steps hanging onto the rope and then climbed back to the airship."

"I heard Andre say they couldn't land," Sally continued. "I knew something was wrong, then. The engines picked up a little, and we went a little faster, but we didn't gain much altitude."

"That would indicate a leak in a gas bag," Charlie said.

"Yes," Sally agreed. "I bolted the cabin door on the inside and took out the gun I carry in my traveling bag. I had a bad time then worrying what had become of Dad. Had they killed him and thrown his body out? I almost went crazy imagining the worst. Two hours later, the ship struck the ground with a jar that rolled me out of my berth. I heard Max and Andre shouting. The gas bag jerked this way then that. I had to hold on to keep from being thrown to the floor.

"I knew I must get away. I put on my coat and hat, took my handbag and my gun, and looked for some food to take. But all the food was stored in the rear cabin. I finally found four candy bars and stuffed them in a pocket.

"I went out the door, saw Max and Andre were outside, trying to rope the bag so it wouldn't roll. I jumped to the ground and started running. I expected to hear them coming after me, but they didn't. They must have been too busy to notice. I ran until I came to the edge of a lake. Then I turned and followed the shore until morning.

"When it grew light, I saw I was leaving a plain trail of footprints Max and Andre could follow and find me if they wanted. I ran until I could not stand and then sat down beside a tree. I ate the candy, tried to get a drink from the lake by lifting some water in my hands, but I didn't get much. I knew better than to eat snow.

"I ran again for I don't know how long, then I crawled under a fallen tree and lay down in the snow. My coat kept me warm, and I remember thinking it had been a good investment after all.

"I went to sleep with the revolver in my hand. It was nearly dark when I awoke. I knew nobody was following me then. I started along the lake shore thinking somebody must live close to it. Finally, I saw the path that brought me here."

She had twisted her fingers continuously during the story, and now she grew more openly agitated. "Why did Max and Andre kidnap me and steal the ship? Where is Dad? Did they drug him or did they kill him? Why did they turn off our planned course? Can you help me figure these things out?"

"You're asking a lot," Charlie said. "But I think I can answer some of it. First, stop worrying about your father. I don't think he was on the ship when it left Winnipeg. I think the hijackers took off before he came aboard. I don't think they wanted to kidnap you, either. They probably got quite a jolt when they heard your voice in the speaking tube. When Max answered, did he sound surprised?"

"Why yes, I believe he did."

"Then your father is safe in Winnipeg. You would be there, too, if you had waited for him."

"Oh, I hope you're right," she cried. "But it still doesn't explain why they did this. The ship is worth a lot of money, but it wouldn't do them much good to steal it. They would eventually have to land at an airport for fuel. There would be no way to disguise such a craft, and they would be arrested. I can't understand what they hoped to gain."

"I can," Charlie said. "There are men who would stop at nothing for the prize your father dangled before these two. This is deadly business, Sally, and you can thank Heaven alone that you are still alive."

Chapter 4 – Only Fools Deny Their Fear

"If this camera does what you claim," Charlie continued, "a dozen countries would not hesitate to commit murder for it. There's a world war going on. Do you know how valuable accurate maps of enemy country are in wartime? This camera has tremendous military value. You say this camera shows elevation? All right, suppose a plane flies over enemy lines today and photographs the layout. They repeat tomorrow. A comparison of the two films will show if any changes have been made—gun emplacements, trenches, tank traps will all be revealed, maybe even after efforts have been made to camouflage them from the air. Why, this invention could be pure dynamite. I'm surprised your father didn't know that. You said he's a colonel."

Sally nodded. "A colonel in the first world war. Perhaps he did know, but maybe he just didn't tell me."

"If he knew," Charlie told her bluntly, "he would have had more sense than to let you go along on a test flight."

Her eyes flashed angrily. "You can't talk about my father that way, and anybody able to invent such a camera must have sense."

"I meant the common variety," Charlie said dryly. "If we hadn't happened to build our cabin here, you would never have made it out. No, I don't think your father realized, or he would have had government protection for this flight. Where did he pick up Max and Andre?"

"Max is an expert on optics. He worked with Dad in developing the camera. I don't know where Father met him. Andre is the mechanic. His only job is to keep the engines running. I believe he came with the dirigible from the factory."

"Sounds about right," Charlie said. "Such agents are always embedded in key industries. How long was Max with you?"

"Three months."

Charlie nodded again. "Okay. I'll stop now. I'm not running your dad down for the fun of it. But I think you need to know he needlessly risked both an invaluable invention and his daughter."

"Well, maybe he was careless," Sally admitted. "But how does knowing that help me now? It doesn't recover the camera."

"No," Charlie admitted. "It doesn't. And the beans are burned no matter whose fault it may be. But won't your father be able to send out an alarm and planes to search for you?"

"Of course. But you say we are hundreds of miles north of the route between Winnipeg and Ottawa. He won't know to search here."

"That's true. But he'll never stop until he finds you."

"Why did Max and Andre go so far north?" she asked.

"That part isn't hard to figure. We are on a direct line with the North Atlantic. They were headed for the southern tip of Greenland. Maybe Iceland. A boat is probably waiting there hidden among the icebergs, to take the pair and the stolen camera back to Europe."

Anger filled Sally's eyes, and she jumped to her feet.

"They can't do that! The camera must be recovered."

"I knew it," Lew groaned under his breath. "Just as soon as that fur coat walked in through the door, I knew we were in for it."

Lew watched his companion's face, searching for a clue of what he was thinking. But Charlie stared impassively into the fire.

Sally could restrain her impatience no longer. "You are going to help me, aren't you? Why don't you say something? Of course, if you're afraid ..."

Lew turned slowly on the bench.

"Lady," he said firmly. "That won't get you any place with us. We don't take bait. Sure, we sympathize with girls in distress. But we don't stick our necks out just because some cutie taunts us. And, yes, to be honest, I am afraid. Only a fool denies his natural fear before getting involved in this kind of business. Foreign agents are plenty hard. If they weren't, they'd be in another game."

Sally sat back down, fighting for control of her feelings. Then she said softly, "I'm sorry. I can't seem to do anything right. But I feel so helpless, so desperate. I'm in a pretty bad jam myself, but I'm thinking of Dad and his camera most. I'll do anything to have you help me recover it from these thieves. I mustn't let my father's work be used to kill our own Canadian soldiers. You can have this coat! It will bring a thousand dollars from any fur buyer. I also have some money, not much, but a little. You can have that, too. And this ring." She jerked a diamond solitaire mounted in platinum from her finger. Then, as they still regarded her silently, she added in a low voice, "Please."

Charlie smiled then. "That last part covers a lot of ground with us. You are in earnest, and that is all I was waiting to hear. Well, here's what we want. First, put that ring back on your finger. Second, dismiss all notions that you pay us if we decide to help. Is that straight?"

She nodded, flushing under the gaze of his steady eyes.

"All right, then," Charlie resumed. "Now I want you to tell us all you know about the dirigible. How badly was it damaged?"

"Just a moment," Lew interrupted, turning to Charlie. "I got to know something, too. Are we or aren't we taking on this business?"

"Well," Charlie replied, "I don't know, yet. But let's go over the ground and see how things stack up."

"That's all I need to know," Lew grinned. Then he jumped up, went to the corner and returned with a rifle, cleaning rod and gun oil.

"What are you doing?" Charlie asked.

"I'm getting ready," Lew answered. "I've heard that old gag about 'seeing how things stack up' often enough to know what's coming next. I can clean a rifle and listen at the same time."

"Don't mind him," Charlie told the girl. "Lew is merely being Lew, so eager to jump headfirst into this thing he can't sit still. Now, go on. Do you think the dirigible is too badly damaged to fly?"

"I don't know," Sally confessed. "But something serious happened or Andre would never have let himself down on a rope to examine from the ground. If compartments are leaking, they have material to patch them. But if too much gas escapes, they can't take off again."

"They could lighten by cutting a cabin loose." Charlie suggested.

"Yes, that's possible."

"How far is the ship from here?"

"That is awfully hard for me to answer. I guess I walked somewhere between eight and ten miles."

"Any guns on board?"

"Not that I'm aware of, but Max and Andre may carry arms."

"It is safe to assume they do," Charlie agreed. "Now, tell me what they look like. And be as precise as you can."

"Max is tall and thin—the educated Nordic type. He claims to be a Swede. Andre is dark and short, powerfully built. He looks like a Frenchman, and I suppose he may have been before the war. But if he is working for the enemy, he can hardly be one now."

"It's still possible," Charlie said. "You can find men with a price in every country on earth. The camera, it is big and heavy?"

"Yes. About two feet wide and high and three feet long. It weighs over 200 pounds."

"A stiff load to pick up and carry away," Charlie reflected.

"Especially while a pair of torpedoes are taking pot shots at us," Lew added.

"The airship is radio-equipped?" Charlie asked.

"Wireless."

"That might help," Charlie said thoughtfully. "If we can send out a call for help, tell a search plane where to come. Do you know how to operate the set?"

"That's one reason Dad took me with him."

"The trouble will be to get at it," Lew suggested.

"Yes," Charlie agreed. "But the real complication comes from a different angle. Max and Andre can send out a call themselves, to other foreign agents. Such men may be on the ship I suspect is waiting off the East Coast, or they may already be here. Regardless, a fast plane could get them here even from the North Atlantic in one day."

"Which means anything we do must be done in a hurry." Lew added. "Better hope Max and Andre can't give their exact position."

"But they can," Sally said. "Andre is a trained navigator, and the ship contains the latest instruments that take latitude and longitude. You are still going to help me, aren't you?"

"Why do you suppose Lew is cleaning that gun? " Charlie said, smiling. "I couldn't keep him out of this business now if I wanted to. And I don't. My sympathies are naturally with you and your country. We, as Americans, are supposed to be neutral. But I can't see any breech of neutrality if we help you recover something stolen."

"Oh, I'm so glad." she sighed. "Thank you."

"Better hold the gratitude until we actually do something," Lew suggested. "All our efforts might wind up with us shot and you carried away to Europe as a prisoner. But now, you better get some sleep."

"I suppose so," she said, and her eyes grew wide as she sent a quick glance around the one-room cabin.

Lew chuckled at that. "I'll hang canvas around the bunk. You climb inside and get ready for bed. We'll sit out here ... looking the other way."

"But I don't want to take the bed," she protested. "I can lie beside the fire. I slept in snow last night."

"All the more reason for you to get some real sleep tonight," Lew asserted. "Don't worry about us. After you are settled, we'll make a bed on the floor. We have plenty of wild hay stored in the attic for emergencies. Now don't argue. Climb in and get busy. Tomorrow," he added, "we'll try to get the rest of your clothes back from the dirigible. Is there a lot?"

"Just one bag. Could you bring my vanity, too? It's a leather case this big," she said, spreading her hands. "I need it so much."

"I guess I can carry both," Lew said.

"You going to bring the camera, too?" Charlie asked.

"You needn't get sarcastic," Lew answered. "Sally needs her things, doesn't she? More clothes could be pretty handy with this kind of cold weather on the way."

"Have you any idea how you are going to get them from the dirigible?" she asked curiously.

"Not yet," Lew admitted. "But I'll figure out something. These fellows will think I'm only a bush trapper. No reason at all for them to suspect any different, is there?"

"I guess not," Charlie agreed.

"So, I'm going to wander over there in the morning and have a look around. Then I can plan some sort of action."

Charlie arose early the next morning, built a fire and put water on to boil. Lew took the axe and went out to cut the daily quota of wood. A second light snow had fallen in the night, and he frowned when he saw it. Lew had hoped to follow the girl's trail back to the dirigible, but now he would have to guess more or less at its location.

Charlie came out to help stack the wood beside the cabin door. Then, after some noisy stamping of feet, they went in. Sally was bent over, tending the fire. The curtain had been taken down from around the bunk. It and the feather robe were neatly folded. She turned around and said cheerily, "Good morning!"

Then she saw Lew's frown. "What's wrong?" she asked quickly.

"Plenty," Lew said and then let out a low whistle. "You have taken away my one good excuse for staying single. I always claimed the bad thing about being married was you had to look at your wife when she first woke up. But now I got to figure something different."

"Silly," she said, and then laughed for the first time.

"Tell me," Lew asked in a serious tone, "how is it done? Where did you get that color, the glow I see in your face?"

"This is my secret," she confided. "But I'm going to trust you. First, I washed my face in the warm water someone so thoughtfully started to heat. Then, I opened the door and rubbed my cheeks with fresh snow. Simple enough even a man could do it."

"Not with my three-day's growth of whiskers," Lew replied.

"You better take them off before they're too long for a razor," Charlie advised.

"No," Lew said. "Not today. I don't want to look too clean and sharp when I visit that airship today."

"Going to play the dumb trapper?"

Lew nodded.

"Well, that shouldn't be hard," Charlie grinned. "How about both of us going?"

Lew shook his head no.

"If I walk into something I don't expect, I will be better off if you stay back here. Besides, if we both go and get in a jam, what would happen to Sally?"

"You're right," Charlie admitted.

"I would have started breakfast," Sally interrupted, "but I didn't know what to make."

"With a long day ahead," Lew said, "I nominate hot cakes and wild honey. With coffee, of course, and some dried meat. Which reminds me, Charlie, we've dug pretty deep into our stock of jerked venison. Maybe I'll bag a deer on my way home."

Lew mixed the hot cake batter, but when he approached the fire, Sally took the skillet firmly from him and made him sit down at the table. He obeyed but rattled his knife and fork like a hungry youngster.

When she slid the first cake on his plate, he cut into it gingerly. Lew was very particular about his flapjacks. He liked them big but not thick, and always evenly brown on both sides. The color of this one appeared excellent. He speared a chunk, smeared on wild honey and shoved it in his mouth.

As Lew chewed, Charlie saw the lines between his eyes smooth out. Finally, Lew spoke, "Sally, you're a wonder. How would you like a steady job cooking for us this winter?"

She looked at him quickly. "I'll be glad to cook all the meals—until the plane comes to take me home."

Lew sighed. "I always get turned down. Still, that should be long enough for me to pack on a few pounds."

When he finished breakfast, Lew put the .30-30 barrel on his combination gun, slid a dozen extra shells in a pocket, paused in the doorway long enough to say "so long," and then strode across the little clearing towards Shadow Lake.

Charlie went to the door and stood looking after him. "Maybe I shouldn't have let him go alone," he said soberly.

Chapter 5 – Hold It, Fellow!

As he walked, Lew searched the snow for footprints made by Sally Bern in her flight from the grounded airship to their cabin. But fresh snow had drifted them over. Still, Lew was confident he could find the dirigible. It had landed rather close to the shore of the lake, if Sally could be trusted to judge distance, and Max and Andre, the men who had stolen the ship, would have to make a fire in this crisp weather. Lew knew his nose could pick up the odor of smoke a considerable distance away.

He stopped once to test the ice at the lake's edge. It was a quarter-inch thick. He wondered how long they must wait before they could fish through the ice and add some variety to their meals. Meals based solely on venison, rabbit and grouse had grown monotonous.

Out in the open water, Lew saw an animal swimming parallel to the shore. "Looks like an otter," he thought. "And I bet that fellow's hide is prime. We must start trapping as soon as we get this camera business settled for Sally. She's really a swell girl and needs our help. Maybe I can finish it up today. All I need do is wait in the woods until I see these fellows and then let them have a couple of slugs from my .30-30. They don't deserve any better."

He swung along briskly, savoring the thought.

"But of course I won't do it," he finally muttered. "I'm no cold-blooded killer. Besides, suppose there is some mistake about this business? Sally told us the truth—I think."

Lew had walked hardly more than two hours when he caught the first scent of burning wood. Then he caught a glimpse of the big, dark bag rising above the trees. It looked like the back of a monstrous whale as it swayed gently in the wind. Lew's pulse quickened.

There were no unusual sounds in the woods. This seemed strange, and it made him cautious. He was close enough to see that the dirigible was in an open space too stony and barren to permit more than an occasional stunted tree and a few clumps of brush. "They were lucky," he thought, "to drop down here and escape being wrecked."

The balloon had slid in between scattered trees in a way that indicated extreme good luck or extraordinary piloting skill.

Lew paused behind a tree. A fire burned a safe distance from the gas bag, and he saw where saplings had been chopped and trimmed. Some lay on the ground, others had been built into a sort of staging around the end of the ship. Lew saw this end was less rounded, and he suspected that was where one of the compartments was leaking. The stage had been constructed to reach and patch the leak.

"If there's nobody home, I might as well get Sally's clothes," he thought. "Anyway, I must not hide here behind a tree. I'm supposed to be a Northwoods trapper without any reason to suspect these men. They might think different if they catch me spying on them."

Lew walked boldly out into the opening and toward the airship. It was larger than he had first judged, with a gas envelope at least 150 feet long. Both ends were blunt like a football. Lew knew they were braced inside by a frame of light metal trusses. Under the bag, which swelled and rolled easily under a dozen lines tied to saplings or driven stakes, hung the two metal cabins.

The rear cabin was settled to the ground, weighted, Lew supposed, by the heavy engines. But the front cabin was tilted precariously with the door several feet up in the air. The bottom was battered, and the sleek sides showed scratches and gouges from a forced landing.

Lew went to the rear cabin and looked in through one of the windows. He saw two engines with enormous eight-cylinder blocks of gleaming steel, a dynamo, steering controls with cables running back to the outside rudders, and a board packed with instruments and gauges. At the opposite end was a double bunk and a small galley containing cupboard, sink and stove. The cabin was empty, and he saw no place where someone might be hiding

Lew walked beside the narrow catwalk that connected the cabins. It had been twisted and bent and looked unsafe. He paused before the door of the forward cabin, raised his hand and was reaching for the knob when a voice spoke from behind.

"Hold it."

The voice was low, almost hoarse. Lew dropped his hand and turned. The man had been standing behind one of the cabins, in fact hiding there while he approached. Lew did not like that. But he forced a grin and said, "Howdy."

The man was short with thick, powerful shoulders. He wore a coverall suit and an aviator's cap with flying glasses pushed above the beak. One of his hands was shoved into what is generally used as the pistol pocket in such a suit. Noting this, Lew carefully kept his rifle down at arm's length, muzzle pointed away.

"What were you going in for?" the man asked, nodding his head towards the cabin.

"I wanted to see if anybody was hurt," Lew replied. "You had a wreck, didn't you?"

"Wanted to see if anybody was hurt?" the man repeated. "Where did you come from?"

"I live here. Or about ten miles that way," Lew said, pointing.

"Ten miles that way." Again the man repeated Lew's words in a most disconcerting manner. Lew was growing uneasy under the cold stare. The dark little eyes played up and down and back and forth over him, not missing the smallest detail.

"Are you a hunter?"

"When I need meat. Other times, I trap."

"You trap." After echoing Lew's words again, the man raised his voice and called, "Max!"

Another man walked around the other end of the rear cabin.

"So, you were both hiding when I came up," Lew thought.

Max was dressed like his companion. But the forceful intelligence in his face left no doubt who was the boss. "He's dangerous, too," Lew thought. "The one I have to watch."

Eyes still locked on Lew, Andre said in the monotonous tone of one reciting a lesson. "He says he traps. Says he lives ten miles southwest. He was trying to open the cabin door. Said he thought somebody inside might be hurt."

Max nodded pleasantly. "Which is perfectly reasonable. I don't suppose you ever saw a wrecked dirigible before."

Lew shook his head. "I never even saw one that wasn't wrecked."

"Are you trapping today?" Max continued pleasantly.

"No, I'm hunting for deer."

"If you shoot one, can we buy some meat? We didn't bring a lot of food, and it may be days before we are able to go on."

"I'll give you as much as you need," Lew offered. "Can this thing still fly?"

"After a little patching," Max replied easily. "Some of the gas has leaked. That may make the ship hard to control. We hope to finish our repairs and test her tomorrow."

"How you going to put gas back in?" Lew asked.

Max gazed at him thoughtfully. "We'll have to figure out some way to restore balance without adding gas. Cut some weight from the front end, I suppose. But getting back to that meat, we don't expect it for nothing. We'll pay. Or," hesitating a moment, "maybe you would trade? We haven't a lot of cash. How about clothes?"

Lew didn't like the way this was going. Obviously, Max was steering the conversation, and doing it smoothly.

Trying to regain the upper hand, Lew glanced down at the high leather boots with fur-lined tops each of the men wore. The leather was Cordovan, and it glistened with a lustrous shine. Lew would have gladly traded a couple of dead deer for a pair of such boots.

"I could use something like that," Lew said pointing.

Max shook his head. "I'm sorry. We don't have an extra pair. But we have other things. You get a deer and bring it in. We'll make some kind of deal that is more than satisfactory."

Lew nodded. "All right. I'll come back before night."

He hated to turn his back on these men. But he simply had to. He didn't dare show any sign of distrust. "If they let me walk off, everything's jake," Lew told himself.

And since that is exactly what they did, his apprehension melted away and he was whistling cheerfully by the time he reached the edge of the timber. In fact, Lew was jubilant.

"They played right into my hand when they mentioned trading clothes," he thought. "If I'm slick enough, I can get all of Sally's stuff. But first, I have to get a deer."

Lew examined the snow for tracks and then worked into thick tangles of brush and deadfall trees looking for any sign that deer might be bedded in the cover. He left the high ground and plunged into a low swale where tamarack, yellow birch and alder grew profusely.

Rabbit tracks ran in all directions, and Lew crossed the trail of two foxes that had been hunting the big-footed snowshoe hares. He found the bones of a deer that had been picked clean by wolves. Lew scowled at the large tracks. "Wish I had brought a couple of number four-and-a-half traps," he muttered.

Lacking such traps, Lew knew only one method by which he could hang wolf pelts in the fur shed. Later, when extreme cold drove the wolves from their swamp fastness to search for ever-scarcer food, he believed he could bag them easily with the flat-shooting .300 Magnum that Helm had left for them when he departed.

Lew walked another mile before he jumped a small buck. The animal cleared a fallen log with one leap. Lew brought the gun up, and the bullet smashed the animal's spine.

"I'm glad he isn't a big one," Lew thought. It was almost two miles back to the airship, and the ground was rough for packing.

He dressed the buck, wiped the cavity with clean snow and then cut off the head, neck, and all four legs at the knees. After waiting half an hour for the carcass to drain, he split out two bands of hide to serve as straps and shouldered the dressed deer like a pack.

Plenty of noise emanated from the dirigible when he approached this time. A voice shouted commands, and then a heavy thud indicated the fall of a tree. Andre was working on the tree, trimming off limbs with a lumberman's double-bit axe that made Lew's eyes shine. He wondered if that sort of tool was standard airship equipment. Or had these fellows brought it for use in such an emergency?

Max stood beside his companion, directing him where to chop. He looked up, smiling, when Lew appeared in the open glade.

"Didn't take you long, did it?"

"Sometimes I get a deer in 20 minutes," Lew grinned. "How much do you want? You can have it all, if you like."

"I think we can use it all," Max said. "But let's first figure out a trade. You said you could use clothes? How about some woman's things for your wife?"

"I guess that would be all right," Lew said. "I ain't married. But I got an Assinoba girl back at camp. Anything would tickle her."

Inwardly, he rejoiced that Charlie hadn't come along. Charlie would have had a lot of fun with that one.

"Come in the cabin and see what we have.

He followed Max towards the airship. Andre sunk his blade in the tree butt and began picking up severed limbs. He did not glance up as Lew walked by.

Lew slipped the deer from his shoulders, easing it down on a log before he followed Max in through the cabin door. He did not set the rifle down. He stopped just inside and waited for Max, who was back between a pair of curtained berths in the opposite end. Lew saw that the cabin was fitted up like a miniature apartment with a rug on the floor and curtains at each window. Besides two berths there was a table, writing desk and two chairs of red leather.

Max drew a bag out from beneath the left berth, carried it back and set it before Lew. When he opened the lid, Lew saw it was packed with a variety of lady's garments. There were dainty negligees, silk hose, slippers and a dress of some dark material. Max lifted some to show him, and Lew wondered if he should bargain.

Max put an end to that notion. "The deer for everything here?"

"It's a deal," he agreed.

Max dropped the lid, snapped it fast and pushed it over.

"That was easy," Lew thought. "Won't Charlie be surprised?"

Max spoke again in his pleasant, low voice, "How about the vanity? Do you want that, too?"

Lew nodded before he realized what he was doing. Then a glance at Max told him he had walked right into a trap.

Max still smiled, but his lips were drawn back, the white teeth looking merciless. Lew had been played as skillfully as a three-pound bass on the end of a baited line.

His fingers tightened on the rifle. His only chance, it seemed, was to shoot Max and make a dash for the woods. But before he could lift the gun something prodded him in the back.

Lew knew it was the muzzle of a gun barrel and promptly abandoned any idea of resisting. Andre's hand came around from behind and took his rifle. Andre, of course, had followed them, waiting just outside the door until needed.

"I played the role of a dumb trapper, alright," Lew thought.

"So," Max spoke. "You're just a trapper who lives ten miles from here? And you came over to see if anybody in the ship had been hurt? Did you think we were stupid enough to believe that?"

Not being able to think of a good answer, Lew kept still.

Max continued, his voice growing sharper, more cutting.

"We knew Colonel Bern's daughter made it to your cabin last night. Andre trailed her in the snow. He listened outside and heard most of your talk. But he didn't hear enough to be sure of your voice.

"You might have been a trapper brought by curiosity. I didn't want to act hastily. So, I waited until I was sure. Letting you shoot a deer for us and bring it in first was a nice bonus. That is going to save us a lot of trouble. When you came back and swallowed my offer to trade for Sally Bern's clothes, I knew."

"You're going to kill me?" Lew asked, already sure.

Max tried to inject regret into his voice. "I fear we haven't any other choice. Andre?"

Lew felt the pressure leave his back. He started to whirl about but something crashed down on his head. He fell forward, elbows unconsciously lifted to protect his face. Lights flashed before his closed eyes; then the lights faded, the pain softened, and his senses ceased.

Lew was out, cold as a frozen whitefish.

Chapter 6 – A Footprint in the Snow

Charlie stood in the cabin doorway for as long as he could see Lew passing through the trees. Then he closed the door and went to the fireplace. The quick blaze used to cook breakfast had burned down. He added two logs of slower, greener fuel that would keep the cabin comfortable until noon.

He stared into the fire, wondering if he had been wise in letting Lew go alone to search for Colonel Bern's grounded dirigible and the two men who had stolen it.

"Maybe I should have insisted on going along," he muttered.

Sally Bern's quick ears heard that. She stopped washing the breakfast dishes and said, "When do you expect him back?"

"Sometime between noon and four o'clock," Charlie replied.

"Are you going to worry all that time?" she demanded.

Charlie smiled. "I'm worrying some now, but Lew has always been able to take care of himself."

Sally nodded. "I would feel awful if anything happened to him. The only reason he went was to help me."

Charlie laughed. "You don't know Lew. He'd walk 30 miles through a blizzard to see a wrecked airship. Curiosity has always been his distinguishing trait."

Charlie reached overhead and took down from the rafter braces the 4 birch strips they had whittled thin for snowshoe frames. It was time to steam the wood and bend it into the proper shape. The two recent snows were ample warning that heavier snow could be expected any week.

"Why don't you go do something to help Lew?" Sally said. "You can still catch up with him."

"I know," he replied. "I considered it. But chances are he was right when he insisted I stay here. He didn't want to leave you alone. Suppose Max or Andre came here looking for you? And, if Lew does get in a jam, I will be more help if I'm not caught up in it with him. No, I've decided to stay as he asked me to."

"Then stop looking like you're going to a funeral," she retorted. "Your face is long enough to step on."

"It's my serious disposition," Charlie told her. "You have to get used to it. Lew always said I'd make a swell undertaker."

In order to bend a snowshoe frame, some woodsmen wrap rags around the wood and then swab the rags with boiling water. This is effective but tedious, requiring much attention and time.

Trappers living in cabins sometimes use three joints of stovepipe for a steam box. They suspend the pipe from the roof with the lower end fitting over a metal pail of water boiling on the stove. The wood strips are hung inside the pipe, and the upper end is closed to hold the steam. This is easier, but lacking both stove and pipe, Charlie was obliged to work out something different.

For his steam box, he dug a trench in the hard ground some 10 feet long, 1 foot wide, and almost 3 deep. Then he built a fire close to the trench and gathered enough stones to cover the bottom of the trench evenly. Working fast, Charlie laid the four pieces of birch on cross sticks wedged in the trench sides a foot above the stones. Then he covered the trench with sheets of bark and heaped dirt over all.

Next, he bored small holes with a sharp stake down through the dirt and bark at intervals of two feet and poured in boiling water. Every few minutes, he reopened the holes to add more water and keep the trench charged with live steam.

While waiting for the birch to soften and become supple, Charlie worked on the forms about which the strips would be curved. These were simply wide slabs split from the center of short logs. He hewed one face flat and smooth, and nailed to it blocks and cleats spaced to give the frame the desired shape.

Rawhide thongs for lacing the snowshoes already were at hand, cut from moose hide. He would have preferred caribou, but they had not seen any sign of caribou around Shadow Lake. Later, perhaps, a few might drift down before the Arctic snowstorms, but he could not depend upon it.

Charlie had soaked the moose hide in wood ashes and water until the hair loosened. Then he had scraped it bare and trimmed away neck, flank and belly, saving only the thickest, strongest hide.

This he soaked soft again and laced inside a stout frame of poles. When it dried, much of the stretch had come out. The hide was then trimmed oval and cut into a pair of long continuous strips. One strip was half an inch wide for lacing around the frames, for the toe bar and center stays of the shoe. The other was slightly wider than a quarter inch. It would be used for the heel and toe webs. Thorough stretching pulled each thong into the correct width for weaving.

Lacking shellac or varnish to seal the thongs, Charlie knew he must remove every inch of "give" before they were installed in the shoes. Otherwise, they would sag and walking in wet snow would be impossible. Accordingly, he soaked the strips of hide in water then wrapped them about a short spruce log. He scored each end of the log with his axe, split it, and drove a wedge in each crack. This exerted tremendous pressure, spreading the halves of the block and stretching the thongs tight. When soaked again and then laced wet onto the shoe frames, Charlie expected they would tighten and stay that way.

He had made two needles for the lacing. One was bone, the other hardwood. Both were pointed at each end with a thong-size hole burned through the center.

He was making their own modified bear paw design of snowshoe, since their trapline covered so many different kinds of ground. The bear paw is a compromise for timber and open land, hillsides and marshy swales. But since neither Charlie nor Lew thought the conventional bear paw shoe perfect, they had worked out their own shoe that was more oval, measuring 12 inches longer and 5 less in width than the standard bear paw. This compromise gave greater support in soft snow and was also somewhat faster, which was important when a long trail had to be traveled.

After the birch strips had steamed two hours, Charlie uncovered the trench and began bending them about the forms. He had to work quickly before the thin wood cooled, and in his hurry, he did what the amateur builder often does. He cracked one of the frames at its center.

The break was not bad, only a few fibers of wood snapped, but he eyed it with chagrin. The break would be at the forward point of the shoe, where much wear and many bumps occur.

"I don't know why I didn't cut an extra strip," he thought. "There is always a chance to break one." He determined to do that as soon as he had time.

Meanwhile, he repaired the fracture, wrapping it tightly with a piece of soaked green hide that would shrink in drying and make the wood almost as strong as before. Seeing how well this patch protected the tip of the shoe, Charlie decided to wrap all of the frames similarly to increase their durability.

When the last strip had been bent and blocked to its form, it was still only an hour before noon. Mindful of Lew's warning about their diminishing supply of dried meat, he decided to go hunting. The dry meat should be saved for emergencies when the weather was bitter and most of the game holed up.

He would stay close to the cabin so Sally could call for him if needed. He had no hope of seeing a deer close to the cabin, but the brush swarmed with rabbits. He found a fresh trail and followed it east towards the lake.

His favored way of hunting rabbits was to watch the cover and spot them as they crouched in a burrow pushed out of snow or among the leaves. Since a northern rabbit blends nicely with its surroundings, it is difficult to see one even when very close. The betraying point is the dark eye, and Charlie had trained his own eyes to spot that pupil no matter how well the rest of the rabbit was concealed.

He saw one less than 15 yards away, lifted the 20 gauge and blew the sitting animal's head off. He was not hunting for sport; he was shooting food. Charlie dressed the rabbit and stood holding it until it ceased bleeding and he could tie it to the back of his belt.

Then he caught sight of a footprint in the snow behind a wide-bo led tree. Charlie bent over to examine the mark. It was one Sally had left on her way to the cabin. What brought the exclamation to his lips—and sent a shiver up his spine—was the second footprint about a foot away. It did not belong to Sally, and it was smaller than Lew's boot and more pointed at the toe.

There was only one explanation. The footprint had been made by one of the foreign agents from the grounded dirigible. He had trailed Sally, probably followed her right to the cabin door, may even have listened as they talked last night.

Lew would last about as long in that camp of wised-up wolves as a snowball in a furnace. Charlie started running back to the cabin.

He hung up the dead rabbit on a peg driven into an outside wall joint and burst in. "I've got to eat lunch right now," he said.

Sally sensed his anxiety at once. "Something wrong?"

He told her about the footprint and asked, "Does Max or Andre wear pointed-toe boots?"

"Both of them."

As Charlie opened a can of corned beef and another of tomatoes. he said, "Lew won't have a chance. They will be expecting him. He may have found part of the double trail himself. If he did, he knows what that means. But I can't chance it. I've got to go."

He ate hurriedly while Sally made tea. Then, turning around, she said, "I'm going with you."

Charlie shook his head. "You're going to stay here where you'll be safest."

"Why will I be safer here?" she demanded. "Both Max and Andre might be on their way here right now. You want me to be alone when they arrive?"

"You will be all right," Charlie insisted. "You can shoot a gun. I'll leave my rifle. Keep the door barred and no one can surprise you. A pistol bullet won't penetrate these walls."

Despite his assurances, Charlie began to wonder if the girl really would be safer alone in the cabin. Somehow he failed to convince himself, and he emphatically failed to convince Sally.

"They can break through that window without a bit of trouble," she told him. "I won't stay here to be murdered. I'm going."

Charlie finished his food in silence. "When," he thought, "did anybody ever get anyplace arguing with a woman?"

"I'm not going just because I'm afraid to stay," Sally added, "but because I am the only one who can do something that must be done."

He raised his brows in question.

"Can you operate the wireless in the dirigible?" she asked. When he didn't respond, she continued, "I thought not. While you handle Max and Andre, I'll send out the SOS. I'll burn up the air with calls for help that will bring planes thick as geese."

"OK," Charlie agreed. "You can come. But since you're so full of ideas, can you suggest a way for me to handle Max and Andre?"

She smiled. "You don't need my help there."

"No use to flatter me now," Charlie retorted. "You already got your way. And flattery is not one of my weaknesses."

"Then you're different from every other man," she replied.

Charlie decided it was time to change the subject.

"You have assumed that the wireless set still works. Where does the power come from?"

"A dynamo belted to one of the engines. We must start the engine, and I can do that, too."

Charlie emptied his teacup and stood. "I'm going to take some grub. I don't know when we'll return." He put five cans in his pack along with tea, a pot and skillet. The weight wouldn't hinder him. He knew he would have to slow his gait to accommodate Sally.

She put on her galoshes and leather jacket. "Better take the fur," Charlie warned. "You might have to sleep in the snow tonight."

He dismounted his single shotgun and put the stock in the pack. "I haven't time to hide the gun," he explained. "And I mustn't leave it here for those fellows to find if they do come. Two barrels are no good without a stock."

He picked up the .300 Magnum, slung the pack on his back, glanced at the fire and saw it was safe to leave.

Charlie paused just outside the door, gave the snug little cabin a swift look of regret. "I hope nothing happens while I'm gone," he thought. Then he started towards the lake with Sally following.

Lew's trail was plain to see in the snow. Charlie anticipated some of the turns and cut straight across to save every possible step.

Sally was carrying the fur coat. Before they covered a mile, Charlie glanced back and said, "Can't you keep up?"

"I'm trying," she panted.

He took the coat from her. "I can carry that."

"I'm hurrying as fast as I can," she insisted. "I'm just as worried about Lew as you are."

"Is that so?" Charlie asked. "You seem to be awfully fond of him all of a sudden."

"Save it," she said shortly. "I can't waste my breath arguing."

Charlie grinned as he turned back around. He had succeeded in getting the girl a little mad, and he knew that would make her walk faster and feel the fatigue less.

They reached the place Lew had turned inland from the lake and paused a few minutes for Sally to rest. She was badly winded, for Charlie had not spared her. He feared any delay might prove fatal for Lew. When they came to the place where Lew had caught the odor of wood smoke, Charlie smelled it, too, and stopped.

"We go slow from here," Charlie whispered. "Don't talk, and don't make any sound with your feet."

Sally nodded.

When Charlie caught sight of the big gas bag of the ship, he started to detour around. At times he crept close, making the girl hide back behind a tree. He was looking for cover that would permit him to creep even closer to the ship without being seen. He needed to study the situation before acting. Just what that action might entail still was not clear to him. It would depend upon so many circumstances out of his control that he saw no point to thinking about it yet.

He could hear men speaking, but the voices were too faint to catch any words.

When he was almost on the opposite side of the camp, he found a clump of thick cedars that extended close to the ship. He dropped his pack and ordered Sally to stay hidden until he called.

Her eyes were wide when they met his. "What will I do if something happens to you?" she asked.

"Nothing will," he tried to assure her. "But take this, anyway," he added, handing over the stock of the combination gun. "If I don't come back, return to the cabin and bar the door. Put the gun together and shoot anybody who tries to get in."

Then Charlie crept in on his knees, holding the Magnum rifle above the snow. The last cedar shrub was 150 feet from the dirigible, and when Charlie reached it, he pushed aside some of the fragrant green branches to look ahead. What he saw pleased him. He smiled grimly, and standing up, stepped out from behind the cover.

Chapter 7 – Is This a Hold-Up?

"I couldn't ask for a better setup," Charlie thought as he approached the front of the grounded dirigible, the end that was partly enclosed with a scaffold of poles and tree trunks now almost 40 feet high with a ladder of nailed limbs reaching to its top.

The reason for Charlie's satisfaction was the two men perched near the top of the ladder working on the cloth envelope. They were patching a rip in the skin with pieces of fabric, holding bottles of cement and small brushes in their hands.

"That pair is worse than out on a limb," Charlie muttered.

He walked in, expecting any moment that one would glance around and see him. But neither did, and he kept advancing until he stood within 20 feet of the scaffold. To go any closer would put him at a disadvantage.

The shorter man, whom Charlie already had identified as Andre, leaned out to apply cement on one of the gas bag seams. The brush slipped from his fingers, and when he turned about to catch it, he saw Charlie standing below. A sharp exclamation escaped his lips. Then one hand jerked back towards his hip.

"Stop!" Charlie ordered. "Take your hand away from that gun."

He raised his rifle to cover the man. Max also had spun about on the precarious footing and now stared down at Charlie. The two were close enough Charlie could cover both without shifting the muzzle.

Andre pulled his hand slowly back and let it hang straight down before him.

"That's better," Charlie said. "Don't make another mistake like that. This rifle shoots a magnum load. It would splash you like spilled paint all over the ship."

"Is this a holdup?" Max demanded.

"No," Charlie told him. "Although I'm going to hold you up there until you answer some questions. First, where's my partner?"

"How should we know?" Max asserted.

"I know he's been here," Charlie replied. "Nobody else butchered the deer hanging from that tree. I would recognize Lew's knife work anywhere."

"I shot and butchered that deer," Max declared.

"Shot it with what?" Charlie asked.

"My pistol."

"That meat was killed with a thirty-caliber rifle, or something similar," Charlie said. "But now we're just wasting time. I know Lew came here. Where is he?"

The pair stared down at him in almost contemptuous silence. Max's pale eyes, deadly as the lidless orbs of a rattlesnake, were slowly filling with rage. That cold anger worried Charlie more than did the hot, flushed passion of Andre.

"If something has happened to Lew," Charlie continued slowly, "it will be just too bad for both of you."

Fear for his companion's safety grew with every second. He raised his voice and shouted, "Lew, where are you?"

Silence weighed down the little clearing. His hopes were dimming when he heard a muffled sound coming from the front cabin of the dirigible, and his face cleared as he realized the sounds were the heels of a tied man pounding his feet against the cabin's metal floor.

He called, "Sally!"

She ran out of the timber so quickly Charlie suspected she had not stayed where he had left her but had instead followed him in. Charlie reached in a pocket with one hand and tossed his knife to her. His eyes did not leave the men on the scaffold.

"Go in and free Lew. I think he's on the floor of the forward cabin." He added to the men, "You better be praying he's OK, only tied and gagged."

They did not answer. Charlie saw their eyes follow the girl as she ran and then wrenched open the door of the tilting cabin. In a moment her voice cried out, "I found him! He's okay!"

"Cut him loose," Charlie ordered.

"I have. But he says his muscles are so stiff he can't walk."

"That's all right," Charlie called back. "I don't need him now." Then he said to Andre, "Pull that gun from your pocket. Use just your thumb and forefinger. Don't grip it in your hand. Do it slowly, and drop it to the ground."

"Go to the devil," Andre said, his voice choked with anger.

"I'm not fooling," Charlie countered. "Drop that gun!"

Andre merely scowled down at him.

"All right," Charlie said. "You asked for it." He fired without further warning. The .300 bullet shrieked past Andre's head, missing his ear by less than 3 inches. The shock almost knocked him off the scaffold. Charlie worked another shell into the chamber. He knew of few things so apt to put fear into a tough man's heart as a high-power bullet ripping by his face.

Charlie was ready to send another shot alongside Andre's opposite ear, but it wasn't needed. His face now livid from shock, Andre forced a trembling hand into his back pocket and slowly produced the gun. His fingers shook so he could not have fired it straight if he had tried. But he didn't try. The weapon fell to the snow below.

"Your turn," Charlie nodded at Max.

"You won't scare me shooting past my head," Max said tonelessly without any change of countenance.

"You get a bullet through the knee," Charlie replied.

Max stared into Charlie's eyes for several seconds. Then he drew his gun and let it fall beside the other. Charlie stepped forward, scooped up the pistols with one hand and then stepped back. He saw that each was foreign-made and bored for the 9mm shell.

"Good," Charlie said, speaking more to himself than to the disarmed men. Sally stood in the cabin doorway, watching.

"Come over and get these guns," Charlie told her. "Give one to Lew, and keep the other yourself."

She obeyed, and when she had run back, Max asked. "Are you going to keep us here all day?"

"Just until Lew can walk," Charlie replied. "If you hadn't tied him so tight, he would be here already. I want him to put the ropes on you two. I have a notion he will do a good job of it."

Sally jumped out of the front cabin and ran back to the other. A motor coughed then started running in a steady, muffled roar. She had started the dynamo to put her message for help out upon the air.

"Swell girl," Charlie thought. "She isn't wasting a second."

Watching Max, he saw the man's face go taut. His keen mind had, Charlie knew, grasped the significance of what the girl was doing. Then, without any sign, without even a shift of hands or feet, Max dropped from the top of the 40-foot scaffold.

Charlie jumped back. "A drop like that will kill any man," he thought. But he was wrong. When Max hit the ground his body curled forward, legs doubled underneath. Instead of crumpling into broken bones, Max rolled across the snow like a human bowling ball. He rolled twice, the motion redirecting the impact of landing, and on the second turn, his feet struck Charlie in the midsection with a force that sent him sprawling backwards on the snow.

As he tumbled, Charlie realized his opponent was a tumbler of incredible skill. He had seen professionals jump from heights almost as great as this, but now he knew he had something more vital to think about than tumbling skill.

He felt a surge of sickness—Max's feet had landed a punishing blow on his belt—but he choked back the impulse to retch and rolled swiftly to the left.

He moved just in time, for Max next landed in the snow exactly where he had been lying. Whirling over, the man lunged with both hands grasping for Charlie's throat.

Charlie rolled to his knees to ward off the deadly hands. He had retained his grasp on the rifle, and now he jabbed the rifle out muzzle first. The end caught Max under an eye and ripped a gash in his lean cheek. But before Charlie could strike again, Max clamped both hands around the barrel. Charlie gave a little ground and then struggled to his feet. Max followed, helped by Charlie's pulling to free the weapon.

They stood toe to toe in a grim game of tug-of-war.

Charlie pulled with every ounce of his considerable strength, but Max's grip held. Looking sideways, Charlie saw Andre sliding down the ladder like a monkey. He knew he had to hurry. In a few seconds he would be helpless with one of them before and the other behind.

He tried to lift the muzzle in line with Max's body. But his adversary's grip held like steel. Charlie knew, then, that Max was stronger than himself.

He heard Andre's feet thud as he dropped the last few yards. Charlie swung hard, and lunging to one side tried to change places with Max and put him with his back towards Andre. He partly succeeded and saw that Andre had picked up a short, heavy piece of wood and was running with it raised above his head.

Charlie glanced at the face on the other side of the gun barrel and saw the eyes were flashing with a deadly light. Again, Charlie tried to swing around out of Andre's reach. But Max was ready this time, his feet firmly braced. He did not give an inch.

Charlie did not dare step sideways. That would give Max dangerous leverage on the gun. He found himself desperately wishing he had kept one of the pistols. Andre was directly behind him now. Charlie determined to release the rifle and use his fists. That seemed like the only way he might save himself.

At that instant, a pistol shot rang out. Andre cried sharply, and his club missed Charlie's head and instead struck him on the shoulder with little force. Andre stumbled sideways, clutching at his shoulder. Blood streamed out between his fingers.

Then Charlie did what he should have thought of before. The safety catch had been slipped from the rifle, and his finger was inside the trigger guard. He tightened that finger and the big rifle roared like a cannon. The recoil jolted Max's steel grasp loose, and Charlie jerked the barrel free. The recoil had also driven the buttstock into Charlie's side, and he was gasping for air as he staggered back clear of Max's clutching hands. Then he covered Max with the muzzle and shot a swift glance toward the airship.

Lew's head was sticking out a window. In his outstretched hand was one of the captured pistols, and he was holding it steady as a rock.

"I can't walk," Lew said, "but that don't mean I can't shoot."

Max, seeing he was covered from two points with no viable options, raised his hands in surrender.

Sally ran out of the engine cabin. "Are you all right?" she cried. She was holding the other pistol in a businesslike way.

"I'm okay," Lew assured her.

"I started on the message," she said. "Then I heard a shot."

"Go back and finish it," he told the girl. "That is the most important thing now."

Lew hobbled out of the cabin, wincing every time he put weight on his cramping feet. But he kept coming. He stepped up behind Max, and reversing the pistol, brought the butt down on the man's head with a smashing blow that was too much even for Max's iron strength. He wilted in the snow.

"Had to do it," Lew stated simply. "Hate to take a cheap shot like that, but this fellow isn't even winded. We can't take any chances with him. Besides, if he tried another trick, I would have had to shoot him."

"I don't like it, either," Charlie agreed. "But as you say, that blow may have saved us having to kill him. Here, take this rifle. I'll look after Andre, and then we'll tie them both up."

Andre sat on a log. His face gray with pain, loss of blood, and, Charlie suspected, shock. But he snapped like a vicious dog when Charlie approached. "Get away from me!"

Charlie menaced him with the pistol until he consented to sit still and let his coat and shirt be cut away. The jacketed ball had gone cleanly through his shoulder, and it was bleeding out both sides. Charlie went to the rear cabin where Sally was bent over the wireless key.

She greeted him with grave eyes. "The receiving part is damaged. I can send out, but I don't know if anyone is answering."

"Just keep on repeating your message over and over," Charlie said. "Is there a first aid kit?"

She left the key long enough to get him a fiber case. Charlie went back out to Andre, sponged both punctures with disinfectant, plugged them with gauze to stop the bleeding, and wrapped a lot of bandage material about to hold the plugs in place.

Andre complained bitterly as Charlie worked. Lew finally grew weary of the protests and said, "Listen, fellow. We aren't doing this because we love you. And I'm getting awfully tired of your voice. Just one more word, and I will gag you."

Andre finally went silent then.

Charlie finished his work and got up. He felt weary, every muscle aching. His feet were so heavy it was difficult to lift them.

Max was regaining consciousness. Charlie quickly cut some of the thinner rigging rope from the dirigible and tied both men with it. He pulled Max's bonds secure but left Andre's a little loose. Even untied, Andre could hardly be much of a menace for several days. His wound seemed to have shot his nerves quite badly, too.

Max was now awake, but he lay quietly while Charlie finished tying him. Then Charlie saw him stealthily test the ropes, using all of his tremendous strength against them. He did this only once. Afterwards, he lay on his back, eyes staring into the sky.

Charlie went into the rear cabin again. It was warm and stinking with exhaust fumes from the eight-cylinder motor. Sally worked the key with hardly a pause between repetitions of her call for help.

"I guess I've sent it 30 times," she said.

"Stay at it a little longer," Charlie urged. "We'll be leaving soon."

"Leave? I thought we would wait here until help came."

"I would rather not," Charlie replied. "The sky looks bad, and a winter storm would toss this ship all around, maybe blow it out into the lake. It would be dangerous for us to be on board then. Besides, our own cabin is so much more comfortable."

"It's so much farther away, too," she said. "What are you going to do with Max and Andre? Take them with us?"

"Hardly. I've seen too much of that pair. But we must do something. I'll see what Lew has to say."

Charlie started to go, paused and added, "I want to look at the cause of all this trouble. Where's the topographic camera?"

Sally pointed to the front of the enclosure and resumed tapping the key. Charlie inspected an almost square box covered with black crackle-finish metal. The bottom sat flush on the floor, inside four metal guides so it could be lowered to hang below the cabin or raised up inside. A crank, chain and gears operated this. Three sides of the box were covered with controls, buttons, switches and levers.

Sally said, "That is the reason I want to stay."

"What would happen if it was damaged?" Charlie asked.

"Dad would lose a lot of money."

"Still," Charlie persisted, "he could make another like it?"

"Yes," she admitted, "I think so."

"Then," Charlie declared, "the sure way to keep it out of foreign hands is to smash it now. I'll go get the axe."

Her eyes went round. "Smash it?" she cried. "Dad spent fifty-thousand dollars before it was finished."

"That isn't the point," Charlie said. "You're making a big mistake if you don't let me smash it now. I got a feeling that camera is going to cause plenty of grief yet."

He started for the door.

"Where are you going?" Sally cried. "Don't you dare bring that axe in here."

"Take it easy," Charlie replied. "I won't smash the thing, unless you say I can, first."

Lew was walking back and forth, stamping his feet and rubbing circulation back into his hands. Every time his eyes fell on one of the captives, he scowled. Charlie motioned him away to where neither of them could hear and asked, "What are we going to do with them?"

"Leave them tied up for a week," Lew said promptly.

"We can't do that. They would freeze on a cold night."

"Guess we turn them loose, then," Lew said. "They probably don't have any other guns. I don't think they can take us armed."

"I fixed Andre's ropes so he can work them loose if he tries hard enough. I'll tell Max about it."

He went over to the chief secret agent and said, "When we're gone, start Andre working on his ropes. He should be able to undo them in about half an hour and then release you."

Max looked up with a half-smile. "You're taking quite a chance leaving us now, aren't you?"

"Maybe," he agreed.

He went back to Lew and whispered, "Did you get that? I think Max wants us to stay. There's something about that I don't like."

Chapter 8 – A Tiger by the Tail

"Yes, there's something screwy about all of this. I'm pretty sure Max wants us to stay here. But why?"

"I'm not guessing," Lew replied. "But whatever the reason, it can't be good for us. That guy is plain poison. Since Max wants us to stay, the safest thing is to leave immediately. Let's go."

Charlie went to the rear cabin where Sally still hammered away at the wireless key, sending out her plea for help.

"That's enough," Charlie said. "If you haven't got through by now, you never will. Come on, we're leaving."

"And don't forget your bag of clothes," Lew reminded her.

"I'm so sorry," Sally cried. "Let me bandage your head."

"Not now," Charlie ordered. "If you want to help, walk fast. We must get away from here as quickly as possible. I think we're in more danger every minute we stay, and I don't want any more messages to go out over the wireless. Can we disable it without breaking it?"

"All we need do is unbolt the transmitting key and take it with us," Sally replied quickly. "There is no backup on board."

Lew went to help her, and Charlie walked slowly around the grounded dirigible, wondering if there was anything else he should do before he left. Lew and Sally came out with the key, and Lew picked up the double-bit axe Andre had used to chop the scaffold timbers.

"Can I have this, Sally?" he asked. "It's too good a weapon to leave with these fellows, and how I could make the chips fly back at the cabin woodpile."

Sally, of course, assented. "I wish we could bring the camera," she added. "I don't like leaving it here where they can destroy it."

"Don't worry about that," Charlie replied. "The last thing Max will do is damage it. His job is to get it back safely to Europe. I've been wondering why Max didn't just take the blueprints and plans instead of the camera itself."

"There aren't any," Sally declared. "Dad told me he worked it all out in his head."

Lew took out his compass and studied it.

"What are you doing?" Sally asked.

"Checking the course between the dirigible and the lake. When we reach the lake, I'll blaze a tree so we will know exactly where to turn away from the shore if we have to come back. I'll mark the direction, too, so there won't be any chance of missing it."

"I thought woodsmen navigated by the sun," Sally said.

"Some do, but I find a compass easier and more sure. But the sun is useful when you don't have a compass. If you know how, you can determine any direction and estimate the hour of day by the sun.

"Why," Lew continued, warming to his subject, "I knew an old trapper who was part Indian, part French and the rest plain dirt. He would squint up at the sun and say, 'Camp's three points east of south and eight miles away. This is Saturday, January tenth, twenty-one minutes past three."

"I don't believe it," Sally declared.

"I guess I don't believe it all myself," Lew agreed, "but it's still a good story. But this I know is true by checking the sun: it is one hour before sunset. So we better move right along."

"How do you know that?" Sally asked.

"Simple finger measurement. When the sun has started down it sinks the width of one finger every 15 or 20 minutes, depending on the size of the finger. So, we hold our fingers out horizontal at arm's length to see how many finger widths are needed to fill the space between the sun's lower edge and the horizon. I get four fingers now, which means an hour. Charlie has wider fingers, so he would have measured three fingers and allowed 20 minutes apiece, for the same hour."

"What other clever things can you do?" Sally asked dubiously.

"You might be surprised," Lew said dryly. "Folks who fight the wilderness for a living have to stay sharp. If not, they don't last long. For instance, I have developed my hearing until I can catch sounds inaudible to most people. Right now, my ears are telling me an airplane approaches. Coming out of the east, I believe."

That brought them all to a halt. Sally searched the sky. But it appeared empty save for thin, curling white clouds.

"Are you sure?" Charlie asked.

Lew listened for several seconds more then nodded.

Sally's eyes shone. "My message got through. I knew it would. They're coming to help us. Hurrah!"

Lew kept his eyes fixed on the sky. Charlie and Sally could also hear the drone of the powerful motors now. Then they caught the sight of a plane approaching rapidly from the northeast. It was flying so low and so close to the top of the tall timber it remained hidden before suddenly flashing into open view.

"Maybe I ought to run down to the shore and wave my arms so they will see us," Lew said.

But Charlie caught his sleeve. "Wait. They won't miss us because they'll see the airship much sooner than they could see you."

"Watch that baby fly," Lew gloated. "She isn't going a foot less than 300 miles an hour. Talk about service. Why, Sally only sent her message out an hour ago. Her dad must have had this plane all warmed up and ready to go."

The craft came straight across the widest part of Shadow Lake and passed about a quarter-mile north of where they stood. Then the pilot cut the motors, gunning them with a roar afterwards, banked sharply and passed right over their heads. The plane cleared the tops of the bigger trees by less than 50 feet, roaring like a million angry hornets.

"Say," Lew cried, "what kind of a plane is that? I never saw one built that way before."

"No, and you can thank God for that," Charlie replied grimly. His face had darkened when he saw the insignia painted across the under surface of the wings.

Lew had seen it, too. "That isn't help for us," he said slowly.

"Don't say that," Sally cried. "It's got to be."

"No," Charlie told her. "Lew is right. I have been afraid of this. That plane came in answer to a call from Max, not you. He probably sent his call yesterday. And it brought this fighting craft from the deck of a foreign navy boat hiding out in the North Atlantic."

"So, this is why Max wanted us to stay," Lew muttered. "So his friends could meet us, too."

The plane had disappeared, headed towards the grounded dirigible. Then they heard the motors roar out signal blasts as the throttle was shoved back and forth.

"It'll have to come back to the lake to land," Lew said. "It had pontoons instead of wheels."

The plane was already returning, skimming along at reduced speed. It flashed over them a second time then swung out over the lake, turning abruptly and then setting down in a perfect water landing. The pontoons ripped through the thin skim ice, sending up a succession of splashes until the plane finally came to rest 400 feet from shore.

Sunlight shimmered from the blunt, metal wings. They were very low, the cabin merely a thicker part of the wing structure, completely streamlined into it.

"Looks like a bat," Lew said, then added, "out of hell."

"Looks more like a long-range scouting plane to me," Charlie replied dryly. "Small and fast with almost all of its lifting power needed for the fuel tanks. But plenty dangerous, just the same. We better get away from here," he added.

But Lew did not move. He stared at the fighter, fascinated by its deadly trimness. The black muzzles of twin machine guns protruded from an armored turret set high in the cabin. A hatch door swung open on the port side and something dropped out upon the lake.

"That's a rubber raft," Lew said. "They're coming ashore."

He shoved his rifle and axe toward Charlie. "Give me that magnum," he demanded.

"What are you going to do?" Charlie asked.

"Stop them," Lew replied, "while it's still easy."

"Don't be crazy," Charlie said. "Don't you suppose I thought of that? It might be easy enough if they all came ashore in the portable boat. But they won't. These are trained soldiers. They'll leave someone up in the gun turret to cover the landing, and he can cut you into hamburger with one blast of those guns."

"He may, anyway," Lew said grimly. "Only now the element of surprise gives me some sort of chance. We started this business, and we're going to finish it. I won't let them load the topographic camera in that plane and take it back to Europe."

He grabbed the rifle out of Charlie's hands and dashed away.

"Stop him!" Sally cried. "He'll be killed."

"You've never tried to stop Lew," Charlie told her. "It never works. I would go with him if I thought it would help. But two men on the edge of the woods make a target twice the size of one. I'll be more use to Lew if I keep out of sight and out of range of those guns."

"He will be butchered," Sally sobbed.

"Don't worry about Lew," Charlie answered. "He has come through some pretty tight places without a scratch."

He spun the crying girl into the timber and away from Shadow Lake. Then he ordered her to double-time it back to the cabin. As they walked, Charlie listened with nerves drawn tight, waiting for the first shot of the battle he knew was coming.

When he had gone a hundred steps he said, "I wanted to smash that camera before I left the dirigible," he said. "If I had, Lew would have stayed with us."

The camera, it appeared, was a sore subject with the girl. Her demeanor again flared up into anger. "You're not going to smash Dad's invention," she repeated. "Lew will save it. I know he will. He'll show those stink cats where to go."

Charlie grinned at that despite his anxiety. "The word probably fits them, all right," he admitted, "but it hardly belongs in the mouth of a nice girl like you."

"I know words that are worse," Sally said.

"I'll take your word for it," Charlie replied.

They started walking again, back into the timber. A shot crashed out behind, the sharp ping echoing over the face of the thinly frozen lake, reverberating back among the trees and hills.

"That," said Charlie, "was the magnum."

* * *

Lew's mind worked swiftly as he ran back toward the lake.

"This rifle shoots a clean, smokeless load," he told himself. "So they can't locate me from that when I fire. I won't shoot from in front of the plane; that is the place they're going to first rake with their guns. I'll stop about 70 feet to this side."

When he reached the last of the larger trees, Lew got down on his hands and knees to creep forward through the low brush. Up ahead was a fallen tree with a splintered end that had been blasted off by lightning. Broken limbs and bark lay all around. The log was almost 3 feet through, and while it had likely rotted a bit, the heart, Lew thought, would still be sound. He made for it because it was the only protection in sight.

When he reached the log he raised his head to peer out across the lake. Two men wearing helmets stood on top of the narrow ladder that hung above the inflated fabric boat. He poked his rifle out through the twisted tendons at the log's jagged break.

One splinter was just high enough to provide a shooting rest, and he adjusted the rifle so the support came where his hand gripped the forearm. Resting any gun by the barrel could harm the accuracy.

He saw with much satisfaction that the ground out in front showed sandy through the thin crust of snow. He saw, too, that the front side of the log was banked with sand deposited there by offshore winds. Bullets would not ricochet up from that banked sand.

"It will take a direct hit to penetrate both sand and wood," he thought as he thumbed back the safety on his rifle and cuddled the stock against his cheek. Then, one of those inexplicable happenings which so often spoil human plans occurred, something Lew could not possibly have foreseen, and even if he had, there would have been nothing he could have done to prevent it.

A big jay swooped out of the woods and hovered above Lew's head, uttering hoarse cries of alarm.

"Son-of-a-gun," Lew growled. "You trying to sign my death warrant? I'm a goner if any of those fellows are woodsmen."

He waited, muscles tense, but nothing happened. The men on the ladder maneuvered the boat into a better position to board. One leaned down to smash the ice with a long double-ended paddle.

Lew sighed gratefully and corrected his aim. He was not an aviation expert, and he had never seen a plane just like this one. But he knew enough about such craft to know approximately where the motor, fuel tanks and controls should be located.

The idea foremost in Lew's mind was to prevent the men taking Colonel Bern's camera back to a foreign power. He could have shot both soldiers standing on the ladder, but that was too cold-blooded for Lew, and he doubted it would accomplish his purpose, anyway. So he aimed not at them but at one of the fuel tanks in the wing. If he could drain the gasoline from the plane, it could not leave Shadow Lake, and the camera would be saved.

Lew's eye had already selected a likely location for each wing tank. He fired, heard the unmistakable sound of a high-speed bullet hitting liquid, threw in another shell, changed his aim point and fired again. "This is more fun than shooting cans with a .22," he thought.

Then it felt like every hellish storm brewed by infinity burst about him. Machine gun fire poured out of the gun turret, blasting the beach. First, the gunner swept the timber along the edge with a 50-yard arc of fire. When the gun swung toward him, Lew ground his body against the earth and instinctively covered his head with an arm.

The gunner lowered the muzzles level with the log and swung them up and down, blasting away. The hail of bullets sent geysers of sand and snow into the air. Bits of wood, bark and leaf mold showered down on Lew, and he felt the massive log shake as chunks of wood went spinning away like sawdust from a high-speed saw.

For a half-minute Lew was blinded by the dust. He wiped his eyes and saw his hand was bloody. His face smarted and stung in a hundred places. He felt it carefully, decided the pain came only from small breaks in the skin made by slivers and sand.

The shooting ceased, and Lew thanked God the log had been stout enough to absorb the blast. Then he felt a shock like cold hands touching the back of his neck. Less than a foot from his face, and about the same height from the ground, he saw the point of a jacketed bullet. It protruded about a third of its length out of the wood. Lew swallowed hard. He had missed death by that narrow a margin.

He gripped his rifle again and then let his trigger finger relax. He decided not to risk another shot that might give away his position. He saw the men were not on the ladder anymore. They had leaped into the lake and were splashing around the plane, trying to hide behind it.

"I know both tanks are hit," Lew thought. "Now, if I can only get away from here." He looked overhead. "Guess I won't have to worry about that jay bird anymore. If he's got any sense at all, he's on his way to the Arctic Circle by this time."

It looked as if Lew would have to stay behind the log until night-fall when darkness would cover his retreat. That thought brought a keen worry. While he was well-screened by the log, he was plainly exposed to anyone approaching from the rear. A man coming through the trees could spot him at once, and if that man happened to be Andre or Max, he could signal Lew's position with fatal results.

"Looks like I stuck my neck out a little too far," Lew muttered. "I'm like the guy who held a tiger by the tail—too scared to hang on but more afraid to let go."

Chapter 9 – Death Outside the Door

Lew considered his position as he lay behind the log on the shore of Shadow Lake, covering with a rifle men who had landed in a foreign fighting plane equipped with machine guns. So far, he had done quite well, shooting a hole in each of the plane's wing fuel tanks. He could smell the gasoline leaking steadily into the lake. The aviators' gunman had tried to blast him with machine-gun fire, and that had failed. Save for sundry small cuts and scratches, Lew was unhurt.

The two men who had flung the rubber boat upon the lake had abandoned their attempt to paddle ashore. But Lew was uneasy about the pair of secret agents they had left back at the crashed dirigible. Charlie had left them tied loose so they wouldn't be at the mercy of the wilderness for long. Charlie would never countenance such cruelty as leaving men bound to freeze to death.

But the arrival of the plane had complicated the situation. If the two men who had been tied got loose and came up behind Lew where they could signal his position to the waiting gunner in the plane, it would be over quickly.

Lew sniffed the taint on the air with satisfaction. Gasoline was pouring out of each tank, flooding the wings and pouring into the lake. Then an idea brought hope. "Once the plane is saturated and the lake is covered with gas, those guys won't dare shoot. Too much flame streaks out of those muzzles. They'd blow themselves and the plane sky high."

Something was going on inside the plane. Lew heard the men talking in low, guarded voices, saw figures darting by the cabin windows. He decided the two men who had jumped into the lake when he fired had climbed back in from the opposite side. He decided, too, that they might be trying to plug the leaking tanks and save the fuel.

"I can't let them do that," Lew thought, shoved his rifle forward again and put another bullet through each wing. Again he heard the satisfying sound of speeding balls penetrating liquid.

"I hope the bullets came through on the other side and made two more pairs of leaks," he thought. "Anyway, the shots will tell Charlie I'm still alive." His companion, he knew, would recognize the report of the magnum rifle.

His last shots, however, did more than reassure Charlie. Lew heard splashes and saw water fly up behind the plane. Apparently, the two men had jumped back in the lake as the safest spot when bullets cut into the wings. They were dog paddling to stay afloat. "That'll wear those fellows out after a while," Lew chuckled to himself.

He dug down hard against the earth, braced for the blasting he thought might follow. But no barrage shattered the sunset settling down about the lake. "I must have been right," Lew said to himself. "They don't dare shoot."

The smell of gasoline grew stronger with each passing minute. Lew supposed he could stand up, thumb his nose at the baffled airmen and walk off if he wished. But he didn't. He realized, now, that he must stay on longer. As long as he lay there, the men would not dare climb back on the plane and try to stop the leaking tanks. Lew wanted every drop of the high octane gas to pour out.

But he couldn't wait too long, either. He didn't fear Max and Andre anymore. They were unarmed and any signal from them could not help the stalled airplane gunner. What did matter was that the gasoline fumes could evaporate if he waited too long, and that would make shooting safe again. How fine dared he cut it?

Lew pulled back the toe bolt of the .300 and looked into the magazine. "Oh no," he muttered. Only one shell remained. He wished, now, he had paused long enough to relieve Charlie of the extra loads his companion always carried in his coat.

He felt that he must save this remaining load for an emergency. Then, as he lay pondering this development, nature solved his problem for him. He had survived a bad break when the Canada jay hovered over his hiding place sounding bird warnings. Now, a puff of breeze caught up sand and powdery snow, swirling it into the air. The blow increased, and the column of debris grew thicker.

Lew had seen these little whirlwinds before, but they mostly occurred in the dead of winter when the snow was dry. "There is a Providence that looks after babies and fools," he muttered.

The moment the little whirlwind of sand and snow blotted the plane from sight, he knew they could not see him, either. He jumped up and ran crouching into the timber.

Even when he was safely out of sight he kept running, hoping he could catch up with Charlie and Sally. He ran about 300 yards then heard a sharp whistle.

"It's me," Lew answered.

A half-minute later, Charlie was whacking him on the back.

"Was I glad to hear those last two shots from the rifle," Charlie said. "After all of that machine gun fire, I never expected to see you again." Then his voice grew sober. "Must have been hellish."

Lew shivered. "In high gear."

Sally had been clinging to his arm with wide eyes. Now she saw a drop of blood run down his cheek, and she cried, "You're hurt!"

"Just a scratch," Lew assured her.

"I wanted to go," Charlie said earnestly. "But I didn't see how that would help."

"It wouldn't have," Lew said. "Two men couldn't have done a bit more than I did. And there was no sense in us both getting killed if it turned out a bust."

"What did you do?" Sally demanded.

Lew described the battle with characteristic vigor. He put plenty of color into the story, and Sally's eyes grew bigger as he talked. A soft flush flooded her cheeks.

"With four holes punched in each fuel tank," Lew concluded, "that plane hasn't any more chance of lifting off the water than a goose with two broken wings. It can't get back to its mother ship on the Atlantic, and your dad's camera is safe, Sally. So you see ..."

But then Lew went silent, and his chin dropped.

"I forgot," he said, "about the fuel in the dirigible. They can carry it over to the plane and get away after all." He felt weak, wondering if he had faced death in a futile effort.

Charlie clapped him on the back again. "No chance," he said. "I fixed that. The last thing I did before I left the airship was open the drain cocks of each tank. They won't find any fuel there."

"That's great!" Lew cried, hope hitting a new high. "And we disabled the wireless, too, so they can't send out a call for more reinforcements. We haven't done so badly, have we?"

"All right, so far," Charlie agreed. "But we didn't make any friends today. There's Max and Andre with their plans smashed to nothing. There's the crew that came for them, now stranded in a plane without gas. Every one of them knows we're to blame."

Lew's face sagged. But Sally was indignant.

"I think you're mean," she scolded Charlie. "Lew was splendid, and I'll have my dad get him a medal for bravery."

"I'd rather have a corned beef sandwich right now," Lew grinned. "But Charlie is right. This business has just begun."

All this time they had been walking along close to the shore of

Shadow Lake. Charlie halted and said, "There's grub in the packsack. Do you want to stop and eat?"

Lew considered this for a moment. "No," he finally said. "I don't know that any of those fellows followed me, but it is possible."

Sally was badly exhausted when they finally reached the cabin. Charlie made her sit beside the fire while he cooked supper. Lew helped a little, but he was nervous and jumpy. He opened the door every few minutes to look out into the forest.

Night had fallen. A pale, thin moon threw a silver glow over the trees, creating an illusion like low-hanging mist. After eating, Lew cleaned the two automatic pistols captured from Max and Andre. He checked them carefully, noting they were built differently than any 9mm he had seen before. The guns used an outside hammer, which was cocked for the first shot by pulling back on the trigger exactly the same as a double-action revolver.

Lew shoved one of the guns into his pocket, handed the other to Charlie. "If we keep on accumulating firearms," he said, "we'll have enough to open a gun store someday. I wonder if we couldn't sneak that two-barreled machine gun out of the plane?"

Sally opened the traveling bag Lew had got her and spread most of the contents on the bunk. She looked at the clothes, then around the cabin. She frowned. The rough pole shelves were already piled to overflowing with food, utensils, tools, pieces of leather and wood, candles, wire, and all of the stuff a trapper accumulates for winter.

"Where can I hang my clothes?" she asked.

Lew yawned. "On the wall, anywhere."

Sally rubbed a finger along one of the logs then examined it closely. "It's too dirty," she declared. "Dust and soot all over everything. I don't see how you stand it."

Lew sat up indignantly. "This dirty? Let me tell you something. This is a model home compared to every other Northwoods cabin. You haven't had a shoe pulled off by a muck floor yet, have you? There weren't any mice trucking across your pillow last night, were there? You have a nerve calling this dirty. What if there is a little soot? It puts a glaze on our clothing to help turn water when we trail swamp deer."

Sally held up a pair of turquoise lounging pajamas trimmed with narrow bands of white fur. "I don't need any glaze on these, if you please, and I don't expect to wear them tracking down deer. I am going to give this place a real cleaning in the morning. I will need 10 pails of hot water and all of the soap and cleaning tools you can find. I want them early, too." She started humming a tune under her breath.

Lew groaned. "You remember me telling you how you spoiled my alibi for staying single? Well, you just fixed me up with another. This house-cleaning stuff. I guess I'm safe, after all."

"That's the way they all talk ... at first," Sally said, speaking impersonally to the fire.

Charlie and Lew took precautions to guard against a sneak attack that night. They blocked the door with an extra bar and barricaded the oiled cloth window with inside shutters made of stout slabs. The chimney could be counted on for enough ventilation in the cool weather.

After Sally had retired behind the curtain that screened her bunk like a Pullman berth, Charlie placed their three long guns on the floor between their own beds. Then he put the automatic pistols under the rolled-up coats that served as pillows.

After waiting long enough for Sally to doze off, Lew whispered, "We got to be careful, fella. This is bad business."

"Worse than juggling a buzz saw," Charlie agreed. "It's death without warning. I'm not so worried about the first part of the night. But if you happen to wake later on, take a look outside. And stay inside the door. Understand?"

"Okay," Lew promised.

"I wish you would stop whispering," Sally said from the curtained bed. "If you want to talk, do it out loud."

"We were just figuring out some way to head off that epidemic of house cleaning," Lew explained.

The hoot of an owl out in the forest awoke Charlie. He sat up in bed, reaching out for one of the rifles. It had been a long time since an owl had aroused him this way, because his subconscious mind had long since grown accustomed to the familiar sounds of the forest.

Then he wondered if it really had been an owl and laid the gun across his raised knees. He knew it wasn't when he heard a sound like fingers brushing over the door. He waited with raised gun. Almost a minute passed before he heard it again. This time it was at the window, the noise of a knife slitting cloth.

Charlie fired through the lower part of the shutter about where he thought a man cutting through the window fabric might stand. As soon as he shot, he jumped to the bunk, grabbed Sally's arm and dragged her onto the floor. The waking girl struck out at him instinctively, her eyes wide with fright.

He retained his grip on her arm until she ceased to struggle and lay panting on the floor. Lew had sprung up the instant Charlie fired. He was crouched beside the door listening.

"Don't anybody sit or stand," Charlie said.

"What happened?" Lew asked.

"Somebody tried the door. Then they went around to the window and cut the cloth. I hope I hit him, but I'm not sure."

"What are we lying here for, then?" Lew demanded. "Why don't we go out and see if you started something that must be finished?"

"Do you want to commit suicide?" Charlie retorted. "Don't you know machine guns can be dismounted from an airplane? Chances are this gang of goons brought theirs along and have it trained upon us from the woods. They sent a man up to test the door and window to see if they could slip inside and cut our throats while we slept. Now they know that isn't a go. So I'm expecting ..."

The owl called again. "That's no owl," Lew growled. "It's a man signaling. Gosh, that's an old trick, older than ..." he glanced over at Sally whose big, round eyes were shining in the dim light of the fireplace coals, "... a man's instinctive fear of females rigged out in sky-blue pajamas."

Sally tried to muster a look of disdain, but fright worked against her. Still, she whispered back, "Color-blind fool. These are turquoise, not sky-blue."

Then the machine gun began firing. Bullets smacked against the cabin's stout walls with a force that buckled the chinking poles from the joints. Dust showered upon them. The big logs at the bottom were too thick for bullets to penetrate, but many still found their way through the thinner edges where log joined log, and some of the smaller logs up near the eaves splintered. The three flattened their bodies against the floor. One ball struck the aluminum coffeepot with a clang.

"Darn them," Lew growled. "That was the best coffeepot I ever had. It never boiled over on me."

The fusillade stopped abruptly.

"Well," Lew said, "how did you like that, folks? I'm getting used to it. They're probably putting in a belt of fresh shells."

"I hope they're finished," Sally faltered, trembling with terror.

"If I can get her mad about something," Charlie thought, "she might forget her fear. She mustn't get hysterical."

But this time he couldn't think of anything to say.

The east wall had been hit by the volley of bullets, which showed the attacking party was off in the timber a little south and east of the path running down to the lake.

"If I could get a chance to shoot back," Lew growled. "What are we going to do, Charlie? We can't just lay here until they chop the place down to kindling."

"There doesn't seem to be much else we can do," Charlie replied. But after some thinking, he said, "Maybe there is."

He crawled to the ammunition shelf and took down a box of .300 loads. Then he crawled towards the door with the rifle.

"Come help me slip out."

"What?" demanded Lew. "You must be crazy."

"I don't think so. They're on the east side where they can't see the door. I can slip out and not be seen. Now slide the bar back and open it about a foot. Then shut it quietly after I am outside."

Lew hesitated, dubious about such a venture. But he thought, "Charlie must know what he's doing. Anyway, he always lets me try the stunts I dope out."

"All right," he whispered, and reaching up, lifted the bar. The machine gun blasted away, not in a continuous roar but in short bursts of several shots each. Lew wondered if their enemy might be running low on shells. "Hurry, Charlie!" he urged. "I don't want to sit up any longer. I felt much safer flat on the floor."

Charlie pushed through the door and disappeared. Lew swung the panel back and dropped the bar back in place.

Chapter 10 – Gentlemen, It's Too Late!

Charlie slipped through the door and around the cabin wall without being discovered by the men attacking them with the machine gun. At least he assumed he had not been seen, for the short bursts of bullets made no shift to follow him.

He knew he had to stop the barrage before someone inside the cabin was hit. They had escaped so far by lying flat upon the floor. But eventually, a bullet was going to rip through the thin edges of joined logs or through a chinked joint and find its human target. The law of averages all but guaranteed that. So, Charlie had decided to climb to the roof and locate the rapid-firing guns by the flashing muzzles. Then, he would try to silence them with the magnum rifle.

He was taking considerable risk, since the thin cabin roof offered scant protection against machine gun fire. If his enemies found him by the flash of his rifle, one burst of their more potent weaponry would surely finish him. Realizing this, Charlie planned to shoot quickly then slide back to the ground where the cabin walls and fur shed, together with the rank of firewood, would protect him.

The notched ends of the corner logs made an excellent ladder, and he started to climb with the rifle slung over his shoulder. At the eaves, he lay flat and squirmed up until he could look over the roof ridge. He saw the machine gun blast as hoped and pushed the rifle out over the top of the roof.

It is hard to estimate range in the dark, but Charlie knew the shot would not exceed the flat-shooting range of a .300 magnum. Any allowance for bullet drop was unnecessary.

He looked into the low-power scope, its high-grade lenses acting like the best night glass, doubling the clarity with which he could distinguish objects back among the trees. He thought he could see the outline of a man when he trained the crosshairs above the flashing twin muzzles. But he was not sure of this, so he aimed directly at the top of the flames and took a shot.

Wham! The rifle recoiled viciously into his cheek. Lying down behind the peak of the sloping roof, Charlie had been unable to direct the recoil away from his face. He threw a second shell into the chamber and fired again.

The machine gun went silent, and Charlie rolled diagonally down and across the roof as swiftly as he could, rifle pressed against his chest and protected by his elbows. At the eaves, he turned and dropped to the ground behind the rank of firewood.

The dash to the cabin door came next. Lew had fastened the door after him, and he hoped he would anticipate his coming and get the bar up the moment he reached the door. There was plenty of risk yet to run. Even if the machine gun was crippled, the enemy hiding among the trees would have service rifles shooting the same high-velocity load.

Charlie tapped against the cabin wall with the butt of his rifle. After a short silence, he heard an answering knock from within. He got his pocketknife out and cut at the wooden strip nailed over one of the wall joints. He cut the strip in two, pried up an end, and with his mouth close to the crack whispered, "I'm coming in."

Two taps answered.

Charlie went to the corner and waited several seconds to give Lew time. Then he ran for the door. A shot crashed across the little clearing, then another. One of the bullets thudded into a log less than a foot from his head. A third smashed through the slab door as it swung wide, and then Charlie tumbled in and fell sprawling across the floor behind the doorjamb.

"That was rifle fire," he grunted. "And not very good shooting."

"You aren't nicked, are you?" Lew asked.

"Not a scratch."

"I think you took out the machine gun," Lew continued. "Without rapid-fire, that bunch is whittled down to about our size. Shucks, what can five of them do with only rifles, especially when one of them has a busted shoulder?"

"Don't get overconfident," Charlie cautioned. "These fellows are dangerous, and they haven't quit, you know. They are just figuring out something new to try."

He looked over and saw Sally flattened on the clay dirt floor almost in the center of the room. "You roll over into a corner," Charlie ordered her. "You're right in line with the door."

She obeyed but complained that her pajamas were being ruined by the dirt.

"That's nothing," Lew retorted. "Think of my coffeepot with a hole punched through both sides."

Two bullets ripped through the rough slab door and smacked against the stone fireplace chimney. Two more followed, and then another two. This firing continued. It looked like four men were working bolt rifles in pairs. Every bullet struck and pierced the door.

"They've changed position," Charlie said, "and are facing the door now. If you hadn't moved, Sally, you would have something more serious than ruined pajamas."

"Why didn't they bring the machine gun around there at first?" Lew asked.

"I've been wondering the same thing," Charlie replied. "Somebody bungled. Maybe they figured the cabin walls were too thin to turn the bullets. Maybe they wanted to quickly kill us in our sleep. You know a lot of those bullets struck about the height of a bunk."

Shots ripped steadily through the door. Only a few ranged straight back and pinged against the chimney. Most of the balls hit toward the corners. The attacking men had separated and were shooting from wide angles to search out every inch of the space within the cabin.

"Darn," Lew muttered.

"Hit?" Charlie asked quickly.

"Just a heel knocked off a boot, but I need that heel."

The clay floor got a lot of punishment now. Bullets smacked into it sending up clouds of dust that made them cough and sneeze.

"I guess we'll have to build a new door," Lew said. "This one will be as porous as mosquito netting. It looks to me like somebody is up a tree shooting down on us."

Lew rolled until his head was almost behind the hinge edge of the door. A group of five bullets striking close together had torn a chunk of wood away, and he peered through the opening. He didn't look long, for two shots struck less than a foot from his nose and sent him rolling back. But before he had left the door, he had seen a streak of flame spurt out from a spot halfway between the skyline and the earth.

"He's in a tree, all right," Lew said. "I wish you were up on that roof now, Charlie."

"Well, I don't," Charlie replied. "I'm comfortable right here, thank you."

"I'm not suggesting you go," Lew said. "But I don't think they could see you shooting up there, either. You were out in the open where the moonlight hid the muzzle flash of your gun. These fellows are back in the shadows where it shows as plain as lightning."

"Still, I'm not making another run through that door," Charlie repeated. He felt the .300 rifle move away from under his hand. "For goodness sake," he said alarmed. "Don't you try it."

"I won't," Lew promised. "I'm just going to peek out through that hole in the door again." But he did more than peek, for the magnum roared a moment later. Lew then rolled swiftly back into his corner, but there was no answering rifle fire from outside. He did hear something out in the trees strike the ground with a dull thud.

"Sounds like he dropped his rifle," Charlie said.

Lew grunted. "Sounds more like he dropped himself. I hope he did. The murdering ..."

"Stink cat," Charlie supplied as Lew floundered about trying to find a stronger term. "That," added Charlie, "is a favorite of Sally's, and she knows them better than we do."

"How can you tell such an awful fib?" she cried out.

"Pipe down," Lew whispered. "You want them to know which corner you're hiding in? I wonder what time of night it is, anyway?"

Charlie crawled over to the fireplace and scratched among the embers until a little glow illuminated the face of his watch. "Just two o'clock," he announced and then smothered the ember with ashes.

They waited in the dark for almost an hour, wondering what their enemy might try next.

"Suppose they've given it up as a bad job?" Lew asked finally.

"I would if I had made as many mistakes as they have tonight," Charlie replied. "If they wanted to kill us, they could have ambushed us from the trees tomorrow when we came outside the cabin. That would have been the easy way. I think they must feel pressed for time. Help may come any hour now, answering Sally's call. When it does, they're sunk, and they know it."

"I'm getting so hungry I'll be chewing on my boot soon," Lew complained. "Could we risk a little fire to make tea?"

Charlie vetoed that firmly.

"I thought it wouldn't go," Lew sighed. "But if I can't eat, what about some sleep? That is, if you're willing to sit up and watch for a couple of hours?"

Charlie agreed, and Lew rolled over on the bed he had laid upon the floor. Then he said to Sally, "Why don't you turn in, too? The shooting has stopped. And remember, you got a reputation to keep each morning. Looking fresh and dewy like a rose, you know."

"You are so silly," she replied, but Lew could tell by her voice she was pleased. Then she added, "I might be able to sleep if I was sure I wouldn't be dragged out of bed again."

Charlie laughed at that. "You won't be, not by me, anyway. Once is enough. My chin still hurts where you socked me. It was worse than pulling a bobcat off a limb."

Sally grabbed the first thing in reach and flung it at him. The missile happened to be the bullet-pierced coffeepot, and it clunked against the wall above Lew's head before dropping down upon his nose. Then they heard her climb back into the bunk.

"You kids make a lot of racket," Charlie warned. "If the shooting starts again, I know who to blame."

But it did not start again. The only sound was Lew's heavy breathing, for he had fallen asleep almost at once. Charlie felt himself dozing at times, but he snapped his eyes open and his senses alert. Twice he stood up and got a drink of cold water. He doubted if there would be any more attacks on the cabin that night. The enemy might as a last resort try to rush in and batter down the riddled door, but Charlie knew they were aware of the risk that would bring.

When two and a half hours had passed, Charlie awoke his companion and changed places. Sometime later, Charlie himself was aroused when Lew stirred up the fire and laid kindling on the coals. Charlie looked at his watch and saw it was 6:20.

Lew started cooking breakfast. The water supply was short, but he quickly scooped up snow from just outside the door and melted it for tea. When Sally joined them in front of the fireplace, he looked her over critically.

"Is there anything the matter?" she demanded.

"No, you're holding off old age pretty well. But since I know you missed the snow rub this morning, did the complexion come from the make-up kit?"

"I'm not telling any more secrets," she replied with a sly smile.

Lew and Charlie took turns periodically looking out through the door and the window, searching the timber for any sign of the enemy. After eating, Lew began to fidget on the bench.

"What are we going to do?" he asked finally. "Stay penned up here the rest of our lives?"

"I want to be sure Max and his gang have gone before I do any walking around," Charlie replied.

"How can we find that out if we don't walk around?" Lew asked.

"We can't," Charlie replied, picking up the rifle.

"I'm going, too," Lew said quickly.

"No, you stay here to guard the cabin and Sally."

Charlie stepped swiftly through the door and pushed it shut behind him before Lew had time to argue. He knew there were risks to such a move, but there was at least equal risk in doing nothing.

Charlie was familiar with the lay of the land around the cabin. He knew exactly where a sniper might find a good stand. The best cover was in the eastern woods where the machine gun had been set up last night. So, he walked around the cabin and the big rock against which it was built to approach that area from the rear.

He walked slowly, trying to keep a tree before him as often as he could. He searched the snow for footprints. A concentration might indicate danger, whereas an absence would indicate that the near ground was probably safe.

It took him more than an hour to reach where the guns had fired from the night before, in behind a small blowdown of pines. The ground was littered with casings. Charlie picked one up and saw the head was stamped 8x56, which identified it as an 8mm load.

Then he saw something that brought him grim satisfaction. The snow was stained with drops of red. And mixed up in it by the trampling of many feet were fragments of machined steel, undoubtedly from where his high-speed rifle round had hit the rapid-fire gun. He had disabled it and also, he hoped, one of the gunners.

Charlie approached every thick clump of brush and every fallen treetop with caution. Another quarter-hour passed before he found the tree from which the sniper had fired through the cabin door. More grim satisfaction came here, for again he saw blood-stained snow trampled by footprints. There was a trail made by two men carrying a load, and judging by their irregular tracks, it was quite heavy.

"Somebody had to be carried away," Charlie thought. "Counting Andre and the man wounded behind the machine gun, three of the five are likely disabled. The attack last night was a costly blunder."

It was reasonable, now, to assume that the entire party had left with the wounded. The timber should be safe enough for them to resume their daily routine, so Charlie turned toward the cabin to tell his companions. But he had taken only a few steps when loud shouts poured from the timber behind, whirling him about.

"Help! Help!" The words were repeated over and over.

Charlie's first thought was of a trap, and he jumped behind a tree. The shouts continued as he looked out and around. He saw nothing but snow and brush and timber. He frowned when he heard Lew's voice up at the cabin. "Charlie! I'm coming!" his companion yelled.

Charlie shouted back, ordering him to stay, but Lew did not hear, for his encouraging cries came nearer. The voice up ahead that called for help went silent. Charlie didn't like that.

Again, he shouted for Lew to turn back to the cabin, but Lew mistook the order as an appeal, and he kept on coming.

Charlie left the tree and ran forward a dozen steps. He saw a man lying on his face in the snow. He dodged behind another tree and covered the man with his rifle.

"If you can yell that loud you are able to sit up," he said. "But don't move your hands. I'll shoot if you do." Then he raised his voice and shouted, "Lew, run back to the cabin, now!"

The man in the snow sat up facing Charlie. It was Max, with a confident smile on his thin face.

Lew had arrived, and he asked, "What's this about?"

"You heard me," Charlie replied. "Go back—now!"

A premonition of disaster filled him with rage. Then his worst fears jelled around three piercing cries that came from the cabin, with the last one smothered at the end.

"Too late, gentlemen," Max spoke suavely. "Much too late."

Chapter 11 – A Cure for Insomnia

As Max rose from his prone position in the snow, Charlie followed him up with the muzzle of the rifle. Then he answered the secret agent's smug declaration that it was too late for him to do anything about the screams that had come from the cabin.

"Maybe," Charlie told him. "Now get up."

The man arose at his leisure.

"Start running," Charlie ordered, motioning towards the cabin with his rifle's muzzle.

"I can't run," Max protested. "I sprained an ankle last night dodging your shots." He seized a small sapling and leaned on it.

Charlie was sure he lied. Quite likely, Max had helped carry the man away that Lew had shot out of the tree. Still, if the others had carried Sally off, and he was quite sure they had, Max might be the only chip he had, offering an exchange of captives.

Charlie motioned again with the gun. Max took a step and tumbled in the snow. Charlie went up, kicked him smartly in the ribs, and stepped back. Max rose slowly, his face twisted with rage. He muttered threats in a foreign language. The kick had been brutal.

Max hobbled slowly ahead several steps and fell again. Charlie kicked him a second time, again making no attempt to soften the blow. Max's face was blacker and more twisted when he stood up.

"He sure can take it," Charlie thought. There wasn't the least doubt in his mind that Max was faking to gain time and delay.

Max walked almost a dozen steps this time before he tumbled. Charlie came up and lifted his boot, but the kick was never delivered. Airplane engines shattered the morning stillness with three short blasts that swelled into a steady roar.

Charlie stepped back, slightly sick with the realization of what was happening. Max sprang up nimbly and faced him, his weight balanced between both feet. His face smoothed out into a confident smile that contrasted oddly with the glint in his eyes.

"We can stop this silly business now," he said quietly. "I'll run if you wish, but you can see there isn't any reason to hurry. As I said before, it is too late for you to do anything."

Charlie simply motioned him on. He didn't want to talk, and he wasn't sure which angered him more, the knowledge of how neatly he had been tricked or the sneering smile on Max's face. Together, they were almost intolerable.

He walked behind his captive with clenched jaws. It was one of the very few times Charlie nearly lost his self-control.

Lew met them some 50 yards from the cabin. His face told Charlie that the worst had occurred. "I got to the lake too late," Lew spoke. "They had taken off in the plane and were so high up I didn't waste a shell shooting at them."

"They took Sally?" Charlie asked.

Lew nodded. Then he turned on Max and demanded, "What do you want her for? She hasn't done anything."

Max raised his brows. "Are you really that dumb?"

The question didn't make Lew feel any better. But here was an outlet for his rage, and he stepped forward determined to thrash the man. Charlie stopped him with a hard grip on the arm.

"Stand back," Charlie ordered. "You know why they took Sally. Max will trade her for the wireless key. He needs that to send out a call for more gasoline. I'm right, am I not?" he asked.

Max smiled. "With one exception. Now you are going to trade the key *and* me for her."

"I thought you had an out planned before you started yelling," Charlie replied. "How did you know I wouldn't shoot you?"

Max shrugged. "I take risks. It is part of the work. But I felt fairly safe. You are the type of weak man who gives an enemy more than an even break. Besides, I knew you would want to question me before you shot. That would give time for my men to take Miss Bern. I figured it was ten to one I would have time to offer the exchange."

"I'm wondering why you didn't use the radio in the plane to call for fuel," Charlie asked. "It has one, hasn't it?"

"The best in the world. Only it was damaged in the shooting yesterday afternoon. Another thing I have to thank you for."

And then his mask of polite condescension slipped so abruptly the change startled them. In a hard, cruel voice he continued, "You're mixed up in something too big for you. The quicker you see that the better it will be—for you. Why not drop out while you still can? Give me the key, and I promise Miss Bern will be set free."

Charlie studied the man's face for several seconds before he spoke. "Suppose we go inside the cabin? We can talk there."

They started walking again, and Charlie continued, "How did

you bring the plane without us hearing it?"

Max answered curtly, impatiently. "We took her up to 12,000 feet, cut the engines and coasted in. Then, early this morning, we towed it closer with our collapsible boats. What difference does that make? Are you ready to give me the key?"

"I'm thinking about it," Charlie replied. Max reached the cabin first, went in and sat down on a bench. He sighed with feigned fatigue. "I have had a very long night," he told them.

"And a bad one," Charlie couldn't resist adding. He stayed a few feet from Max. Lew stopped in the doorway.

"I suppose you found the blood in the snow," Max said. "I argued against that clumsy night attack, but Lieutenant Wilk insisted. He believed he could blast you out of the cabin with his machine gun. I argued for more subtle methods."

How Lew and Charlie both hated that smug, sneering smile.

"What happened to the man I shot out of the tree?" Lew asked.

Max's smile faded. "He was hit in the chest. We had to carry him all the way to the plane."

"That isn't all, either," Charlie said. "Somebody got hit with shrapnel or a ricochet when I hit the machine gun. I saw blood in the snow there, too.

Charlie was talking for two reasons: first, to gain time while he figured some way out of the apparent stalemate; second, the more information he obtained from Max, the more effective any plan he evolved might be.

Max seemed willing to answer his questions. The secret agent seemed to be trying to sound agreeable in order to sell the idea of trading the key for Sally.

"Sergeant Brenner lost two fingers," Max said. "You shoot well, but I knew that. It was another reason I protested the frontal assault."

Lew stepped into the cabin. "So, you are the one who figured out this stunt of kidnapping Miss Bern?" he demanded.

Max smiled.

"And you called me dumb," Lew said, shaking his head.

"What do you mean?" Max asked quickly.

"I'm thinking about all the trouble you took. Why didn't you just grab the key in the first place? It's right there in plain sight," and Lew pointed to the shelf where the instrument lay.

Max's face grew pale, but he answered, "I ordered them not to search the cabin. I was afraid they wouldn't have enough time. I was sure, too, that the key had been hidden. But suppose we did go to needless trouble? We still achieve our aim."

"Yeah?" Lew asked.

Max nodded firmly. "There isn't any doubt of that."

"You believe we're going to give you the key and turn you loose? Then take your word no harm comes to Miss Bern?" Charlie asked.

Max nodded and then said, "You can't do anything else, not if you want to see the girl alive. You'll do just as you're told. One life, a dozen lives, what does it matter to me? Don't be fools. Give me the key. The quicker I get back with it, the better condition you'll find the girl in when I turn her free."

Charlie watched Lew's face go white with rage, and then he stepped in a little closer to the secret agent.

"Seems to me," he began in a low drawl, "you've been taking too much for granted. You're a long way from winding up this dirty work. Already we've disabled three of your gang. With you here, that means only one sound man back on the job. I don't think we'll have much trouble handling him. We stood five of you off last night."

Without warning, Charlie's right fist struck Max's jaw a mighty blow that hurled the man from the bench and sent him in a heap to the floor. Max's head rolled against the cabin wall, and he lay still. Lew gaped in surprise.

"I noticed that one of Max's hands had slipped half inside the pocket of his coat," Charlie explained.

Lew bent over, reached in the pocket and brought out a queerly shaped weapon. It had a blued steel barrel and a thick, bulging breech. It was hardly more than 6 inches long. "A gas pistol," he muttered. "One more second, and he would have let it off."

Lew laid the dangerous device on the table. "How did you know he was going to pull it?"

"I was watching his eyes," Charlie explained. "I knew Max was too clever to telegraph his thoughts. But I also thought he was clever enough to know that his eyes might give him away. So, when he looked away, I figured he was going to act. I stepped in and slugged him. Even if I had guessed wrong, it would have been all right, wouldn't it?"

"Absolutely," Lew agreed. "Wonder if I could take a crack when he comes around?"

"Don't talk nonsense," Charlie ordered sharply. "Get some of those thongs we cut for snowshoes and tie him up. Really tie him, too. He's got to stay here until we get back if that takes a week. I'm not ..."

Charlie gasped as something struck him in the stomach and sent him reeling. Max had bounced out of the corner like a rubber ball, arms flailing. An elbow had struck Charlie just below the belt. A fist had cuffed Lew on the side of the head and spun him against the wall. They caught a brief glimpse of the man as he shot out the door.

"Get him," Charlie gasped, arms hugging his middle. Lew grabbed a rifle and followed, but Max had disappeared before Lew cleared the doorway. Following around the nearest corner of the cabin, Lew heard him crashing through the brush to the north.

Lew ran as fast as he could. But he had to stop and listen to follow the escaping man's course. He still ran faster than he had ever run before, and presently, he was close enough to catch glimpses of Max coursing like a hound with head stretched out and shoulders low.

But then Lew began to tire, and Max built his lead. Lew hung doggedly on the trail until all sound of Max died away. Then he stopped, looked out through the bare trees for several seconds, and started back to the cabin.

Charlie stood in the doorway waiting.

Lew shook his head. "He's too fast on his feet."

"We've been a pair," Charlie said bitterly. "Everything that fellow planned turned out the way he wanted."

"He didn't get the key," Lew reminded Charlie.

Charlie glanced over quickly to assure himself the instrument still lay on the shelf. "It's a wonder," he said. "This is all my fault. I should have remembered Max is an extraordinary athlete. Heaven knows he gave me enough proof yesterday.

"He must have seen my blow coming and rolled with it. I doubt it even hurt him. He was waiting for the right moment to make a run for it. When I told you to tie him up, he didn't dare wait any longer."

"He struck you pretty hard, didn't he?" Lew asked.

"Caught me unguarded," Charlie nodded. "With warning, I could have flexed my stomach muscles and not been knocked windless."

"Can you walk?" Lew demanded.

"Give me a minute."

"We've got to hurry," Lew said. "Didn't you hear what he said about Sally? The sooner we turned him loose, the better shape she would be in when she came back? We can't waste a second, Charlie. Maybe we can head Max off before he gets back to his camp."

"I doubt that," Charlie replied. "He has too much of a start. Besides, the airplane may have come back to pick him up somewhere along the lake. He is smart enough to think of that."

"If they hurt Sally, I'm going to hunt him down," Lew said matter-of-factly. "I'll get every one of them if it takes a lifetime."

"Get all of the rifle shells," Charlie said. "Put them in the pack sack with some dried venison."

"You think I'm going to waste time eating?" Lew asked.

"You'll be starving by the time we get there," Charlie said. "A hungry man can't think clear, so pack the meat."

Lew stuffed the provisions and then the shells in the pack. He looked around for what else he might bring to a showdown.

A special knife already hung on his belt, not the kind carried by woodsmen but one with a wide blade balanced expressly for throwing. Lew had acquired a nice skill with it, and that knack had served him well in other perilous places.

They each picked up a rifle, pocketed a pistol, and left the cabin. Lew took the lead, and several times Charlie called to him to cut his pace. It still lacked two hours of noon.

Lew protested each time, "We have to hurry, old-timer. We don't know what's happening to Sally."

"Regardless, we can't arrive winded," Charlie reminded him. "We're up against the deadliest combination of brains, strength and ruthlessness we have ever faced. Besides, I don't think anything will happen to Sally, not today. She is the only card they have to play. And they're going to play her close to the board."

"That reminds me," Lew said. "Did you get the key?"

"I've got it, alright" Charlie answered. "It may be our only card to play when we meet up with Max again."

Chapter 12 – Blitzkrieg!

As they hiked along the shore of the lake, Lew said, "I hope you've figured out some way to sort this mess out."

"I have a couple of ideas," Charlie replied.

Lew waited for more and then said, "Would it be asking too much if I wanted to know the best of them?"

"Right now, yes," Charlie said.

Lew kept silent for several minutes after that. Then he asked, "Could a couple of the gang be waiting along the lake to dry-gulch us in the back? They would expect us to follow the beach."

"It's possible," Charlie conceded. "We'd better turn inland."

Because they had to proceed carefully and not expose themselves, it was well past noon before they reached a point in the forest opposite the site of the grounded airship. But instead of turning towards it, Charlie started back for the lake. Lew frowned and whispered, "Why that way?" They had long since ceased to talk out loud.

"I want to see if the plane is there," Charlie replied. When they reached the edge of the woods they saw it moored some 200 yards out. Two collapsible rubber boats were pulled up on the beach with a double-bladed paddle in each.

Lew started toward the boats, but Charlie jerked him back. "You crazy?" he demanded.

"Nope. I just thought I would like to take a look inside that plane. Everybody is on shore; the second boat proves that."

Charlie sighed. "Curiosity is going to get you in the doghouse, yet. Those boats are most likely a trap."

"A trap?"

"Sure. The boats prove nothing. They could have left a man aboard when they came to shore. I'd be willing to bet somebody is out there with a service rifle, and wouldn't he have fun cutting loose about the time you were halfway out? You wouldn't have a chance."

"Okay," Lew said. "So, what are we going to do instead?"

"Plenty," Charlie replied and then drew Lew back into the timber. Indicating a very tall, straight spruce, he said, "Sling the rifle over your back and shin up that tree."

"What do I do when I reach the top?" Lew asked.

"When you're halfway up, shoot a hole in each of the plane's pontoons. That is just as effective to ground the plane as shooting the fuel tanks. If you had thought of that yesterday, the ship could never have taken off the water."

Lew's face lengthened. "It is a wonder I have lived this long," he admitted. "Want to kick me, Charlie? You'll feel better; I'll feel better; and the boost will start me up this tree."

"I'm not kicking anybody," Charlie replied. "Except hopefully Max in the ribs again. Go high enough so you can shoot down on the pontoons. That will put a hole in the top to let air out and one in the bottom for water to come in. Once the pontoons fill, the plane will settle so deep only a wrecking crew could get her out."

"The shots will let Max know we're on the way."

"What of it? He expects us."

"After I shoot holes in the pontoons, then what?"

"We go give Max the wireless key—if he still wants it."

Lew climbed until he was 40 feet above the ground, unslung the rifle, trained it upon the inside pontoon and fired. Reloading swiftly, he aimed at the second float. This one was harder to see, and he realized he should have shot it first when there was no need for haste.

Before he got off that second shot, a bullet from the plane buried itself in the tree about 6 feet below the limb on which he stood.

"He's got my range pretty well read," Lew muttered and then took his second shot, scoring another clean hit.

The next shot from the plane cut green twigs less than a foot from Lew's head. He reslung his gun and slipped nimbly around behind the tree. "That was close. The sun must be glinting off my barrel."

He slid down as fast as he could. Two more bullets cut deep into the spruce before he dropped the last 6 feet and landed on his hands and knees. Then he got up and said, "See how that guy followed me down the tree? He isn't dumb, and he isn't a bad shot, either."

"They don't send incompetent men out on jobs like this," Charlie reminded him. "And they are all crack shots."

"I am glad you sent me up a big tree," Lew said. "But hardball 8mm military rounds can penetrate 5 feet of wood. Why didn't those bullets come through?"

"The wood is still alive, green and full of knots. Every knot spreads a bullet and slows it."

"I hope you thought of that before you sent me up there," Lew replied. "Anyway, that takes care of the plane. Max next?"

"Not yet. Now, I want you to build a fire back away from the lake out of rifle range. I'm winded, so I'll let you do the work while I watch and protect you from surprise attack."

"What good is a fire going to do?" Lew asked.

"Get a blaze going," Charlie ignored the question. "Then smother it with green pine. I want a big column of smoke in the sky."

Lew nodded. "I get it, now. You're thinking of the rescue party coming for Sally. A smoke signal will help them find us."

"Right," Charlie said. "The only reason they haven't found her yet is there's too much country and they don't know where to search. I'm sure they didn't lose any time starting out after her message came."

"You bet they didn't," Lew chimed in. "Her father must be half nuts with worry. Maybe it'll do him good, too. He'll take better care of his impulsive daughter next time, and the experience should make the daughter a little less headstrong, too."

Charlie went a hundred yards deeper into the timber to watch and listen. Lew built the fire with dry limbs wrenched from a deadfall. The blaze crackled and snapped, and the smoke brought four wild shots from the man in the plane. Lew began breaking off green pine branches and laying them on the blaze. The fire sputtered, but presently, a white twister of smoke soared upwards. Three more shots came out of the plane before Lew joined his companion. These hit much closer.

"That fellow's no slouch as a rifleman," Lew grumbled, "even at that range. Twice I heard balls singing over my head, and that's a song I never care to hear."

"It was a mistake starting the fire within even long rifle range," Charlie admitted. "But I thought the trees would shield you."

"I'm awaiting more orders," Lew said quickly.

"All right. Go back and see if the rifleman has tried stepping down on the pontoons to patch the leaks."

Lew got a box of cartridges from the pack, filled the gun and a pocket. When he reached the edge of the woods, he saw no one standing on either of the floats. Lew was disappointed at the lack of a target. But his disappointment eased when he saw how badly the ship was listing. It wouldn't leave the lake under its own power.

"I must let him know we're still around," Lew thought. "I think I'll send a slug through the motor, might even strike pay dirt there."

The big rifle boomed and kicked back into his shoulder with a stiff jolt. "I hope I learn how to face this stock properly before too long," Lew grumbled.

The man in the plane sent two fast ones back, but neither came close. Lew trotted back to join Charlie.

"She's settling, fast," Lew said. "Not a chance she'll take off. I wonder why Max hasn't showed up to investigate this shooting?"

"I suspect Max wants us to come to him," Charlie replied. "So let's go."

"Our luck's been swell, so far," Lew said. "I hope it holds out."

Charlie hoped so, too.

Lew piled more green stuff on the fire to keep the smoke billowing up into the sky. Then they started toward the grounded dirigible.

"What do you figure on doing when we get there?" Lew asked.

"I will have a talk with Max."

"Boy," Lew said, "you sure don't mind sticking your neck out. Going to walk right up to the lion and look at his teeth. Then what?"

"I will offer him the wireless key," Charlie said simply.

As they drew closer to the airship, they could hear men talking and caught glimpses through the treetops of the big gas envelope of the sky cruiser. Charlie stopped and drew Lew close. Then he whispered in his ear for almost a minute. As Charlie talked, Lew's eyes began to shine. They also widened a little.

"I'll hold up my end," Lew promised. "We can't do any worse than take a shot." Then he walked into the timber.

Charlie waited motionless. When 10 minutes had passed, he started walking toward the enemy camp. He could hear someone breaking dry tree limbs. When there were only about a dozen trees intervening, Charlie stopped and called out in a loud voice, "Max!"

The camp talk ceased. After a short silence, Max replied, "Did you bring the key?"

"I've got it, and I'll trade it for Miss Bern. What do you say?"

"Yes, of course." The secret agent's voice had become warm, almost friendly. But Charlie still kept his body shielded behind a tree.

"Don't try any tricks," Charlie began. "My companion is covering both of us with the mag. There isn't a chance of anyone slipping up behind me. The key is on the ground in front of me, but if I suspect a trap, I'll smash it with a bullet of my own."

"All right," Max said. "We won't try any tricks."

"Bring Miss Bern with you," Charlie continued. Just you and her, nobody else. When I see you coming together, I'm going to pick up the key and back off. Stop when I tell you to, and I will toss the key to you. While it's in the air, release her so she can run to me."

"Then you put a bullet through me?" Max asked dryly. "Do you really think I'm a fool?"

"No. But you need the key. So you must take the risk. I give you my word of honor I won't shoot, and my companion won't, either. You've seen we play fair. You're going to have to trust us that far."

Max didn't reply for almost a minute. Then, "All right. I'm starting with Miss Bern. She will walk directly in front to shield me."

"Fair enough," Charlie answered. He had already started to back away, following a course previously fixed upon. He heard Sally and Max coming. They made no attempt to walk silently. In fact, Max scuffed his feet on the ground rather noisily.

"Where are you?" he called out.

"Come a few more yards," Charlie replied. He stopped and waited, his body screened by a tree.

Max was talking to Sally. "You know what to do? Stop when you see him. Then, when he throws the key, I'll release you. Run straight to him, not to a side. I want you between us so he can't take a shot at me. If you veer off, I will put a bullet in your back."

Sally's indignant voice did not hold a trace of fear as she replied scornfully. "You would do that, too."

Charlie could see them now. Max behind the girl, head and shoulders stooped until he was scarcely any taller. It looked like the agent was gripping the back of her jacket with one hand, for the garment was pulled taut over her heaving chest. The other hand was hidden. Charlie didn't like that, but he merely said, "Stop. You're close enough."

They halted.

"Ready?" Charlie said. "Here comes the key."

He flung the key out around the tree. They were still some 25 feet away, and the key fell short, landing at Sally's feet.

"Let me go!" she cried. "Let me go!"

But Max jerked her back, this time more tightly than before.

"Not so fast," he snarled. "I haven't got the key, yet. He didn't throw it high enough to catch. You pick it up and hand it to me. Then you can go."

Sally stooped for the key. Max backed away and bent over with her so his body was protected. She handed the key to him over her shoulder. "There it is. Now, let me go."

Max laughed. It was an ugly sound.

"Hold still or I will shoot you," he said.

She stopped trying to jerk free. Charlie knew, now, that Max's other hand was pressing a handgun barrel into the girl's back.

"Did you think I was really going to let you go?" Max said, his voice venomous. "You little fool. You're going to Europe with me. We have a few things to talk over, you and I."

Then he spoke louder to Charlie, "Don't make a move," he raised his voice even louder, "You or your partner. I'll shoot her through a kidney if you do. You'll be committing murder just as surely as if you held the gun yourself."

Then Max started backing away, forcing the girl to step backwards at the same pace. She screamed, "Let me go!" Then she winced, jerking forward. Max had jabbed the gun painfully into her back.

Charlie watched Max's deliberate retreat. When they were 50 feet away, Max said, "Don't move until I get back to the airship. You'll have a dead girl to carry home if you do. Then you better start running. My men will hunt you down like rats. I told you this morning this thing was too big for you. Perhaps you agree now."

"Perhaps not," Lew muttered silently to himself. He was lying flat along the thick limb of a tree almost directly over Max's head, holding his pistol straight down. There wasn't a chance of missing when he pulled the trigger.

The bullet struck Max's hand just back of his own handgun. The weapon flew out of his fingers, and Max reeled back, clutching his mangled hand with the other, which had unwittingly released Sally's jacket. She darted away with a cry.

"Keep running, baby," Lew yelled to Sally and then dropped directly onto Max's shoulders. He landed hard, and they both went down in a heap.

Max regained his feet, but Lew's fingers were around his throat, squeezing with all of his strength. Yet Max's physical power was still prodigious. He heaved and spun around in a circle, Lew's swinging feet clearing the ground.

Max's purpose, Lew saw, was to crash him into a tree and dislodge the strangling grip. The chances were good, too, for trees grew thickly on every side. Lew's foot struck one with a jar that numbed him to the knee. He was beginning to wonder if he shouldn't drop, roll away and use the pistol he had thrust in his pocket before he jumped. But the pistol no longer weighted his coat. It must have dropped out.

Before Lew's worry had a chance to mount, Max went limp and slowly slunk to the ground. Charlie stood in front of Max, pistol butt raised for a second blow, but it wasn't needed.

Max was truly out cold this time.

Charlie took the key from the man's pocket, and pulling Lew along, began to run. Lew didn't need any urging. Shouts rang out behind them. A gun fired, and Charlie turned to snap a shot back at the camp, hoping it would slow any pursuers and buy them time to escape. Sally was still 100 feet ahead of them, but Charlie didn't want a pitched gun battle among the trees with her so near.

Then, before a real battle could ensue, the roar of multiple planes filled the sky. Motors blaring, five big silver ships circled around like a swarm of eagles. Charlie halted in amazement. It was a magnificent sight, and nothing compared to what followed.

The planes cut their motors and began wheeling overhead in short circles a thousand feet or more above the treetops. Dark objects by the score dropped from the planes. The objects blossomed out like billowy white flowers. An entire troop was bailing out in parachutes, dropping into the clearing and among the trees all around.

Any pursuit ceased. Charlie still yelled to Sally, "Get behind a tree, and keep your head tucked in."

He motioned to Lew, and they ran back, rifles at the ready. They knew how vulnerable men suspended from parachutes would be to riflemen on the ground. Help had come, and this help had courageously leaped out despite the danger that waited below. Charlie and Lew intended to cover these men until they stood firmly on their feet.

They saw one of Max's men raising a rifle. Both fired. The man fell, reaching for his knees. This, apparently, was the last of the five to remain unwounded. Now he was off of his feet, too. Lew ran up and kicked the rifle from his hands.

The men floating down from the sky wore Canadian service uniforms, pistols strapped to their belts and rifles slung over their backs. Charlie climbed up onto the dirigible. Andre was standing beside one of the cabins, but he was cowed, not even armed.

Some of the paratroopers became entangled in trees and brush, but most reached the ground of the little meadow. They unsnapped themselves from the clumsy chutes and ran up, affixing bayonets to rifles as they came.

Lew sank down to the ground\. "Am I tired," he groaned. "I could sleep for a week."

A soldier came up, menacing Charlie with a rifle. "Drop that pistol," he ordered.

Charlie laid the weapon down. "Sure," he said. "It's your turn to take this business over. I'm plenty sick of it. These are the fellows you want," he pointed out the enemy.

The soldier looked at him doubtfully. Then Sally ran up, flung her arms around Charlie's neck, and kissed him on the cheek. "Don't you dare touch him," she cried. "He saved my life a hundred times."

She glanced around. "Where's Dad? Where's my dad?"

A young lieutenant saluted smartly. "Colonel Bern? He's up in the tri-motored bomber. We came prepared. After command received your message, they ordered out five planes with bombs, light cannon and machine guns. The War Office finally realized just how critical your father's invention could be in a time of war."

Sally saw Lew slumped on the ground. She ran over and knelt beside him. "What's the matter?" she cried. "Are you hurt?"

"Just tired," he told her. "Gosh, but I'm tired."

Sally's arms went around and pulled his head against her bosom. "Poor baby," she murmured. "Poor baby."

"Say, what is this?" Lew demanded. "Don't you see all those men watching us? They'll think I'm a baby or something."

Sally's eyes were big and round. "I think you are a sweet baby," she crooned. "One I'm never going to forget."

"And," she continued, before he had a chance to protest, "just so you won't forget me ..." She leaned down and kissed him slowly on the mouth. Sally had finally got the last word.

The End

Danger at White Goose Bay

Chapter 1 – Too Nice a Day to Die

It was unusually nice for so late in fall. The sun burst through a morning cloud bank, and a keen wind made short work of the fog that crept across the lake. Canada jays quarreled in the aspens, but their bickering sounded more like habit than bad temper.

It was too nice a day to die, yet two men were already doomed before the sun cleared the timberline around the shores of Shadow Lake. Charlie and Lew knew nothing of any of this. But they were soon to learn, and the knowledge would plunge them into grave danger, too.

Lew shifted his weight from one aching knee to the other. Both were sore from pressing against the bottom of their homemade boat. He scowled at the hand line running over the gunwale and then shifted his eyes to the single fish lying on the slat floor. "Eleven inches of tough skin and bone," he muttered bitterly. "That's all I get for sitting out here three and a half hours."

Lew glanced towards the bow. Charlie was kneeling with his own hand line, composed and calm. Lew decided his companion's face might even be happy—too happy. "How much more time are we going to waste trying to catch fish?" he growled.

"I'm ready to quit," Charlie replied. "You caught the only fish."

"And I'm not proud of it," Lew scowled again. "One bite each, maybe two. I used to think I was pretty good at fishing, but you won't hear me bragging anymore."

"Then our forenoon's not been wasted," Charlie said grinning. "Suppose we paddle home, get the guns and try hunting."

"Fine," Lew replied, pulling his line up until he could see the hook baited with a soft rubber imitation worm. "Only I want to try fishing deeper, first."

They were both jigging the only artificial lures they had brought in an outfit put together for a winter of hunting and trapping.

Lew let out line until his finger touched the knot marking the 35-foot depth. He let out 10 feet more and began jigging the line gently up and down.

His face was serious, now. It wasn't really a matter of life or death that they catch fish. Still, meat had begun to grow scarce, and it seemed that despite their industry and frugal meals, they were making no headway in piling up a surplus for the lean times to come. Thirty pounds of dried venison was their only reserve. It hung high in the loft of their cabin where the smoke that drifted out from the stone fireplace dried and cured it a little harder and blacker every day. Long ago, they had realized that the wilderness life was largely a daily struggle to procure food.

There had been weeks at Shadow Lake when they saw deer every day within a mile of the cabin. But lately, animal life except for the predators had vanished. The deer that had browsed along the shore were gone. The wildfowl migration had passed over, and the rabbits and grouse that had furnished so many meals could only be found through hours of tedious hunting.

Not that either of them minded long hours spent stalking game. Their muscles were tough from the daily hiking and wood chopping. Charlie, at least, had the limitless patience that marks most successful hunters. But the last three days had yielded a single rabbit, and they had turned from the woods to the lake, which before had never failed to yield at least enough fish for the day's meal.

They were accustomed to the changing distribution of animal and bird life in the Northwoods. Game, they knew, migrated as the weather changed. But they had been keenly disappointed with their luck upon the water.

Lew leaned back against the side of the boat to ease his aching back. *Zing!* The cord jerked sharply and then burned through his fingers. His fingers clamped down, and he jerked back to set the hook. Then he began pulling the line in hand over hand, coiling it neatly on the bottom of the boat. There was no finesse in this fishing. They were out for meat not sport, and the lines were strong enough to "horse" even a good-sized fish up to the boat without having to play it until it was tired and tame.

Lew worked fast, for a poorly hooked fish might slip the barb and escape. When he saw the catch his hand shot down, fingers locked in the gills and he dragged it aboard.

"Look, Charlie. Isn't he a dandy?" It was a deep fish some 18 inches long. "Three pounds, maybe four," Lew chuckled, his eyes glistening. Then he hit the fish smartly on the head with a short wood club and removed the hook.

"What is it?" Charlie asked.

"Darned if I know. Never saw one just like it. I'd say whitefish only I didn't know they lived in this lake. Holy smoke! I got another."

Again the line burned through Lew's fingers. He checked it as before, and in another minute had a second fish flopping in the boat.

"Just like the first one only bigger. Drop your line down farther, Charlie. There must be a school feeding down there."

Charlie gave out line, and something started to run with his bait. He dragged his first fish to the surface as Lew hooked his third. The next few minutes both were as busy fishing as they had ever been. Fish snapped up the soft rubber worms as fast as they sank to the 45-foot depth. The heavy line was rasping the skin from their hands, but they worked on, oblivious. Neither could have said just how long the run lasted. It might have been an hour; might have been 30 minutes. But the bite ceased as suddenly as it had began, and they leaned back in the boat, wiping sweat from their eyes.

Lew began untangling a snarl. He had been working too fast to lay the line smoothly and evenly. They started to fish again. But there were no more takers. Lew paddled in a slow, wide circle while Charlie worked both lines. That failed, too. The bite was over.

Lew put the paddle down and looked at the fish piled around his legs. He pawed them over, counting. There were 53. Charlie counted his catch and announced, "Forty-eight! It's a good thing the run stopped. We'd have swamped the boat."

Lew looked with alarm at the gunwales. They had only a couple of inches of freeboard. A hard wind might capsize the overloaded craft, and should that happen, they could lose 300 pounds of fish.

"No wonder my arms are tired," he thought.

They paddled quickly but carefully to shore and unloaded. Each spread his catch in a circle, heads pointing in. They took out their knives and began cleaning. "That," Lew declared, "is what I call fishing, when you can pile them up in ricks like stove wood."

They strung the cleaned fish on lengths of cord, making three heavy bundles each. When they had packed all of the fish home, they got out axes to cut stakes and long, slender poles.

They carried these inside the small fur shed built against one cabin wall, drove the stakes into the dirt floor and placed the poles across to make a rack.

Charlie got the salt sack. It was more than half empty, for they had used many pounds tanning deer hides. So little was left Charlie decided they couldn't spare enough to make brine. So he decided to just dust a little salt inside each fish and lay it on the rack to dry. Salt was not really necessary for drying. The Eskimos dry their fresh fish without salt or smoke curing. But the taste is strong, so much so practice is required before even a hungry man can really relish it.

As they worked, they glanced outside every few minutes to check on the pile of cleaned fish heaped on the work table by the fire. An eagle might swoop down and carry a fish or two away in its talons, for the wild predators had also been feeling the pinch.

When the rack was finished, they salted each fish and laid it belly down to drain. They saved three fresh fish each, and Lew dropped two in the skillet to fry. Charlie made tea and got out a half-dozen biscuits left over from breakfast. The meal may have lacked variety, but each picked the last bone of his three-pound fish clean.

Late in the afternoon they scraped away the brine-soaked earth beneath the poles and started a small fire. The fur shed was tight enough to also make an excellent smokehouse.

Lew took his shotgun and set out for an afternoon hunt. But the bore was clean when he returned and found Charlie kneeling before the fireplace cooking supper. The skillet was again heaped with fish, and a pan of fresh biscuits leaned in front of the fire browning.

After dinner, Charlie tended the fire smouldering in the fur shed/smokehouse. It had burned out, but he still sprinkled the ashes with water to be absolutely sure. He decided they must begin soon building the small emergency cabin planned as insurance against being burned out of the main cabin during the long winter. They planned to build this second cabin small but tight, and stock it with matches, kindling and surplus garments. This cabin would not have a fireplace.

Charlie kindled another little smoke fire in the fur shed early the next morning. He used finely chopped birch for this.

"I've been wondering," Lew said, "how other people eat smoked fish. We always just peel off the skin and break the meat off the bones. Can't we find another way to cook them?"

Charlie nodded. "We could soak out part of the smoke flavor and fry them like fresh fish. And I think the meat flaked up and made into a sauce with deer fat and flour would be pretty good."

"Every time I eat smoked fish," Lew said, "I wish I had a big hunk of rye bread."

Charlie glanced at his watch. It was almost 9 o'clock. "How about a pail of water?" he suggested.

Lew started towards the little creek that ran beside the cabin. But an unexpected sound brought him up short, and he ran back into the cabin. "I heard a big splash out on the lake, Charlie. I'll walk down and look around." Then the quiet was shattered by a roar of rapid explosions. "Good grief," Lew said. "Is that a plane engine?"

Frowning, he went to the wall and took down the magnum bolt rifle. Charlie followed him out the door. "If that is a plane," Lew wondered aloud, "how did it get this close without us hearing it come in?"

The pair jogged down the trail toward the lakeshore.

But it was a plane, a silver twin-engine monoplane riding the waves about 200 feet out. The motors were idling smoothly, ticking like a pair of big watches. Then the engines picked up, and the plane skimmed in towards them. Forty feet out it veered with a sharp turn that sent the tail almost up on the beach. The motors went dead, and the little ship rocked on the swell it had made.

They could see the cabin, skillfully blended into the wings for perfect streamlining. Lew waved his hand and started forward, eager to see who had dropped such a swell plane down in a lake he had begun to regard as his own.

He lifted his hand again in salute, and a window slid back. Then a face appeared in the opening—peering over the muzzles of a double-barreled shotgun pointed straight at his chest. It was a small bore, 20 gauge he guessed, but quite capable at that range.

"Don't touch the plane," a voice warned. Then the gun moved a little and he got a look at the face behind it. Lew's eyes widened, for the leather helmet and thick frame goggles pushed up above the eyes couldn't disguise the certainty of this being a woman.

As Lew backed slowly away, he mused,"What's wrong with me, Charlie? Every woman I meet up here sticks a gun in my face. Sally did the same thing. She wouldn't let me shut my own cabin door."

"Sally?" the woman repeated quickly. "Sally who?"

"Why, Sally Bern. You know her?"

"Yes, I know her very well."

Then they heard her murmur something that sounded like "Thank goodness!" The shotgun dropped from the window, and the woman stripped off the helmet and goggles then leaned out. "Sally told me all about you," she said. "I suppose I should have recognized you. You are

Lew, and the man with you is Charlie."

"Right," Lew replied. "But who the dickens are you?"

"That can wait. I see a boat on shore. Get in it and paddle under my plane wing. Hurry, every moment counts."

Lew didn't move, but Charlie, sensing something urgent behind the request, ran over to the boat and shoved off in it. He maneuvered the craft under the left wing, which set so close to the water he had to duck down almost level with the gunwale.

"See if the tank is leaking," she called, and Charlie caught the odor of gasoline that instant. He discovered a tiny trickle of fuel seeping along the curved underside of the wing. He traced the stream back to the drain cock, turned the valve and the flow stopped.

"Find it?" she called.

"Yes. The valve was open a quarter."

"Check the one in the other wing, will you please?"

Charlie grasped a pontoon strut and propelled the boat past the bottom of the cabin and under the right wing. He frowned when he saw a second trickle of gasoline. One leak could be accidental, but two?

He turned the valve up hard. Then he pushed the boat out into the clear and met the pilot's gaze thoughtfully.

"Both tanks were leaking," he said.

"Thanks," she said. "That's why I landed. There was less than half as much gas in the tanks as there should have been. I was lucky to be over a lake. I couldn't set this plane down on anything but water."

"I can," Lew said. "I can set them down anywhere. Of course, there may not be much left …"

"Did you lose much fuel?" Charlie interrupted.

Lew, he knew, was talking nonsense while he appraised the situation. The sillier the comment, the harder he was thinking.

"More than I could afford to lose," she answered.

He studied her face carefully. The eyes were very dark, and he wondered if he had ever seen hair so totally black. She was young and pretty, too, despite the haggard circles under her eyes and the sharp lines on each side of her mouth. A vein was throbbing on one side of her neck, and he realized she was laboring under intense strain.

"I haven't enough gas to go on. I must fly home." She looked at her watch. "Can you be ready to come with me in ten minutes?"

Chapter 2 – They Wanted Me to Crash!

It was unusual enough that a monoplane had landed on Shadow Lake. But when the pilot turned out to be a woman who insisted they immediately fly somewhere with her, that rocked Lew.

"Get ready to go in 10 minutes?" he repeated. "Go where? You can't just pull a shotgun and expect me to elope with you."

Lew was pleased with that little pun. But his enjoyment evaporated before Charlie's admonishing eyes.

"Cut it," Charlie told him softly. "Can't you see she's suffering, half crazy with grief or fear?"

"Sorry about the bum joke," Lew said quickly. "Really, I am. But I still need to know why you want us to go with you."

"Because you are the only ones within a thousand miles who can save me," she replied without a moment's hesitation.

She saw Lew's doubt and continued passionately. "You saved Sally. She told me all about it. I'm in worse trouble. So much worse it almost kills me to think about it. Why do you just stand there? Every moment is precious. Get the things you need—and hurry!"

Lew still didn't move. Charlie asked, "How far is it?"

She glanced at her wristwatch. "I flew here in two hours. That means the distance is under 600 miles."

"Got enough gas to make it back?"

"Just enough. I can stay up high and glide in the last 10 miles or so if we run out."

"Suppose you run out before that?" Lew asked.

She bit her lip, clenching the teeth down hard.

"I don't know. You're not afraid, are you?"

Charlie ignored that. "If you're a friend of Sally's, we'll help you. But 600 miles is a long way to go even if we can fly it in two hours. We trap for a living, and we plan to begin in earnest next week. I think it only fair you tell us about the jam you're in and what you expect us to do to help."

"I will tell you all about it," she said quickly. "But it would take too much time now. Can't you trust me?" She leaned farther out the window of the plane, both hands gripping the sill. Then she reached down, grabbed a leather handbag and tossed it to Charlie.

"Open it," she said, "and count the money."

He found a dozen $50 bills and two tens.

"Is that enough?" she demanded.

"Easily," Charlie said.

"Then keep it. That's your wages."

"Okay," Charlie agreed and put the folded notes in a pocket. "You will fly us back when the job is finished?"

"I promise."

"All right, we'll go. Give us 10 minutes. Come on, Lew," he turned and started trotting to the cabin.

"Don't forget to bring guns," she called after them.

"Uh-oh," Lew grunted. "She's in a real jam. But not bad-looking. Maybe in her early 30s?"

"Save your wind for packing," Charlie told him.

They moved swiftly in the cabin. Lew already held the magnum rifle. He took one of the .30-30 combo shotguns and both of the 9mm pistols captured from Max and his gang of secret agents. Changes of underwear, socks and shirts went in the canvas bag with them.

"Will half-smoked fish spoil before we get back?" Lew asked.

"It won't, if we return inside a week. I'll make sure the fire under is out before we go."

"If this woman didn't know Sally, I'd be suspicious," Lew said.

"I am anyway," Charlie replied. "There was a hole in the bag she tossed me. About the size of a 30-caliber bullet. It went through the folded money, too."

"Isn't that interesting," Lew's face was thoughtful. Then he grinned. "Well, we can't say we weren't warned. And six hundred bucks is a lot of dough."

"Depends on what we have to do to earn it," Charlie replied.

The window in the plane cabin was closed when they returned, but a narrow door in the fuselage was open and a short, folding steel ladder dropped to the water. Lew spun a propeller, and that motor sputtered and fired. When Charlie spun the other, it fired, too.

The cabin was very narrow, and the woman sat in the forward seat behind the controls. They wedged themselves in the other seat behind. It was a tight squeeze for their wide shoulders. Charlie laid the canvas pack behind the seat. Lew stood the rifles up between his knees.

The motors picked up, and they taxied out onto the lake. Charlie noted how carefully she fed the gas and wondered if she really did believe she had have enough fuel left to make it back home.

They taxied 100 yards more and then lifted quickly off the water with a burst of speed that slammed him back into the leather seat.

But after the first steep climb, the plane slowed to a more leisurely rise. Charlie looked at his watch. It was 11 minutes past nine. Much had happened in less than a half-hour.

She looked around, tried to smile but the corners of her mouth only twitched. "I was incredibly lucky to land in the only place I could have gotten help. And I will take that as a good sign. And we do have enough fuel to fly home."

"How did you start out with both tanks leaking," Lew asked.

She didn't try to smile now. "It wasn't an accident—they wanted me to crash. That's why the valves were only opened a little ways."

"Who are 'they,'" Charlie asked.

"The men who took George and Hugh and ..." her voice died out queerly. She shook her head, tried to push her shoulders back, and then with a sigh that drained the air from her lungs, slid sideways off the seat and crumpled to the floor.

The plane dipped sharply but straightened when the autopilot took over. Charlie reached his long arms over the back of her seat, and took the leather-covered wheel. The plane kept flying, and he made no attempt to change course. He merely stood holding the wheel.

"Pull her out of the way," he ordered. Lew seized her under the arms and slid her limp body down the aisle until there was room for Charlie to squeeze into the pilot's seat. He knew next to nothing about flying a plane, but he knew it would practically fly itself and maintain a straight course if he didn't move the rudders.

"See if you can bring her around," he told Lew.

Lew lifted the woman's arms so her head would receive more blood. He patted her gently on one cheek and then the other. Her eyes fluttered but did not open. He slapped her a little harder this time. The lids raised, and she looked at him vacantly.

"Who are you?" she whispered. Then she sat up suddenly.

"The plane!" she cried. "Are we ... are we falling?"

"Take it easy," Lew said. "Charlie's holding a straight course."

"Can he fly a plane?" she asked anxiously.

"No. But he's doing all right just the same."

"Help me, please," she said, straightening the flying helmet, tucking several strands of hair back under the edge. She wiggled, trying to straighten the flying suit that had twisted around her body when Lew slid her along the floor. "How silly of me to faint," she finally said.

"When did you last eat?" Lew asked. Food was his first thought to remedy almost any ailment.

"Last night, I had tea."

"No wonder you passed out," Lew remarked.

Color seeped back into her thin cheeks. She stood and said, "I'll take over now."

"We jerked to the right," Charlie told her as they changed seats. "So better check the course. Then, when you're feeling able, we'd like to hear what this is all about."

"Have you ever heard of George Malverson?" she asked.

"I don't believe," Lew replied. "Still, it sounds familiar. Wait—I saw that name in one of the newspapers Colonel Bern left us when he and Sally went home. Didn't he invent some kind of explosive? Something he hoped would help the Allies defeat the Germans? But it flopped. The papers played that up big."

"They always do," she replied bitterly. "George Malverson is my husband. He was working with the Canadian military. He would have succeeded, but some general wouldn't let him have enough time. He insisted on a test before George was ready."

She changed the rudder a little, and that sent the ship climbing higher. "Malvorite is what George calls the explosive. It will make a 500-pound bomb as powerful as the 1,000-pounders now in use. George works slowly, but Malvorite will be worth the wait."

They cut into some fleece clouds and then flashed out above them. "When Malvorite failed to do more than regular TNT," she continued, "he lost faith in George. My country lost a valuable war weapon just because one man was short-sighted."

They had been flying on a two-thirds throttle. Now, she jammed , it wide and the plane rocketed forward. She remembered their fuel situation a second later and pulled the throttle back where it had been.

"I'm sorry. But I get so mad when I think how they treated George. They lost faith in him, but he didn't lose faith in himself. When he got over the disappointment, he began working on a new device. This time a tank. Then he invented an anti-tank gun for the Malvorite. He worked the designs out on paper. My brother Hugh helped, and they nailed every detail. Then they had the various parts of the tank and gun made in scattered machine shops, some in the United States. Twice, parts of George's designs were stolen. That made us thankful we had divided the work, and also wary."

"I should think so," Lew said.

"George knew he had something," she continued. "And he wanted our country to benefit. The tank is good, but the gun and load are revolutionary. You'll find that out when we arrive."

"Funny place to test a tank," Lew remarked.

"I know. But the theft of the designs told George he was being watched, and he knew we would be alone up here. Or at least he thought we would be."

Her voice grew bitter now.

"We packed our tools and the finished parts into a coastal sailing ship and came up to White Goose Bay. That's where we are going, a narrow neck of Hudson Bay. George had been there before to hunt geese. He got the use of the lodge without any trouble because all of the club members are busy with war work. George, my brother Hugh, his wife, Kirta, and I came up on the ship. Kirta also brought her maid Anna, and George brought a machinist who had worked with him seven years. Anton Zack is a Czech, intensely devoted to George's work because we face a common enemy in Germany. I am Joan Malverson."

She glanced at the fuel gauges and compass, turned the plane's nose a little to the left and tilted it higher. Lew glanced over at Charlie, shrugged and grinned without much humor. They knew she was gaining altitude so they could glide farther after the tanks went dry.

"Everything was going fine," she spoke again. "They finished the tank and the gun. Then they began working on the new load. Then, yesterday morning, George, Hugh and Anton all simply disappeared."

"Sounds incredible," Charlie murmured.

"But it happened. They went to the log barn we use for a shop. When Kirta and I went down to the shop to watch them work, all three were missing."

She throttled the speed down a little and checked the compass and gauges again. "We thought that odd but weren't overly alarmed. They might have gone out into the timber for some testing. We worried more when they didn't come back for lunch. When they failed to return for dinner, we searched the building but couldn't find a clue as to what had happened. I didn't sleep more than an hour last night."

The port motor faltered but then droned on steadily.

She continued speaking, anxiously eyeing a gauge.

"This morning I went down to the shop and searched again, looked in every bin, behind the machinery. I climbed to the loft above, and a foot from the top of the ladder I saw a puddle of blood. It was almost black, but I could tell it was blood from the smell."

She choked after that sentence.

"I looked around and saw the loft was empty. I don't know how I got down that ladder. But I knew I needed to go get help."

She eased off the throttle, watching the altimeter. "Before I left the house, I opened the safe that holds George's data and blueprints. Only he and I know the combination. We trust the others, but the fewer who know a secret the better that secret can be kept."

"Amen to that," Lew said softly.

"I carried all the papers from the safe straight to the plane. They were intact and in good order. There's a sandbar about 100 yards out from the boathouse, and I had to turn to miss it. As I did, the handbag fell from my lap to the floor. I saw the bullet hole when I picked it up. Somebody had taken a shot at me while I was leaving. I didn't hear it over the plane motors."

"Who?" Charlie asked.

"I don't know."

"Why didn't you take your sister-in-law with you?"

She flew in silence for several seconds. "I didn't think of that. But I may not have asked her, anyway. I like Kirta, but I don't trust her—with men. I think she's a two-timer."

After another thoughtful pause, she said, "I'm sorry I said that. She has been very good to me. But sometimes I think she is making a play for my husband. No woman trusts another who could do that."

"You only distrusted her because of the way she acted with George?" Charlie asked.

"What other reason could there be?"

"I don't know. Go on."

"That's all. I flew until I looked at the fuel gauges and saw how low they were, and then I landed on your lake. I thought maybe another bullet had punctured the tanks. I was getting ready to climb out on a pontoon to see when you appeared."

She glanced at her watch and said, "We're only 20 miles out. Looks like we'll make it."

Then the 12-cylinder engines missed in unison, picked up, faltered, and went dead.

She set her shoulders with resolve. But they knew the plane was too heavy and the wingspread too small to glide in for 20 miles.

They were too high to see the ground. There were even a few thin clouds under them. But two minutes later they flashed down through those clouds. Charlie thought he saw the thin, light streak of a river and wondered if it was wide enough to let them land.

Joan clutched the controls with desperate strength. But when she turned they saw panic and fear in her dark eyes.

"She knows we're not going to make it," Charlie thought.

He looked around for parachutes, didn't see any and asked her where they were.

"Somebody took them," she said. "The same person who opened the gas tank valves, I suppose."

Then the plane lifted unexpectedly, as if both motors had started to fire, but they hadn't.

Joan flashed a smile over her shoulder. "We just hit a headwind. It may lift us enough to get within gliding range."

The headwind buoyed them for almost five minutes before it died. Now they could see a streak of pale blue against the horizon. "White Goose Bay," Joan said pointing.

They were coming down but still moving smartly ahead. Charlie saw three buildings at the edge of the water, widely spread out, rambling and weather-beaten. Joan wheeled in a wide corkscrew to lose altitude. They circled over the house twice, and when they came around to it again he heard a gunshot, distinct and loud because the silent engines did not muffle it.

There was a second shot, and Lew felt something tug at his leg. There was a clean hole drilled through the floor.

"That shot about ruined my boot," he yelled angrily. Then he picked up the magnum, slammed a shell in the chamber and slid the window open.

Charlie looked at his watch.

It read 11 o'clock.

Chapter 3 – This Setup Smells!

Lew got the barrel of the big rifle out through the plane's window and thrust his head out beside it without any difficulty. The trouble after that was nothing to shoot. All he saw was the greenish blue water of White Goose Bay, the log and stone buildings beside it and dead grass tundra stretching to where timber began a mile inland. There wasn't a sign of whoever had just fired two shots, one into the plane.

Lew pulled his head back inside. "Nice welcome, all right. Who do you think it was?"

Joan didn't answer. The last circle had brought them skimming over the bay, and a sharp lift of the nose checked their speed and then they set down with a splash. They were floating about 150 feet from shore. Joan turned and faced them, frowning.

"We're out of gas, so I can't taxi into the hangar."

"That's easy," Lew said. He stood his rifle beside Charlie, took the pistol out of his pocket, peeled off coat and boots and dropped out through the cabin door. The water was icy, so he swam rapidly to the hangar, found a small boat with a paddle in it and pulled himself over the stem. He saw an outboard motor clamped to a timber nailed across two posts, but he didn't want to take the time to install it. Instead, he started paddling for the plane.

Back in the plane Charlie was regarding Joan with steady eyes. "You didn't answer Lew's question. Who shot at us?"

"I didn't answer," she replied, "because I haven't the slightest notion who it was."

"No suspicions?" he persisted.

"Not a one."

"Who was in the house when you left four hours ago?"

"I told you. Kirta, my sister-in-law, and her maid Anna. Of course, I don't know who may be inside now. Somebody could have entered after I left."

"Any settlements near? Seen a stranger or heard reports of one?"

"The closest settlement is an Indian village a hundred miles down the shore. We haven't seen any strangers or heard of any." Then, after a short silence, she added, "But there must be one."

"Why?" Charlie asked.

"Why?" she repeated. "My husband and my brother have disappeared, haven't they? Anton, the mechanic, is also gone. They didn't just walk off in the woods. Somebody shot at me as I left this morning. And someone fired at us just now!"

Charlie looked out the window, saw Lew rowing towards them and motioned for him to hurry. He hadn't worried about the sniper taking a shot at Lew because the hangar shed lay between Lew and the house. The shots must have come from the house, and he wanted to search it as quickly as he could.

The boat bumped against one of the seaplane pontoons. Charlie dropped down and helped steady the craft while Joan climbed down. Charlie brought the rifles with him, and he gave one to Lew as he picked up the other paddle. "Can you wait a few minutes before changing those wet clothes?" Charlie asked.

"Sure. Everything is wool. I won't even feel a chill as long as I keep moving."

"You're going to be moving, all right," Charlie assured him. "The instant this boat hits ground I want you to run around behind the buildings. Go at least a hundred yards so you can see anyone who may try to slip out a back door or window. If you see someone making for the timber, you know what to do."

"They fired first," Lew said grimly. "Did you bring my pistol?"

Charlie handed it to him.

"What are you going to do?" Joan asked, alarmed.

"Smoke out the gunman," Charlie replied. "He is in the house or shop. You stay in the hangar until I call for you."

She flushed enough to put some color in her pale cheeks. It made her look decidedly pretty. "I won't stay in the hangar. I'm going in with you. It's my home."

Charlie's cheek muscles hardened. "Mrs. Malverson," he said, "you begged us to come here and help you. You paid us over six hundred dollars, so you must have had some confidence in our ability. I don't like the setup, and from what I've seen, something smells.

"But either we handle this in our own way, or we don't touch it at all. Now, you stay in the hangar until I call you to come out. If you can't do that, fill up the plane tanks and fly us back home. I'll give you back all of the money."

He pulled out the wad of bills with the bullet hole through it and held it in his hand, waiting.

Her eyes flashed in a way that made them seem even darker than ever. It might have been anger, maybe a gleam of admiration. But she only nodded and said, "I want you to stay."

The prow of the dinghy bumped up against the plank dock inside the hangar, and they jumped out. Lew ran past the three buildings to a spot from where he could cover the rear of all. Charlie handed his rifle to Joan, drew his pistol and ran up to the wide porch that fronted more than half of the lake side of the house. He went up three steps, across the salt-stained boards and grasped the knob of one of the two doors leading into the house. It was unlocked, and he shoved it wide. He went through into a large living room lined with low-placed windows. The bare wood floors were dark with tanned skins scattered across the wood. Other hides hung on the walls, and straight ahead was a rough stone fireplace big enough to take six-foot logs. Three gigantic polar bear skins were laid out in front of the hearth.

Charlie ran lightly into a short hall with three closed doors. He opened the nearest, saw a bathroom with old-fashioned fixtures, backed out and opened the next. This disclosed a chamber with twin beds and dressers. There was a closet with a closed door. He flung that wide. It was filled with men's suits and women's dresses. He looked under each bed then ran out and through the remaining door.

This revealed a chamber fitted like the first except that the closet was empty. Apparently, it was a spare room. He went back to the living room. Another opening led him into a dining room and then into a kitchen directly in back of that. It was equipped with a massive wood range and hot water tank. The double sink was cast-iron.

A door led out of the kitchen into a small hall where he again faced three doors, all shut. Another bathroom accounted for one. The second led into another bedroom, also empty. He started towards the third and last door, but before he got there, it opened and a very tall, thin woman faced him. The hair piled high in thick masses over her forehead was quite gray, contrasting strangely with the almost wrinkle-free face. Gray eyes fastened on Charlie, spilling hatred.

"What do you want?" The voice had a tone of toughness. He knew by her dress and age that this had to be Kirta Lang's maid.

"I want to know who is in that room," Charlie said.

"Get out. You have no right to intrude."

"You're mistaken," Charlie said evenly. "Mrs. Malverson gave me authority to search. Stand aside, please."

The gray eyes did not falter, and she did not move from before the door. Charlie knew the sooner he searched the better the chance of discovering the one who had fired at them. But he restrained himself long enough to explain, "Somebody fired a rifle at us as we landed. Now, will you step aside so I can go in?"

"Nobody is hiding there," she told him.

Charlie tried to slip past. But she swung her lean body to block the way. Charlie dropped the pistol in a pocket, put his hands against her shoulder and shoved. Her strength surprised him. But then, panting, she gave way, her face livid with rage.

"Sorry," Charlie said shortly. "But I asked you nicely."

He flung the door open and entered another bedroom. Where the rest had been plainly furnished, the beds here were covered with fluffy pink chenille. The dressing table had three large mirrors, and its top was littered with boudoir items. A woman was seated at the dresser, a woman with a well-rounded figure and short, wavy blond hair.

One leg was crossed over the other, and she was drawing on a light tan stocking.

Charlie stopped abruptly. He started to back out, for the woman wore only a thin, pale blue negligee with no sleeves and a low front. Then he remembered the urgency of his search and held his ground.

The woman looked up casually, sweeping him with level eyes. "Don't blush," she said. "It spoils the compliment. Makes me wonder if my age is beginning to show."

Charlie's embarrassment came almost as much from surprise as the liberal view of her plumpness revealed through and above the negligee. But he recovered quickly. She evidently was pretty good at banter. So he launched a direct attack, instead.

"Who is hiding in your closet?"

A little frown came between her eyes, but then she laughed, her voice rich and husky.

"Don't you know the contents of a lady's closet are her secrets?"

"Maybe," Charlie replied. "But I'm afraid you'll have to share them with me today." He started forward.

She shrugged and the negligee slipped, but she caught it expertly with another shrug and put it back in place. "Don't mind me. I'm only dressing in what I thought was the privacy of my bedroom." She reached inside a drawer. Charlie stiffened, hand on his gun. But she drew out a big powder puff and dabbed it over her nose.

Charlie opened the closet door, ran his arm in back of the rows of hanging dresses and gowns. Save for these it was empty. Then he raised the spread of each bed and looked underneath.

"I'm sorry," he apologized. "But I had to do this. Somebody shot twice at us as Mrs. Malverson put the plane down. I thought the gunman might be hidden in the house."

"Joan is back?"

He nodded. "She gave me permission to search. If there had been a bad actor here, I would have got him before he had a chance to hurt you. A beautiful woman should never be exposed to danger."

"That's better," she said thoughtfully. "So, you came with Joan. She would pick up someone so impetuous. And you think I am beautiful?" Her tone was light, but Charlie detected a touch of wistfulness.

"You needn't worried about me. I can handle bad actors."

Charlie was sure she could. A sharp inhale at his shoulder brought him about. Anna stood close, her eyes glowing. "If you are through talking nonsense, maybe you will go away so Miss Kirta can dress before she catches cold."

Charlie started out quickly, but not quite quickly enough. Propelled by Anna's sinewy strength, the door caught him halfway out, striking him hard in the back.

He went back into the kitchen, noticed a small door he had overlooked. It opened into a small utility room. There was a good-sized gasoline engine, a pump, dynamo and well head. He lifted up the board cover over the well, saw that the shallow pit was empty.

The machinery explained why it had been possible to equip a wilderness home with electric lights and plumbing.

Charlie left the house through a rear door and hustled towards the shop about 50 yards away. He saw Lew standing out on the tundra, leaning forward with the butt of his big rifle on the ground. Remembering his companion's soaked clothing, Charlie decided to hurry and finish what he was now sure would be a futile search.

He went inside the shop, saw it was just one big room with benches and machines along each wall. But in the center sat one of the strangest objects he had ever seen. It resembled a sea turtle, only it was fully 25 feet long and almost 8 feet wide. The top of the rounded metal dome was 8 feet off the floor. It had armored caterpillar treads of steel and rubber. This had to be George Malverson's new tank.

Charlie scampered up the ladder to the attic above, a dim place strung with cobwebs and empty. He saw the spot of dark, dried blood. There was no place to hide, but Charlie went around the walls and looked under each bench and machine, anyway. Then he went outside and beckoned Lew.

"I don't suppose anyone ran out while I searched the house?"

Lew shook his head no. Charlie expected that, of course. He told Lew to go and change clothes in the hangar. "Tell Joan to meet me at the house," he added.

"What did you find?" Joan asked when they met on the porch.

"Nothing, or I should say nobody except Mrs. Lang and her maid. Is Anna always that hostile?"

"She dislikes men. I think someone must have treated her badly when she was young. So, there was nobody else in the house?"

"Pretty sure, and somebody shot at us as we were landing."

She faced him belligerently. "You're wrong if you think either of them did it."

"Am I?"

"Absolutely. I admit I don't like Kirta. She will probably make a play for you—if she hasn't already." Her eyes searched his face.

"Her husband has also disappeared," she added.

"She didn't look like she was grieving," he said.

"You can't tell anything with Kirta. She always has that wise-cracking manner. It covers up her real feelings. I think she does love Hugh. And shoot at me? That's absurd."

"Okay," Charlie said. "Let's go in. I want to check the guns I saw in the living room." There was a shotgun on the rack and two .303 Enfields. He checked and found both rifle barrels fouled.

"That doesn't mean anything," Joan explained. "No one ever cleans a gun around here."

"But this means something," Charlie told her. "This rifle is warm. It has been fired within a few minutes."

Her eyes probed his anxiously. "What are you going to do?"

"Nothing, for now," he replied. "Is there a cellar or an attic where a gunman could hide?"

"There isn't a cellar. But there is a small attic over the front bedrooms. All of the other main floor ceilings go to the roof."

She took him to a trapdoor in the ceiling of her closet. Charlie got a ladder he had seen in the utility room and climbed up.

The sun cut through dozens of cracks between the roughly chinked sidewall logs, lighting the space surprisingly well. The place was maybe 30 feet square, just high enough in the center to stand erect. The floor of rough-hewn boards was free of dust. That, he decided, was queer, for dust accumulates thickly in spaces such as this.

Near the far corner he saw a stain on the floor and got down on one knee to examine it better. The knee pressed on something hard and sharp. It was an empty rifle shell. Charlie couldn't see the mark on the head, but the shape and size of the case were .303 Enfield.

He found a second empty shell and then looked at the roof just over the stain on the floor. He pressed his hand against the shingles. One of them moved to reveal an opening plenty large enough to admit the muzzle of a gun. No doubt the marksman had been kneeling there, like he was kneeling now.

The question was, who?

Chapter 4 – I Thought I Was Tough!

No doubt Charlie had found the place from which the gunman had shot at the plane as Joan landed them on the water; it tied the shooter to the house, and he might still be hiding there. Charlie put the empty .303 cases in his pocket and climbed down from the little attic.

Joan was waiting in the living room.

"You told me you put the blueprints of your husband's tank and antitank gun in the plane this morning. Are they still there?" he asked.

She nodded, and Charlie went outside. Lew was coming out of the hangar. "Go back and guard the plane," Charlie called to him. "Don't let anybody near it."

"All right," Lew agreed. "But while I stand watch, can I put the outboard on the dinghy and tow the plane into the boathouse?"

"Yes. But be sure nobody gets in that plane cabin."

Charlie returned to the living room. Kirta had come in and was talking to Joan. "Where have you been? Why didn't you tell me you were taking the plane? I would have gone, too."

"I made up my mind quickly, Kirta. But it doesn't matter, because I didn't get far enough to alert the authorities. The valves of the fuel tanks were leaking, and I discovered it just in time to land and save enough gasoline to fly back. You remember Sally Bern, don't you? She told us how two men helped her recover her father's topographical camera. Well, I happened to land on the same lake, and I brought those same men with me to help us find George and Hugh. This is Charlie. Lew is in the hangar.

Kirta smiled at Charlie. "We've already met," she said. "He said somebody shot at you. Is that true, or did he invent it as an excuse to break into my bedroom?"

Charlie winced, convinced he was never going to hear the last about forcing his way in when Kirta was still dressing.

"It is true," Joan said.

"The shots were fired from the attic through a hole in the roof," Charlie added. "Here are the two empty shells."

"I don't believe it," Kirta said flatly.

Charlie shrugged. She waited for him to argue with that, but he remained silent. "Anna and I were here all morning," she finally said.

"Nobody could get in that attic without us knowing it."

"That's right," Charlie agreed, watching her keenly.

"You aren't insinuating that ... "

"No, I'm not insinuating anything," Charlie interrupted. "Two shots were fired at us. The barrel of a rifle on a rack in this house is warm. And you say you and your maid were alone in the house and didn't hear a thing."

"I didn't say we were alone," Kirta replied. "I said we were in all morning." Her eyes opened to their fullest width, which was considerable. The color reminded Charlie of the sea water in White Goose Bay. She went to the wall rack and touched both of the rifles. She came back and looked at the empties Charlie had laid on the table.

"So, you are clever," she said slowly, "just like a real detective. Aren't you going to tell us who did it? You do know, don't you?"

"Not yet," Charlie said. "But at this rate, it won't be long."

He glanced at his watch. It was exactly noon.

"I've only been here an hour," he added. Then his voice hardened. "Mrs. Malverson asked us to come here. I don't think she knows exactly what she wants us to do. But we'll help her. Right now, I want to know what you think of this business, about the disappearance of your two husbands? Who do you think is behind that?"

"Foreign agents," she said promptly. "Isn't it obvious?"

"It is," Charlie agreed. "And so is your lack of concern over what may have happened to Mr. Lang." Charlie wanted to get her angry, to drop that bantering tone and get serious. He succeeded.

The cold blue eyes flashed.

"Blast your insolence! Do you think I killed my own husband?"

"I can think of a situation where you might want to get rid of him," Charlie said. That, he thought, should start her raving. But instead, Kirta took a deep breath and then smiled. The smile was doubtless forced, but it looked pretty good, just the same.

"No, I didn't kill Hugh or make him disappear, and I'll admit there have been times when I've wanted to do one or the other. But wives don't murder husbands because they're bored. They get over it by smiling at the first man they meet — or the one who crashes into their bedroom while you dress." She arched her brows in his direction.

"Why, Kirta," Joan cried. "I didn't know Hugh bored you."

"It wasn't so much Hugh. It was this wilderness he kept me in. My word, Joan, do you think I like it here?"

"Of course not," Joan replied. "Neither do I. But George and

Hugh have their work to finish. So I make the best of it."

"I tried," Kirta said, weariness suddenly showing in her eyes. "Only God knows how hard."

Then she yawned and said, "I suppose I better speak to Anna about lunch. You must all be hungry."

She smiled at Charlie. "The sooner you find Hugh, the sooner he can finish his work and take me back where I can see people and go places." She executed a leisurely turn and went to the kitchen.

"I don't know how to take Kirta," Joan admitted as soon as she was gone.

"She is either very hard-boiled and trying to cover up a world of worry, or hard of hearing and a liar," Charlie said simply.

Joan sat in one of the big chairs in front of the fireplace. Charlie went over to the other. The frames were handmade from tree limbs, but the cushions and backs were deep and soft. Charlie thought they might be filled with duck down. He glanced over at Joan and was shocked to see how haggard she looked.

"I can't stand much more of this," she admitted. "First the men disappear. Then I find blood in the loft over the shop. Somebody has been killed, I just know it. But it is the uncertainties that are driving me mad. I feel like I may start to scream and keep on screaming until I wake up out of a bad dream. But this isn't a nightmare, is it?"

"I'm afraid not," Charlie said gently.

"Find George and Hugh," she suddenly pleaded. "Find out who was killed in the shop, whoever is responsible for all of this. If you can't, I want you to destroy the tank and gun then help me deliver the plans for both to the government at Ottawa. George's work must not have been in vain, and it must not fall in enemy hands."

"You are a very brave woman," Charlie said quietly. "We'll do all we can to help. Now, suppose you tell me exactly what happened yesterday morning when you discovered the men were missing?"

"Nothing unusual, up until the moment we missed them. We always breakfast at seven. Sometimes the men get up early and work in the shop before we eat. They did that yesterday. When they came in they were excited, for they believed they had found the right combination of powder for the gun. They are working on an idea that could make guns twice as powerful without increasing the internal pressure."

"That would revolutionize armaments," Charlie said gravely. He was also thinking that millions of dollars might be at stake here. Any gun maker would pay a fortune for such a breakthrough.

"The three of them went back to work as soon as they finished breakfast. George said he didn't want to be disturbed. I heard them shoot about a dozen times, I guessed testing the new load. It made an awful noise echoing across the bay. I walked past at about nine o'clock and looked through the window as I passed. They were loading up the large shells used in the anti-tank gun. Kirta was on a walk, and she came home before eleven and went in the kitchen to help Anna cook. She always does that. Then she asked me if I wanted to go to the shop with her to see if the men had finally succeeded."

"Did you see any of the three men come out of the shop? Did any of them enter the house?"

"No. The last time I saw any of them was when I looked through the shop window. When Kirta and I went down the shop was empty. We called without getting an answer. We went out and looked towards the timber, wondering if they had gone there to make some kind of a test. We were surprised, but not alarmed."

"You didn't look upstairs in the loft?"

"No. If the men had been there, they would have answered our calls. Late in the afternoon we began really searching the grounds along the bay. Kirta went as far as the timber but couldn't find any trace of them. We looked in the plane and in the hangar. By night we were both thoroughly frightened."

"You must have been," Charlie agreed.

"I went out very early this morning and searched the shop again. That's when I found the blood on the loft floor. I went straight to the safe, opened it, took out all the papers, got in the plane and left."

"Did you see Kirta or Anna before you left?"

"No. I don't think either had come out of their room."

"Were all three men together when they disappeared?"

"So far as I know."

Charlie gazed into the cold fireplace, thinking hard. "Where do they go to get a drink when they are thirsty?" he finally asked.

"Sometimes they come to the house. Sometimes Anna carries a pitcher of water out to them. Why?"

"I think they were drugged," Charlie replied. "Three men together vanish without any suspicious sounds? You would have heard cries, something, if there had been an attack of some kind. I think they were doped, and the easiest way to have done that would have been putting something in their water or coffee. Call Anna, please."

She got up and went to the kitchen.

Anna followed her but stopped in the doorway, stiffly, silently.

"Can you remember if any of the men came to the house yesterday morning for a drink?" Charlie asked the maid pleasantly.

"They didn't," she replied.

"Maybe you took water or coffee out to the shop for them to drink?" he suggested.

"I took them nothing," Anna replied. She waited a moment for him to ask another question, and when he didn't, she said, "I have a meal cooking on the stove. If there are no more pointless questions, I will go back and take care of it."

"Yes," Charlie agreed. "Go finish lunch."

After Anna was gone, he turned back to Joan. "I didn't expect to get anything out of her, and that is just one of the angles about this business I don't like."

"What do you mean?" she demanded.

"I'm not sure I know, exactly," he evaded. "I agree with Mrs. Lang that foreign agents are likely behind this. But that new gun and load will be priceless if your husband succeeds, and that means any number of other bad actors could be involved. We must not lose the drawings you left in the plane. They have to be guarded day and night. I want you to give them to Lew and me to keep."

"All right. I trust you. If I didn't, I would not have brought you back here. Let's go and get them right now."

Charlie followed her out into the big porch. Lew had finished towing the plane inside, for it was not in sight. They went down to the log structure, which was built partly out over the bay. It was about 50 feet wide and 60 feet long.

The plane was neatly tied up beside a plank platform. But Lew had not remembered or had not been able to turn it around and drag it in backwards, so the nose was pointed into the boathouse and not headed out across the bay ready for flight.

Joan noticed this immediately. "We will have to do it over again so there won't be any delay if we must go in a hurry."

Charlie agreed and said they should to do it at once.

Lew was nowhere in sight, so he must be in the plane. Charlie called to him, and when he didn't answer, Charlie was suddenly very alarmed. He ran along the plank gangway to the cabin door. It was partly open. He ducked through and found Lew face down on the floor, jammed between the seats, wedged in so tight Charlie had some difficulty dragging him free.

He turned Lew face up. Blood was smeared on his right cheek, seeping down from a short but deep gash just above the temple. Charlie lifted his companion's limp body and somehow got him through the tight door and onto the platform outside.

Joan cried, "Oh, no! Is he dead?"

"What makes you think he might be dead?" Charlie asked sharply. "Give me a handkerchief or something I can dip in the water and wash his face. His heart is beating."

Joan instinctively felt at her belt for a handkerchief but found none. She grasped the sleeve of her thin blouse and forcibly ripped the lower half off and gave that to Charlie. Seeing the strength in her fingers surprised him.

"What about the plans?" she asked.

"Gone, I am sure. That was the only reason to attack Lew. But go and see. I'm not leaving Lew until he comes around."

He dipped the cloth in the water and sponged the blood away. Lew was still unconscious, but his heart was beating regularly, and he looked better with the blood wiped off his face.

Joan came back from the plane.

"They are gone," she said, struggling not to burst into sobs.

"Maybe we can get somewhere now," Charlie said slowly. "If Lew saw who hit him, maybe we can break this thing wide open."

Truthfully, he had little faith in that. Would the attacker have left Lew alive if Lew had seen his face?

Lew groaned, opened his eyes and looked blankly at both of them for several seconds.

"Feeling better?" Charlie asked cheerfully.

"No, worse. He hit me an awful wallop. I saw more stars than you find at a Hollywood premiere."

"He's all right," Charlie's voice was relieved. "When Lew can joke, he isn't that hurt."

"That's what you think," Lew said feebly. He touched his temple carefully. "Is that bump as big as it feels, Charlie?"

"Well," his companion said, "folks will think you're packing a potato under your hat."

"Help me sit up." Charlie got an arm under his shoulders and lifted. "I suppose they got the stuff from the plane?" Lew asked.

"Yes. The plans are gone. How many were there?"

"Darned if I know. I didn't see anybody. I was leaning over to tie up the dinghy when I heard a step behind me and started to turn. Then, all I saw was stars. I remember telling myself I must not fall into the water, because if I did I'd drown. I bet you had to pry my fingers loose from the boards, didn't you?"

"You weren't out here. You were inside the plane."

Lew pondered that for a moment. "Why?" he finally asked.

"To get you out of sight in a hurry. Your assailant had to work fast, knowing I might come in anytime."

"They could have just rolled me into the water."

"Cold water might have revived you, made you cry out. No, the person who hit you was too smart for that."

"Guess I flopped. You told me to guard the plans, and I didn't."

"We'll get them back," Charlie assured him. "Now, tell me why you spoke of the attackers as 'they.'"

"I don't really know. I guess I assumed there was more than one because I supposed I was too tough to get taken by one. I won't make that mistake again, believe me."

"I'm not blaming you, of course. In fact, I had hoped to use the blueprints as bait. Let the enemy make a play for them and we'd make a play for the enemy when he did. But that's out now."

"Someone's coming," Lew said. His keen hearing had apparently recovered from the blow. Anna walked into the hangar. She barely looked at them before announcing, "Miss Kirta says lunch is ready."

Something in the way Charlie watched her caught Joan's eye.

"You're thinking she did this, aren't you?" Joan demanded.

"If you are, you're wrong," Lew spoke up.

Charlie glanced at him in surprise.

"I thought you didn't know who hit you?"

"I don't, not exactly. But I know it wasn't a woman."

Lew stood, swayed and clutched Charlie's arm. "You go on up to lunch, Mrs. Malverson," he said. "Charlie will bring me along slowly. I can't walk very fast yet."

"Then I should help, too," Joan said.

"No, you go ahead," Lew repeated.

Joan clearly wasn't used to taking orders. But she went.

Charlie waited another half a minute. "All right, she's gone. What makes you think it wasn't a woman?"

"I heard his voice. I said my last thought was to grab at something so I wouldn't fall in the water. I flung my arms out and one struck him. He must have been leaning close. I couldn't see him. But when I hit him, he said, 'Schweinhund!' That's German, you know, and not exactly a compliment. It was a man's voice. Deep and harsh. No woman could have spoken like that."

Charlie regarded him with grave eyes. "Are you sure, Lew? Remember, you were dazed, about to pass out."

"I'm just as sure as I am about being socked on the head," Lew replied. "Take my word, Charlie, when we get the person who socked me, it will be a man."

"All right," Charlie said. "Even if it knocks some of my ideas and makes this business more baffling than before. Now, what we have to figure out is where this mystery man hides."

Chapter 5 – Dead Men in a Row

"Our mysterious enemy can't be far away," Charlie continued, "because he had only minutes to get in the hangar, knock you out and steal the plans. You're sure it was a man, but there was no man in the house, and I'm sure I searched the place thoroughly. So where does that leave us?"

"He's still got to be in the house," Lew replied matter-of-factly. "What about a cellar hidden under the floor?"

"I would say there isn't one because a cellar would fill up with water, being so close to the bay. But we'll look for one anyway after we eat. Come on, Anna said lunch was waiting."

"What about Anna?" Lew asked. "I only had one look at her, but she sure didn't seem friendly."

"She isn't. She let me know that right away. Mrs. Malverson says she hates all men, that a man may have given her a raw deal."

Joan Malverson was waiting for them on the porch.

"You're sure there isn't a cellar under the house?" Charlie asked.

"Yes, I am," she replied, before leading them inside.

"How about a storage pit, maybe a trapdoor in a floor?"

"None," her tone was positive. "I'm sure because we use skins instead of carpets or rugs. Twice they've been taken outdoors to air while we scrubbed the floors. Now we must go, Kirta is waiting lunch for us."

"Just a moment," Charlie said. "Who does the housework?"

Joan turned impatiently. "Anna and I cook. Kirta helps, but she would rather take care of the rooms. Kirta may be girly, but she doesn't mind scrubbing and cleaning, and she cooks as much as I do, now. Anna was supposed to just look after Kirta. She refused to come unless she could bring Anna."

They followed her into the dining room. Kirta was seated at the head of the table. She looked up and said to Charlie, "Don't you know you must never keep a woman waiting?"

"Or a man hungry," Lew added with a smile.

Kirta swept him with wide blue eyes. He had the feeling they weren't missing any detail. "I suppose you are Lew," she said. "Why a real man like your friend would run with such a punk is beyond me."

Then she waved them towards two chairs on the opposite side of the table from Joan.

There weren't many instances when Lew was at a loss for words, but this was one of them. He went to his place, sat down and stared at the plate. Charlie, grinning at Lew's discomfiture, took the chair at his side. The cloth on the table was white and clean. The china looked expensive, and the silverware gleamed like honest metal. Lew fumbled awkwardly with his linen napkin.

Anna came in with a platter of steaming ham steak. Her features were grim, unchanging. It was an excellent meal despite the fact every ounce had come out of a can. Besides the ham, there were French fried potatoes, asparagus, a salad of mixed vegetables, baked beans, brown bread and peaches. Lew appeared to be recovering quickly. If he was there very long, there would be a pretty big heap of empty tins.

When they had finished with the meal, Anna brought a chrome coffee urn. Lew had recovered from his embarrassment, too, and he watched Anna and Kirta carefully, directing most of his glances at Kirta. She ate as she did everything else, with supreme complacency.

She seemed to have a splendid appetite, and she passed the serving platters to Lew whenever she took a helping. Once she caught Lew's eye and winked—wickedly.

Joan didn't eat much, just stirred her food. The contrast between the women was so marked it made Lew wonder if Kirta was already used to the idea of being a widow. "Her appetite sure doesn't seem to be giving her any trouble," he thought.

Joan began fidgeting, clearly wanting to get away from the table as soon as she decently could. Charlie pushed his plate back a couple of inches, and she immediately stood up.

Charlie and Lew also got to their feet, and Charlie said, "With your permission, I want to search the house again."

Kirta's blue eyes lost their sleepy, satisfied look. "My God," she protested. "Do I have to go through that again?"

Charlie didn't answer. He stood with eyes fixed on Joan. He had been thinking how someone hidden in the many-room house could have slipped from one part to another and kept ahead of him while he searched. He decided to go over it again with Lew and have Joan watch the central living room to prevent it happening again.

"If you think it necessary, go ahead," Joan said.

Charlie asked her to accompany them. Out on the porch, he told her his plan.

"Did you look up the chimney?" Lew asked.

Charlie went back in and knelt before the deep, wide hearth. The flue was two feet across with plenty of room to conceal a man or even two. But it didn't. He looked straight up at blue sky overhead.

"I thought we might strike pay dirt there," Lew said disappointedly. Then he added, "Well, how about the roof? There are wings and valleys between them where a man could lie hidden from view."

"All right," Charlie said. "You go up there. I'll leave that to you."

Lew went around the side of the porch and found the projecting log ends at a corner of the building made an excellent ladder. He climbed up in a few seconds. Then he went straight to the highest peak where he could look down into every valley.

"All clear," he called down. "Go on with the rest of the search."

Kirta stopped Charlie on his way through the dining room. "I always lie down after lunch," she told him. "So if you will search my room first, you won't bother me as much."

Charlie agreed to this sensible request and found her room and closet empty. He went through the bath and the other bedroom, which he decided must be Anna's because of the sparse furnishings. Dining room, kitchen, and utility room also yielded nothing. Then, instead of going on to the living room, he went back to Kirta's door and flung it open without knocking.

She was leaned over, unfastening the ties of her dark red slippers. She straightened, frowning. "I have a good nature," she said, "but you are using it up fast. You looked here already, didn't you?"

"Sure," Charlie agreed. "But I wanted to make sure nobody slipped inside while I was in another room." He watched her carefully as he said that. But she just waved a well-rounded arm.

"Heavens," she said. "How you trust me. All right, go ahead and look under the beds again. But make it fast."

She stood, reached around at the back of her neck and slid a talon fastener open. Then she calmly continued undressing. She was pulling the frock off over her head when he finished and made for the door.

Charlie went directly to Joan.

"I'm surprised Mrs. Lang can sleep at a time like this," he said.

"I told you she never reveals her true feelings. She's as worn out as I am. Anna told me she was in the timber searching for the men all of the time I was away in the plane this morning."

Charlie checked his watch. It read 1:25.

They had been at White Goose Bay less than three hours.

He went into the opposite wing, searched it with no result. Then he went out in front of the house. Lew was still perched on the highest roof ridge. He shook his head, said, "No dice," and started down.

They went back to the plane hangar, looked in the corners, in the plane, in the dinghy and up on the beams that supported the roof.

The shop was next, and Joan joined them as they started towards it. Lew whistled softly when he saw the tank for the first time. "I'd sure like to drive that chariot," he said wistfully.

They looked everywhere but found nothing.

Lew strolled over to the heavy bench on which was mounted George Malverson's prototype of the high-power cannon. It was pointed at a window, which could be pushed to one side.

Charlie came over and joined his inspection.

The tapered barrel was 6 feet long with a 2-inch bore. The muzzle was fitted with a flared funnel-like device to hide the firing flash at night. The breech closed with a sort of toggle arrangement like the old model Luger, only trimmer. Charlie picked up a loaded shell. It held a hard, brightly polished projectile evidently plated to pierce armor. The entire load was about 10 inches long.

Three shock-absorbing cylinders were grouped about the breech end of the barrel, extending down a third of its length. The mounting was extremely flexible. Lew loosened the wheel clamps and spun the gun two thirds of a circle and then raised the muzzle almost straight up.

"The mounting is also experimental," Joan said. "The finished gun will move even faster and cover a wider field. That," she said pointing to the shell still in Charlie's hand, "is the key. There are plenty of anti-tank cannons. But nobody has been able to make a 2-inch shell as powerful as 3-inch field ammunition. Well, this one is."

Charlie regarded her thoughtfully. She had mentioned before how revolutionary the gun and load would be. He hadn't thought a lot about it for there had been other matters occupying his mind. Now he looked at the shell, hefted it in his hand. It seemed impossible to give such a light load as much power and range as a 3-inch gun because as power increases, the propellant must increase in proportion to the square of the diameter and not merely the caliber of the bore.

Joan noticed his doubt.

"Of course you don't believe it," she said. "Nobody does. George knew he hadn't convinced the War Ministry that he was on the track of something big. So, he came up here to finish the work in secrecy."

"How does he get so much power from such a small shell?" Charlie asked. "I haven't heard of any breakthrough in smokeless powder."

"The secret is a blend of several existing explosives. George discovered a way to combine them until the mix was twice as powerful as the same weight of any one powder would be."

"Duplex loading?" Lew asked.

"Better," she said, pride glowing in her no-longer tired eyes. "George calls it triple loading. In order to give a two-inch cannon the power and range of a three-inch gun, first he had to overcome the limited powder capacity in the shell. Then, he had to keep down the breech pressure of such a load. George would lie awake at night going over the details aloud. He told me time after time that he could do it, and I learned the details he shared by heart."

She went over to the door, looked out, closed it and came back. "I thought I heard someone walking outside."

Charlie looked at Lew. If anyone could hear stealthy footsteps his companion could, for his ears were unusually keen. Lew shook his head slightly. Joan pushed the hair back from her forehead.

"I keep thinking I hear George," she explained. "I suppose I'm going a little wacky."

"You were telling us about the load," Charlie reminded her.

"Of course. George said that every other cannon developed too much breech pressure in relation to power. That made it necessary to build bigger-bore guns with thick breech walls and barrels. He believed the right blend of certain powders might give more power without increasing the initial pressure. So he purchased quantities of more than 30 varieties of propellants and powders. It was tedious work. One week he tried 354 combinations and made no headway at all. This is the second barrel, made by hand in a steel forging shop. He wore out the first with his test shooting."

"Sounds expensive," Charlie said. "Why didn't he experiment on a smaller scale with less cost?"

"You have no idea what this has cost us," she agreed ruefully. "He tried working on a smaller scale, but after he found what looked to be a successful load it failed in the larger volume in the cannon. It takes three dollars' worth of powder alone for most shots, and he has fired thousands. Everything we have is tied up in this gun and shell."

"How did your husband overcome the problem of breech pressure?" Charlie asked. "That is if you will trust us so far."

"It's not that I don't trust you," she replied. "But only George knows the formula. And he wrote it down in chemical symbols only a chemical engineer could read. But I can tell you the principle.

"George said ordinary loads developed higher pressure than necessary to start the bullet moving. Most of it pushes out against the walls of the chamber and is wasted. Do you follow?"

"Sure," Charlie said. "We've worked up a few loads of our own."

She nodded and then continued.

"George worked out a combination load that builds pressure in three stages, and that gives the projectile three successive impulses instead of one. The initial push doesn't have to be as strong. This successive action with three different powders, properly mixed and loaded into the shell by a process he hasn't even shared with me, raises muzzle velocity to unmatched speeds."

"Sounds pretty remarkable," Lew said.

"It is remarkable. And with Malvorite, what he calls the new propellent, this small shell may hit with greater destructive force than one fired from a three-inch gun."

"What is the top velocity attained?" Charlie asked.

"I don't know, exactly. We haven't a capable chronograph. George uses a system for calculating velocities by the crushed primer fuses. But that isn't truly accurate because the load has a low initial pressure. He did say he thought the armor-piercing shell had exceeded a speed of 4,000 feet a second."

"Wow," Lew exclaimed. "What a gun this will be for tanks and airplanes. Light enough to be mounted on the smallest fighting ship."

"What is the penetration?" Charlie asked.

Joan pointed at a plate of armor. It was about 18 inches square. A little to one side of center, a hole had been punched clear through. Charlie and Lew lifted it with difficulty it was so heavy.

"Our gun did that," Joan said with pride. "That plate is the same used for battleship armor."

"See what this means, Charlie?" Lew said with building excitement in his voice. "Nobody could build a tank heavy enough to turn these shells. Plant a hundred of these guns along any invasion route and make scrap out of a division of tanks. Put four or five of them on a fast mosquito boat and it could whip a destroyer."

"It is a remarkable breakthrough," Charlie agreed. "Your husband deserves much credit for working it out. Can you tell us anything about the tank? What special features does it have?"

"The tank isn't so revolutionary," she admitted. "Its biggest point is the streamlined exterior. Because of the curvature, George thinks it will turn most shells from a regular three-inch gun."

"That's pretty remarkable, too," Charlie said.

Lew was running a hand up and down over the polished metal.

"This is but a model," Joan said. "It's made from soft steel because we didn't have presses large enough to shape hard steel. Anton is an expert metal worker. He curved and fit all of the plates and then welded the seams by hand. The joints are almost invisible."

"I don't see any gun ports," Charlie said.

"To expose the guns, a section of the tank slides back over another. The crew inside can fire in any direction, even straight up. The turret is worked like the power turrets on English planes. Even when the ports are exposed, the tank body is streamlined and smooth."

"Say," Lew exclaimed. "How do we get in that tank? We never looked there, you know. How'd we forget that?"

The thought had struck Charlie at the same moment. He turned to ask Joan about the door, but she had already run up to show them a small bulge in the side. "Push that!" she cried. "Hurry!"

Charlie drew his pistol, motioned her to stand back. Then he pressed on the swell. There was a little click, and a panel about 28 inches wide swung back. He thrust his head through. Then he pulled it out just as quickly, blocking the door with his body.

"You go on up to the house, Mrs. Malverson, please."

Her eyes flashed. "I have a right to know what you saw in there. You will have to tell me sometime."

Charlie studied her pale face, wondering if she could take it. He decided she could.

"All right. There are two dead men in there, sitting in a row."

He glanced at his watch automatically. The time was 2:30.

Chapter 6 – Signals in the Night

When Charlie told Joan there were two dead men in the tank, Lew stepped up to catch her, sure the shock would be more than she could stand. But she didn't fold. Instead, she said in a firm voice, "Step back, so I can see."

Charlie didn't move. "Are you sure you want to do this?"

"Of course I am sure," she replied. "You can't tell me who it is; you don't know any of the missing men."

Charlie stepped away from the tank door. Her glance inside was even shorter than his had been. When she turned away, she was clutching the side of the big metal machine. But then they heard her say for the second time that day, "Thank God!"

Charlie closed the door.

"It is my brother Hugh and Anton Zack," she said. "Don't misunderstand, please. I love my brother, and his death is a terrible shock. My relief is at not finding George dead, too."

"Hadn't you better go tell Mrs. Lang?" Charlie said.

"Poor Kirta. I wonder how she will take this, especially after saying such awful things about Hugh."

Charlie wondered, too. He had thought of going along to note her reaction. But he decided Kirta had a right to privacy at such a moment, and also too much control to betray her real emotions to a stranger. He walked Joan to the door and then went back to the tank.

Lew had taken a look inside and was backing away, his face colored the peculiar tint of putty. "That is all I can stomach," he said. "I got a queer sensation behind my belt."

Charlie felt the same way, but he also knew the bodies had to come out, and he told Lew so. Lew swallowed hard.

Both of them were shaken badly when the job was finally over. They laid a piece of tarpaulin over the two bodies on the shop floor.

Hugh Lang looked surprisingly young, his hair dark like his sister's. In life, he must have been a very handsome man.

They stepped outside to breathe the cool air off the bay.

"I'm lucky to be alive," Lew said. "The same killer only knocked me blotto."

"They need to be buried," Charlie said. "Lord, what a mess. This is more responsibility than I am comfortable shouldering. We are going to fill the plane with gas and send Mrs. Malverson out for help. She can bring back mounted police or the army.”

“Lew, you stay in the hangar and see that the killer doesn’t get away in the plane. He has the blueprints, and if he should fly away with them we’re licked—and stuck 500 miles from home.”

“Okay,” Lew agreed. “But where do you think George Malverson may be, killed like those two?”

“I’m afraid so. Only don’t let Joan suspect we think that way. I have no idea why these two bodies were put in the tank, much less why they were still in there. Why not drop them in the bay with a weight tied to the feet? Of course, whoever opened the fuel tanks on Joan’s plane never expected her to return. When she came back, somebody may have had to change his plans on the fly. Regardless, Lew, your job now is to see that nobody gets away in that plane. Here’s my pistol, and don’t trust anyone, even Joan. Understand?”

When Charlie went up to the house, Joan was pacing back and forth across the living room. “Kirta took it hard,” she said. “I made her lie down in her room.”

“Was she surprised or just grief-stricken?”

“I don’t think she was surprised. I believe she had reconciled herself to Hugh being dead. She cried quite hard.”

“I see,” Charlie replied thoughtful. Then he continued quickly, “Mrs. Malverson, I want you to leave here at once. You can fly down to the first police headquarters or army post and bring back as much help as you can, as quickly as you can. We’ve got to have official help now. This is bigger than I had any idea.”

“I can’t leave until I know what happened to George.”

“You must. You are the only one who can fly the plane. We’ll search while you’re gone, and you staying won’t help us any. I’m going to be frank now, even if it sounds brutal. I doubt Mr. Malverson is still alive, and finding his body won’t do anything but settle your doubts. We’re licked without reinforcements. The killer has the plans, and if you don’t get away in the plane, he may. No one would be able to stop him then. You know your husband would want you to do everything possible to keep his work out of enemy hands.”

“I’ll be ready to go in five minutes,” she replied calmly. “There are nearly thirty barrels of gasoline in the hangar. You’ll find a pump to draw out the fuel and a hose long enough to run it to the plane.”

“Not a word to anybody about leaving,” he warned her.

She nodded, and Charlie went down to the hangar. The water of the bay was glass smooth. Three gulls rode high on the surface. Two others circled overhead. The only sound was the murmur of water lapping against the sturdy spruce posts that supported the big roof. He wondered about that lapping with the bay itself so calm. He pushed his sleeve back, checked his watch and saw it read exactly three o'clock.

They had been at White Goose Bay exactly four hours.

Lew stood on the board platform facing the door. Charlie saw he was backed up by the west wall, pistol in hand. Lew was frowning, and Charlie didn't like that.

"What's wrong?" he demanded.

"Maybe nothing," Lew replied. "And maybe a lot. When I got here the plane was rocking on the water. And there isn't a wave on the lake big enough to make it rock. So I wonder if somebody was in the plane before I came back in."

"Did you see anybody?"

"Nobody. Anna was walking along the beach a couple hundred yards off, looking down for seashells. Anyway, she bent every half minute to pick something up. I watched her through the door."

"Did you check the plane?"

"Sure. I'm no mechanic. But everything looks okay to me."

"Help upend one of these barrels. We're going to fill the tanks so Joan can leave immediately." They found the portable pump and in a few minutes were sending a steady stream of gasoline into the plane.

Joan came in wearing her wool flying suit. "I feel guilty leaving again without telling Kirta. Can't I take her with me this time?"

"No," Charlie said decisively. "You must go alone. We'll expect you back sometime in the morning. Right?"

"Right!" she said and then climbed into the cabin to watch the fuel gauges. When the tanks were full she signaled them to stop pumping. Then she called, "I'm going to start the motors. As soon as they catch, take the dinghy and pull the plane outside."

"I'll do that," Charlie said quickly. "Lew, you stand here just inside the door. Don't let anybody inside."

They stood waiting for the roar of the big motors. A minute passed. Then the cabin door opened and Joan came out. "I can't start her," she said. "There isn't any pressure in the self-starter. It works by air pressure stored when the engines are running. I flew far enough this morning to have plenty of air. The ignition is dead."

"So, they won't start even if we whirl the propeller?"

"Not with a dead ignition system."

"I should have figured on this," Charlie said. "Somebody was in the plane, Lew. You missed them by only a minute."

He turned to Joan, "Think you can repair it?"

"Maybe," she said doubtfully. "Depends on what's wrong."

"Go and help her, Lew." Charlie said and sat down on the edge of the platform, feet hanging over the water. He needed a couple of minutes to think this out. He hoped Joan could locate the trouble and correct it. But it was not a vigorous hope.

Joan and Lew stood on the narrow walk that passed by the nose of the plane. They opened a small hinged panel and peered in at the engines. "Look here," Lew said. "Something has been removed from this flat base. The nuts and lock washers have been put back on the six studs that held it. On the bright side, it looks like all we have to do is find the part and put it back on ourselves."

"That is the first definite information we have about the killer's plans," Charlie spoke up. "He fixed the plane so we can't use it, but so he still can when he is ready. That means he and his companion are planning to leave with the blueprints. Probably tonight."

"What makes you say companion?" Joan asked quickly.

"A second person is needed to spin the props."

"No one is going anywhere in this plane," Lew asserted. "I'll lock myself in the cabin and wait for them to try."

"You don't have to," Charlie said. "What was taken?"

"Something small, electrical equipment I think."

"Help yourself to something else, Lew. Then nobody can fly the plane until all of the parts are back together."

Charlie stood up and realized he was very tired. It wasn't physical exhaustion but rather nervous strain—the baffling uncertainty.

Lew came up to him carrying a complicated little piece of machinery. "I don't know exactly what it is, but it has something to do with injecting fuel, and I know the plane can't run without that."

"I might as well get out of this suit," Joan said. "What next?"

"I have one idea," Charlie said. "A way to make contact with our enemy. Until we do that, we're helpless. You can't fight someone you can't find. We must establish that contact, and soon."

"How?" Joan asked.

"I'm not saying just yet."

Joan stalked off towards the house.

"She is mad," Lew suggested.

"Maybe," Charlie replied. "This business is making us all half crazy. And she is carrying a heavy load of grief, too."

Then Charlie sighed. "We've been a disappointment to her, too. But now we'll hopefully make some progress using that part you took as bait to catch a killer."

"What about George Malverson?"

"Unfortunately," Charlie replied, "I don't think there is any need to hurry on that one. We'll look for him when there's time."

"Nobody will try to get away with the plane before nightfall," Lew said. "So I'm going to the shop and look at that gun again."

Ever since Lew first glimpsed George Malverson's cannon his fingers had itched to handle it. He went into the shop, walked carefully around the two bodies laying on the floor and stopped beside the cannon. He unlocked the swivel base and swung the muzzle back and forth. Then, he opened the window before the gun.

It faced out across the open bay.

Of course, mere scrutiny of such a gun wouldn't satisfy Lew. He opened the breech, shoved in one of the slender shells, and looked out across the water to make sure there was nothing in line with the gun.

After he fired the gun, his ears ached from the concussion even though he had remembered to hold his mouth open. The barrel of the gun was as nearly level as he could make it, and he watched the water, eager to note how far the ball would get before gravity pulled it down. He looked for more than a minute and didn't see a splash.

"What a gun!" he exclaimed. "It shoots so flat it doesn't drop four feet within eye range. We're lucky the killer didn't use this gun instead of a rifle to take a shot at us when we were landing."

Charlie came in quickly after the shot. He stopped when he saw Lew standing beside the gun.

"You could have warned me you were going to shoot it."

"Didn't know I was," Lew said with a wide grin. "But then I couldn't resist the urge."

He described his failed test to determine point-blank range.

"And the action is sort of semiautomatic. The breech slides back and there's a pocket exposed to drop in a new shell. That trips the action so it closes again ready to fire. Two men could shoot thirty rounds a minute." He counted the shells. There were 18 left.

"Not enough for a rapid-fire test," he decided. "Anyway, I don't suppose Joan wants me to use them up."

"I don't, either," Charlie said. "What you can do is figure out where to hide them. One of those shells is just as important as the stolen formula. Any chemist familiar with explosives could break down the load from a shell and figure out exactly what is in it."

"You're right," Lew said. "We'll find a safe hiding place and put them in it tonight." He closed the window and swung the gun around.

Joan appeared at the door, short of breath.

"What happened?" she demanded.

"Just Lew's curiosity getting the better of his common sense," Charlie repled. "He just had to shoot the gun. I hope you don't mind."

She clearly did mind, but relieved it was no more serious than that, she let it go. As she walked back up to the house with Charlie, he told her why they were hiding the rest of the shells, and she agreed that was wise.

Anna must have started a fire, because big chunks of driftwood blazed in the fireplace, and they sat down to relax before it. But Joan got up to pace after only a few minutes.

"If we could just do something," she declared. "This sitting around getting no place drives me mad."

"I know," Charlie agreed. "And we haven't been very successful helping you. But, I think we'll finally get somewhere tonight."

He still refused, however, to say anything more.

Dinner was another meal of tinned foods, yet every dish was excellently seasoned. "That is one thing about properly canned things," Kirta said. "It takes a really bad cook to spoil them."

Anna sat at the foot of the table, silent and if possible more sullen than she had seemed at noon. Kirta's eyes were red and swollen. Nobody talked much, and all were glad when the meal was finished. Charlie and Lew felt especially uncomfortable.

After a dessert of plum pudding, Joan offered to show them to their room, the rear bedroom in the right wing. But Charlie was already familiar with the layout since he had searched the place twice.

When they were in the room Lew immediately pulled the cotton spread from one of the twin beds. He always liked to check the material he would be sleeping on. What he saw pleased him.

"Look," he said. "Genuine Hudson's Bay blankets."

Charlie set down their pack of clothing. Then he brought in the two .303 rifles from the rack on the living room wall. He decided they should have a corner on firearms and got both of the shotguns, too.

They lay down until it was dark outside and the house was quiet. However, when Charlie went into the bathroom he could hear Joan pacing back and forth on the other side of the partition.

Charlie examined the window at the back of the room. It opened easily, and he rubbed soap over the guides to make it silent. Half an hour later, they climbed through it and dropped to the ground.

They carried their own rifles. The other guns were shoved under one of the mattresses. It wasn't a great hiding place, but it was the best they could do. All of the shells and cartridges Charlie had found in the living room were now in his pockets. When they reached the hangar, he threw them out into the bay.

It was too dark to examine the plane without lighting matches, and they didn't want to risk that. The plane seemed to be just as they had left it. They took seats in facing corners, backs against the walls, waiting in silence.

After sitting that way for an hour, Lew stood to relieve his cramped muscles. The only sound was the gentle rustling of water. Lew went to the door and looked along the beach.

"Charlie!" he called urgently. "See that? Somebody is signaling."

Down the beach a light was blinking on and off. They watched for almost a minute before Charlie realized it was a message in Morse Code, using a short burst of light for a dot and a longer flash for a dash. He was familiar with the code, and started to repeat the letters as fast as he recognized them. "K-I-K-period, that's the end of a sentence. Now it's starting again. S-M-U-L-, that's the first word. "B-L-E-S-K …"

"Doesn't make sense," Lew objected.

"Of course it doesn't," Charlie said. "It's code. Our enemy is signaling someone out on the bay. Come on, Lew, it's time we meet."

Charlie couldn't see his watch, but he guessed the time at 9:30.

Chapter 7 – Disappearing Footprints

They ran swiftly over the wave-packed sand at the edge of the bay, eyes locked on the signal light that flashed on and off. When the light was still a few hundred feet ahead they turned away from the water so they could slip in behind the signaller and block any escape. Now he was plainly visible silhouetted by the flaring light, tall and bulky. The arm holding the light, which appeared to be a small battery lantern, was as thick as a man's lower leg.

"This bird is going to be tough to handle," Lew thought.

Then he stepped on an empty seashell, and his boot crunched it with a loud noise. The light went out, and he heard feet running on the packed sand. Then he heard a loud splash followed by smaller ones.

"He's swimming for it!" Lew cried, raising his rifle and firing two snap-shots in the direction of the splashing.

The splashes continued, and Lew lowered the gun, unwilling to waste more shells. "I never touched him," he told Charlie.

"That's all right, he's trapped now," Charlie replied grimly. "He can't last long in that frigid water. All we have to do is follow along the beach and grab him when he swims ashore. Which way is he going?"

Lew listened intently. "Still heading straight out," he finally said.

They decided to separate and each patrol opposite directions of the beach. Charlie took the beach directly in front of the house and the hangar. As the minutes passed without a sound from the swimmer, he gradually lengthened the space he covered. He began to wonder if the man might elude them after all. But that seemed impossible, for the cold water would surely drive him back to shore.

He was approaching the hangar for the fifth time when he thought he heard movement inside the building. Then there was a dull thud and a gun fired. He reached the hangar door quickly and plunged through, but the interior was so dark he had to stop. Then he moved forward slowly, one hand extended out. He collided with a figure, grabbed and caught his fingers in cloth. The cloth ripped loose, and Charlie stumbled forward, arms spread wide. They encircled someone and clamped down tight. The size, softness and faint odor of perfume told him he was holding a woman. He released his grip, pulled matches out of a pocket and struck one. The match flared, and a white face sprang out of the blackness. It was Kirta Lang, eyes surveying him coolly.

"Good evening," she said. "You are as impetuous as ever."

Her clothing was perfectly dry. It certainly had not been Kirta swimming in the bay. "What are you doing here?" Charlie demanded.

"I'm trying to figure how much damage you did with that bear-hug. I thought I heard something snap," she said. "Probably a rib."

She spoke so leisurely Charlie decided she was trying to cover up something. "Don't stall," he said. "Answer me."

"I don't know why I should, but I came down from the house when I heard two shots. I don't want anything to happen to the plane; it's the only way of getting away from this dreary hole."

"Well, don't lose any more sleep over the plane," Charlie told her. "It was put out of commission sometime yesterday."

"What?" she sounded surprised, and Charlie decided to press that temporary advantage.

"There was a third shot just now. Where were you then?"

"In here," she replied, quickly regaining her customary aplomb. "The shot was outside but close. I think you broke two of my ribs."

Charlie ignored that. "See anybody?"

"Nobody but you."

Charlie saw he wasn't going to get anything from Kirta Lang and let her return to the house. His match had gone out, so he lit another and held it down close to the floorboards. They were dry. The man who had signaled on the beach and jumped in the bay had not entered the hangar. Lew came running up as the second match flickered out.

"Who's in there?" he demanded.

Charlie struck another match. "Just me, but with Mrs. Lang a minute ago. She told me she got anxious about the plane when she heard your shots. So she came down to guard it."

"Sounds fishy," Lew grunted.

"Why don't you go question her yourself?" Charlie suggested.

"No thanks. Where did the third shot come from?"

"Close," Charlie replied and started outside. "I want to look around. Somebody might be hurt out there."

They started over the ground with flaming matches held low. Halfway along the side of the building, he bent lower and picked up a pistol. The barrel was warm.

"That's mine," Lew said. "The one they took when they slugged me on the head."

The breech was jammed, a fresh cartridge wedged in the open

breech. The mechanism was also full of sand.

"Another trick," Charlie said. "The gunshot was to draw us over here. The swimmer came up close enough to toss the gun against the hangar. It was loaded and cocked so the jar would set if off. When I ran up to see what had happened, he probably landed farther up the beach and escaped. And I was thinking we had him trapped for sure."

"We can check on that," Lew said, lit another match and started along the edge of the water. About 200 feet away they found a wet trail leading out of the bay. The shoe marks were imprinted deeply in the sand, the trail running directly towards the front door of the house.

"He can't escape us now," Lew said confidently. Twice they paused to light matches and check the trail. It was still unmistakable. When they paused a third time the trail had run out.

"That's all right," Lew declared. "Maybe his clothing isn't dripping so much now. But we'll see where he walked over the porch."

Yet the porch floor was dry. Where they expected to find wet marks and sand on the scrubbed porch floor there was absolutely nothing. They switched on the porch light and went around the big house stopping at every window and door to light matches and examine the sills and thresholds. Every one was dry. Baffled, they came around to the porch again and stopped just before the door.

Lew clutched his companion. A figure was coming around the corner of the house. Charlie drew his pistol, and they stepped into the shadows. Charlie said, "Where have you been, Mrs. Malverson?"

She started, "Oh. You frightened me."

Her clothes seemed dry, but he grasped an arm to be sure. She pulled away. "I've been down to the shop," she said. "When I heard the shots, I thought somebody was shooting the cannon again."

She glanced meaningfully at Lew. But Charlie ignored that and demanded of her, "Don't you know there's a killer loose?"

Kirta, who had come walking slowly up from the hangar, stopped behind them to listen. She laughed, but Joan's temper flared.

"It isn't us who are being stupid ..."

"I know," Charlie cut her off. "But I haven't time to listen to that right now. Where's Anna? Either of you seen her?"

"I haven't," Joan said.

"Neither have I," Kirta echoed.

"Did either of you see the other leave the house tonight?"

They shook their heads. Charlie's exasperation grew.

"Who fired the shots? And why?" Joan asked.

Charlie told her about the signaller on the beach.

"He jumped into the water then swam all the way to the hangar, tossed a cocked gun against it so it would fire and drew us that way. That gave him a chance to slip out of the water. We tracked him almost to the house. Then the trail ended. I think he entered the house, but how he did it without leaving any water marks I can't figure."

Anna walked out through the front door, and Charlie demanded, "Where have you been?"

Anna tersely replied that she was awakened by the shooting, had dressed and checked Kirta's room. It was empty, so she looked in every other room for her. Then she had sat in the kitchen listening. When she heard voices on the porch, she came outside.

"All right," Charlie nodded, realizing he wouldn't get anyplace with her, either. He looked closely at her clothes; everything was dry.

"I'm going to search the house again," Charlie declared. And without waiting for a reply went inside quickly. He looked in every room and closet but found no one, not even something damp.

Lew had stayed with the three women, ostensibly to protect them but actually watching that no one communicated with an unknown occupant of the house. When Charlie told them he was finished searching, Kirta said, "I'm going to lock my door as soon as I get inside. You better do the same, Joan, if you want any sleep tonight."

She waltzed away with her regal, sweeping gait, Anna trailing.

Joan's eyes were frightened when she turned to Charlie and said, "Do you really think someone is in the house?"

"I don't know what else to think," Charlie replied. "But I'm tired, and you are, too. We can take this up in the morning."

"Who was he signaling to?" Joan stood her ground.

"I have an idea," Charlie replied curtly. "We'll talk tomorrow."

She saw he again didn't intend to explain his statement, hesitated and then hurried away. A few seconds later they heard her door slam and then sobbing from behind the closed door.

Charlie dropped into one of the big chairs that stood close to the still-glowing hearth. "I guess I could have told her what I was thinking," he spoke to Lew, who had taken a chair on the other side of the fire. "But she isn't crying over anything I said. She is crying because her grief and worry are more than she can bear."

He reached for the poker and prodded the coals until a handful burst up in flame. The glare illuminated the face of his watch, and he idly saw the time was 16 minutes after 10.

"Tonight," he continued, "we almost had him. I know he came in this house. He's in here now. There isn't any other place for him to hide, but where?" He poked the coals again.

"This is a mess, Lew, and when we wind it up, I suspect we'll be disgusted. But we will wind it up, all right. Yes, there may be more killing. A regular slaughter, if my suspicions are correct."

Then he got up suddenly, his eyes fixed on the floor in front of the fireplace. Charlie began speaking more to himself this time than to Lew. "Funny, I never thought of that." He knelt on the polar bear rug that covered the floor, running his hands through the thick pelt.

"Come here, Lew. Feel that damp fur?"

Charlie's eyes were calm and clear. He was his old competent self again. "The killer stood on this rug while he changed out of his wet clothing. That's why there are no damp spots on the bare wood floor."

"But how did he get here without leaving tracks?" Lew asked.

"I don't know," Charlie admitted. "Not yet. But I will."

As he walked back and forth in front of the fire, his eyes played over the floor, the walls, the furniture. Finally, they came to rest on the five-foot logs piled neatly to the left of the mantel. "Yes," Charlie said slowly. "I think I know now. Help me move these logs."

Lew helped him lift the logs one at a time onto the floor.

"There it is," Charlie said, pointing to a dark roll crammed down in between two logs at the bottom of the pile. Charlie pulled, and the roll unfolded into a coverall suit made of pure black gum rubber. Lew immediately remembered how monstrous the figure on the beach had appeared when silhouetted against his signal light.

"No wonder he looked so big," Lew said. "He had this on over his regular clothes."

The suit had rubber feet and gloves permanently attached to each cuff. A waterproof talon fastener opened the suit down the front.

"No wonder his trail up from the beach ended so suddenly," Charlie said. "The water just ran off and had stopped dripping by the time he got to the porch. He must have stopped and took the suit off. Then he walked in without leaving a trace. Then he laid it on the rug while he moved enough logs to hide it."

Lew was studying his companion's face.

"You know who it is, don't you?"

"Not for sure. And I can't act yet because I haven't proof. This is going to be a rather delicate affair. It may be awfully hard to prove anything. But I'll try, just as soon as I learn a little more."

Chapter 8 – Lew Walks Out at Night

"You suspect Kirta, don't you?" Lew asked.

He had a few ideas about her himself.

"I suspect them all," Charlie replied.

"But it doesn't have to be one of the three," Lew said. "Does it?"

"No, it doesn't," Charlie agreed. "The person on the beach was signaling to someone out on the bay. That definitely brings in an outside element. Maybe George Malverson was out there. Maybe he killed the other two. We don't know he invented the tank and gun himself and that the others merely helped. The safe thing is to trust nobody."

"Not even Joan?"

Charlie hesitated and finally said, "Not all the way. We can't risk it. But now it is late, and I'm going to bed."

Sitting on one edge of his bed, Lew unlaced his boots and let them drop on the floor. "What about guarding the plane?" he asked.

"Nobody is going to bother it tonight," Charlie replied. "I have a notion the rest of tonight will be very quiet."

At that moment a gun fired behind him. Charlie whirled and saw the door of the room open some 10 inches. He thought he had closed it when he came in behind Lew. He jumped for the switch on the wall and struck it down, plunging the room into darkness. No longer an easy target, Charlie went to the door and flung it wide. The little hall outside was empty. But he thought he heard steps in Joan's room, leaped to the door and jerked that one open, too.

She faced him with frightened eyes. Her hair had tumbled down over her shoulders. She cried out something he did not understand, and her eyes went to the thing she held in two trembling hands.

It was a short, blued pistol.

Lew came running out into the hall. "Search the bathroom and living room," Charlie ordered. They were empty, but he heard voices in the left wing and started towards them. Kirta met him in the small hall. Anna was behind her, peering over her shoulder.

"My God, what is it now?" Kirta demanded. "Where's Joan?"

Lew turned and went back to Charlie. His companion had taken the pistol from Joan's trembling fingers.

"It was an accident," he said quickly. "I was cleaning it and forgot to remove the last shell from the chamber."

Kirta stepped up close, her breath heavy with the sweetish odor of London gin. "You were cleaning a gun in Joan's room?"

Charlie smiled. "Hardly. I came to reassure her about the noise. Now try to get some sleep."

Kirta looked doubtful, but she led Anna away with her. When he heard their doors click shut, he turned back to Joan.

"Why did you tell them that?" she whispered.

"What did you want me to say?" he asked. "That I heard a bullet buzz by my ear, and when I opened your door you stood there with a gun in your hand?"

Lew's mouth fell open. "Joan took a shot at you?"

"I didn't!" she cried.

"Take it easy," Charlie soothed. "I know it looked bad when I found you holding the pistol. Now let me tell you what actually happened. You heard the shot, jumped out of bed, put on the light and started for the door. Just before you got there, the gun came sliding in underneath the door. The crack is 2 inches high. You were so surprised you picked up the gun. Then I came in. Is that about right?"

"How could you know all of that?" she asked, incredulous.

"You had no reason to shoot me," he explained with a grin, "even if I am a bum detective. You could just fire me. No, the intent behind this was to sow doubt—and it was the enemy's first dumb play."

Then he glanced quickly at Lew. "What was that?"

"Somebody closed a door in the back of the house." Lew replied instantly, his keen ears identifying the sound.

"Come on, Lew. We're going out to the shop!"

The moon had risen up out of the bay. Cold and dull, it gave the ruffling waves a sinister look. Charlie switched a light on at the shop door and went straight to the experimental gun. The shelf which had held the cannon shells was empty.

"I thought he was dumb when he shot at me in the house," Charlie said ruefully. "But it was another smart trick, to hold us there while he came down here for the shells."

"Why didn't he just take them before?" Lew asked.

"For some reason the shells weren't important until tonight. Maybe after you fired one it started him thinking. Regardless, he has them all," Charlie concluded bitterly.

"It isn't as bad as you think," Lew replied with a grin. "I came out before dinner and walked away with four shells under my coat. I've got them in a safe place, and anytime you need them, just say so."

Charlie was so relieved he forgot to ask Lew about the safe hiding place. When they got back to the house, Joan looked relieved, too, when she learned Lew had saved four of the shells. "Good. We can still have the charge analyzed if we need to."

"I wasn't thinking so much about preserving the formula as having more loads to shoot," Lew confessed.

"Mrs. Malverson," Charlie said. "I think you're in even more danger now. I wish you could get away."

"How?" she asked wearily. "You know the plane won't fly."

"How far away is that Indian fishing village on the bay?"

"About a hundred miles up the shore."

"I want you to go there tomorrow," Charlie ordered. "We'll put the outboard motor on the dinghy and start you at daybreak."

She shook her head decisively. "I can't do that." Her voice was low but firm. "I would go mad worrying what was happening here."

"Think about it," Charlie advised. "Now, good night. Be sure to lock your door. Don't let anybody in without calling us first. Promise?"

He followed Lew into their room and pushed the door shut, making sure it latched this time. "Wasn't there a lock on this door, Lew?"

"Sure. A bolt on the inside."

"It's gone, now."

Lew whistled softly. "Getting to be a war of nerves, isn't it?"

He started pulling blankets from his bed. "Bring yours, too," he said. "The bathroom still has a lock, and there's plenty of room on the floor. If there isn't, I'll take the tub."

They took their rifles in with the bedding. There was only one small window high in the wall, and they agreed it would be safe to open it for ventilation. Charlie laid his 9mm pistol beside his pillow. Lew got a cloth from back of the tub, and after dismounting his recovered pistol, wiped away all of the sand. He put the gun back together, tested the action several times and loaded the magazine.

Lew fell asleep before Charlie. He almost always did. But he rolled and turned, and after he had been asleep less than an hour, his hand collided with the rim of the iron tub and that brought him sitting up and awake. He slid out from under the blankets and got a drink of water. Then he stepped to the window and looked outside.

Lew could see the outlines of the hangar at the edge of the bay. He looked down at his watch. It was 40 minutes after midnight. Then he looked along the side of the house in the other direction and could just make out the dark mass of the shop.

He thought something moved close up beside the shop wall.

There wasn't a screen over the window, so he thrust his head out for a better look. But the movement didn't occur again, and he figured it had been a trick of the moonlight. He started back to bed. But then he pulled on his trousers instead, picked up his boots and pistol and went back to the bedroom where Charlie had soaped one of the windows so it would open without noise.

Lew dropped his boots out and crawled after them. It took him a minute to get the boots on. Then he approached the shop cautiously. The door was ajar a couple of inches. He remembered Charlie closing it tight after they discovered the cannon shells gone.

Lew backed around the corner where he couldn't be seen but where he could see anybody coming out of the shop. There were two dead men in the shop now; he didn't care to become the third.

He didn't have to wait long. The door creaked a little on salt-rusted hinges. Then he heard steps running lightly alongside the building. Acting on impulse, Lew thrust out a leg. The runner tripped over it and fell headlong. Lew heard a harsh exclamation and felt a thrill as he recognized the voice. It was the same he had heard when he had been knocked out in the hangar. He fell upon the figure, pistol in hand to use as a club. But the figure rolled out with astonishing agility, seized two handfuls of sandy soil and flung them into Lew's face.

Lew staggered, blinded and gasping. He backed against the wall and rubbed frantically at his eyes. But by the time he got one open and working, the figure had vanished. Something lay on the ground a few feet away, a small object but very plain in the moonlight.

Lew picked up a small hypodermic needle. "What the devil?" he muttered. "Is the fellow a dope addict?" He walked around the shop. The door was still closed, and he decided not to enter.

He went back to the house, and woke Charlie. "It's the same fellow who slugged me," he concluded his report.

"What was he wearing?" Charlie demanded.

Lew scratched his head, puzzled by the question. "Darned if I know. But I think it fit rather tight."

Charlie remained silent for several minutes, trying to reconcile this latest incident with what he knew, and what was harder, with what he suspected. And then suddenly it all fit.

"Should we go to the shop?" Lew asked.

"No. We will need our sleep tomorrow. Get back in the tub."

They were awakened by somebody pounding on the door. Charlie looked at his watch. It was exactly 7:30.

"Are you all right?" It was Joan's voice.

"Just sleepy and mad I didn't wake up sooner," Charlie replied.

"I was worried when I saw your door open and you gone. Then I saw the beds had been stripped and guessed you were in here."

"Somebody took the lock off our door," Charlie said by way of an explanation.

Seated at the breakfast table, Charlie looked around at the faces. Joan's eyes were ringed with dark circles. Kirta's looked like she was nursing a hangover. Anna was eating slowly, avoiding his eyes.

Charlie knew he didn't look much better, for he had seen his own face in the mirror when he shaved. But he felt better as soon as he drained a cup of coffee. It was steaming hot and very black. Then he helped himself to bacon and slid four big pancakes on his plate. After that, he took on a dish of canned whole figs.

"They're edgy now," Charlie thought. "But wait until they hear what I have to say."

Kirta looked up and caught his eye. "Well," she said, "what has Scotland Yard planned for today?"

"We're going to take it easy," Charlie replied. "There's just two jobs to finish. One is to find George Malverson. The other …"

Joan's cry interrupted him. "Do you know where he is?"

"I think so," he said. "And also the reason George Malverson wasn't killed like your husband and the machinist."

She met his eyes steadily. But her face lost all color. "If you know where George is," she said angrily, "take me there at once."

"If I'm right, a few minutes more aren't going to matter."

"You said you knew why he was not killed?"

"Yes, and we're going to find him as soon as we finish breakfast."

"Well, I can't eat now," Joan's declared, eyes flashing angrily.

Kirta's eyes had not left Charlie. "You said you had two jobs to do today. What's the other?"

Charlie took a drink of coffee, set the cup down and wiped his lips. He noticed the napkin was beautifully monogrammed with the initials *J.M.* "After we find Mr. Malverson, I'm going to reveal the fiend responsible for all of these crimes."

Chapter 9 – No Bigger than a Grave

"What?" Joan cried. "You have found that out, too?"

Lew had no idea what Charlie was talking about, but that didn't stop him from chiming in. "It's time we got things wound up," he drawled. "We've been here 24 hours. Usually we handle jobs quicker."

Kirta kept her eyes fixed on Charlie.

"You're bluffing," she said coolly.

Charlie laughed. "I suppose you could call it that," he said, and any lingering doubt in his mind eased.

He finished his cakes, drank more coffee and stood. Joan was already on her feet. Kirta was still watching him with her wide blue eyes. Anna's head stayed bent over her plate.

Lew followed him back into their bedroom where they picked up rifles without exchanging a word. Joan was waiting in the living room.

"I'm not letting you out of my sight until I see George."

"Yes, you are, Mrs. Malverson. You must let us handle this the way we think best. That means you stay in your locked room until we come for you. I give my word we'll do that as soon as we find him. Don't let anybody in until we return. Is that clear?"

She nodded dubiously. But she didn't argue when she saw his unyielding eyes. He stood outside her door until he heard the bolt slide home. Then he went with Lew to the shop, and once they were inside, he closed and bolted that door.

"George Malverson is in here," he said simply, "and he is still alive. The person you tripped last night was down here giving him another shot of dope. I'm going to tear this place down one board at a time if I don't find Malverson first. You stand by that wall, Lew, where you can cover the doors and windows. We're headed for a showdown, and it's death for both of us if they catch us napping."

Lew's eyes went to the tank in the middle of the floor. "He might be in there now. We took the two dead men out yesterday. There ought to be room for a live one."

Charlie shook his head at the idea. But he opened the door and crawled inside to be sure. He came back out and said, "Still smells like a slaughterhouse. But it's empty."

Then he walked slowly over the floor, scrutinizing every plank.

He dug down with his knife point into the dirt and grease in any opening between the wooden planks.

"There are just two possibilities left," he said finally. "The floor under the tank and the space below that big lathe."

"Tank's out," Lew said. "It would take four men to push it aside to expose a trapdoor. There was only one man down here last night."

Charlie nodded and walked over to the lathe. It was built in around the bottom with sheet metal that formed a bin to catch the steel shavings. It seemed loose, held between the lathe legs by metal turn buttons. He removed them and the box came easily forward.

"This is it," Charlie said quietly. He got a steel bar from one of the benches and pried at the end of one short plank. A complete section of floor raised a couple of inches. There was a black hole below. He lit a match and held it down. Lew heard him exclaim softly.

"What is it?" Lew asked.

"George Malverson, I suppose."

It was hard for Lew to stay back now. But he remembered Charlie's warning and stood guard. "Is he dead?"

"I don't know," Charlie whirled around. "What was that?"

"I didn't hear anything," Lew said.

"I'm jumpy, I guess. But don't watch me, Lew. Watch those windows. I'm surprised we haven't been stopped before this."

The bottom on which the man lay was damp, his clothing plastered with yellowish clay and his face covered with two days of beard. That was what made Charlie believe George Malverson still lived, for contrary to popular belief, hair does not keep growing after a man dies. It is the shrinking of the skin about the roots that gives an impression of continued growth.

Charlie felt for the man's pulse. It was beating feebly. He picked the limp man up and shoved him up onto the floor. His teeth remained clenched, and Charlie tried to pry the lower jaw open but couldn't.

"Well," Charlie said. "Our first job is done. I'll go and tell Joan like I promised. You stay here and don't let anybody in."

"I won't," Lew promised. "But I don't understand why they went to so much trouble. Why didn't they just kill him like the other two?"

Charlie paused, his hand on the door. "Because George Malverson had to be kept alive at any cost."

The living room was empty when Charlie entered. He went directly to Joan's room. "Who is it?" she demanded when he knocked.

"Me—Charlie."

She flung the door open, eyes begging.

He nodded. "We found him—alive."

"Where?" she cried.

"In a hole under the shop floor."

He let her go then stood looking anxiously out the window as she ran past that side of the house. He waited another minute. Then he went back to the living room.

Charlie shook his wide shoulders as though casting off a load. "This business," he thought, "is practically finished."

He stiffened when he heard footsteps. Kirta Lang came in with her smooth-flowing stride, Anna as always close behind.

"So," Kirta smiled. "Scotland Yard is back. Strike out again?"

Charlie thought he heard someone coming up from the shop. He hadn't told his companion to leave George, but he knew Joan was with him now. "On the contrary" he answered. "We hit a home run."

"You found George?" Her voice sounded a little shaky.

He knew Lew's walk, and when Lew stepped up on the porch, Charlie sprang past Kirta and drove his fist directly into the point of Anna's chin. She went down like a storm-blasted jack pine.

"What are you doing?" Lew yelled.

"Finishing the second job," Charlie said. He leaned over the unconscious form, grasped the piled-up gray hair and gave a savage jerk. With a sound like tearing cloth, the hair came loose in his hand. It was a wig, and it had been glued to the bare, shaved poll underneath.

"It's a man!" Lew said.

"Sure, it's a man. Get a piece of rope so we can tie him up."

"Don't move." It was Kirta's voice, hard as nickel steel. She held a pistol in her hand, the muzzle trained upon a point midway between them where it could be shifted to cover either one. That showed she was a cool and capable hand with guns.

Charlie saw, now, that he had made a serious mistake not telling Lew more of his plan. He had expected his companion to watch Kirta when he struck the man they had known as Anna, but instead, he had followed the action.

"I was wondering how much you were mixed up in this," Charlie spoke calmly to Kirta. "Now I know. Do you intend to murder us like you murdered your husband?"

"Don't mention him again, damn you," she said in a voice thick with emotion. "Or I'll shoot you myself."

Lew hadn't raised his hands when Kirta covered them, but he had held them out from his sides to assure her he wouldn't grab for his own gun. His right hand touched a small end table, and he recalled there was a book lying on it. He moved his hand very slowly until his fingers touched the book. Then he seized it suddenly, and with a side-arm sling flung it at Kirta's gun. He ducked at the same time.

He would have been killed were it not for the book—and a great deal of luck. The ball hit the volume in midair and lodged somewhere in the thick bulk of pages. Before Kirta could shoot again, Charlie seized her wrist with such force the gun fell from her fingers instantly. Lew scooped it up, and Charlie ordered, "Get the rope, Lew."

"Do you know who I am?" she demanded imperiously.

"Just another dirty spy."

"I am the Countess Jurnetschy."

"Well, don't expect any favors from us because you have a title. You're just a murdering cutthroat in my book."

He looked down at Kirta's accomplice. His eyes were still closed but Charlie expected he would come around soon.

"Is he your real husband—or your lover?" Charlie asked.

Kirta lost her composure at that. "Damn you," she whispered viciously. "I wish I had let Hemlich kill you yesterday. But it's going to be a pleasure to watch you die, now."

"Don't count on your friends to arrive in time to save you."

"How did you know?" She was surprised, almost disconcerted.

"I thought all along there was too much gasoline stored in the hangar. I've expected an airplane to drop down from the sky anytime."

"Does it worry you?"

"Sure, it worries me. But we can handle it."

"Yes," she replied. "I believe you think you can."

Lew came in with a coil of rope. "Mrs. Malverson is half wild waiting for us to come back and help her get George up to the house."

"Did you tell her what happened here?"

"Just the highlights."

"Tie him up first," Charlie nodded at the man on the floor.

Lew did a thorough job of it, and when he finished, he said cheerfully, "All right, Mrs. Lang. You're next."

"Don't touch me," she ordered icily.

"Is that any way to act?" Lew grinned. "Come on, baby. Put your paws behind you."

Kirta threw back her shoulders and balanced on the balls of her feet. "I'll bet you could kick a man's hat off his head," he said cheerfully. "Maybe his head with it."

As he talked Lew made a slip noose in the rope, threw it deftly over her head and jerked it tight pinning her arms to her sides and throwing her off balance. "Now," he said coolly, "you can act nice and get tied up without any fuss or you can fight. If you do that, I'll trip you over and sit on you while I rope your ankles."

The countess finally surrendered. Lew bound her hands behind her, pushed her into one of the chairs, tied her ankles together and wound the rope about her body and the chair so she couldn't rise. It was a difficult position, but nothing, Lew thought, could be too bad for a woman who had helped to murder her own husband.

"You fools," she hissed. "You are as good as dead right now."

Something in the way she said that dampened Charlie's elation. Frowning, he thought, "She believes it, too. She knows it wouldn't do her any good to try to bluff us. We must work fast."

He looked at his watch. It read 9:18.

Chapter 10 – Death Out of the Sea

Charlie beckoned Lew to follow out on the porch. "You heard what Kirta said about us being as good as dead? I don't think she's bluffing. She knows more of her gang are on the way, and my guess is they're close. We've got to get away as soon as we can."

"How?" Lew asked.

"By plane would be my first choice. We must find the engine part they removed and hid. Go down to the shop and send Joan here."

Joan came in a minute later with a light step and happy eyes. The happiness faded, though, when she saw Kirta tied in the big chair.

"You, you she-devil!" Joan spit at her.

Kirta shrugged. "You're working for your country, I'm working for mine. What's the difference?"

"Plenty," Joan replied. "I didn't murder my husband."

Kirta didn't answer, and Joan's gaze moved on to Hemlich, still flat on the floor. "I can't believe Anna was a man," Joan said. Then her face grew pink as she realized the man had seen her undressed.

"Get my rifle," Charlie said. "And use it if they even make an attempt to work loose."

"I will," she promised. "It will be a pleasure after seeing the hole they kept George in for two days."

Lew and Charlie carried the man up and laid him in his bed. Lew went back to keep an eye on the captives so Joan could join Charlie.

"I don't know what they gave him, but thanks to Lew he missed his midnight dose last night. My guess is he will come around soon."

"He will look so much better after I've shaved him," Joan said.

"Wait," Charlie said. "There's something more important to do now. Kirta is expecting her friends any minute. We have to get the plane running. I want you to help me find the missing part."

They went to Kirta's room first.

"How are the other spies coming?" Joan asked.

Charlie jerked the blankets off one bed and said, "By air. It's quickest. Otherwise, Kirta wouldn't be so confident."

Joan started taking dresses from the closet. "It was a terrible shock when Lew told me. She was always good to George and me. I remember the time he was sick with appendicitis. She worried over him as much as I did. I never believed she loved Hugh deeply, but even if she didn't, how could she murder him?"

Charlie was slashing the mattress open with his sheath knife. "Her handlers evidently watched your husband for years. Kirta was planted well in advance to gain your confidence. She went the limit, even married your brother. When the time came …"

"She murdered him!" Joan said it fiercely.

"I suppose Hemlich did the actual killing," Charlie replied, "after he had drugged them all. But she's equally guilty, of course."

Joan finished with the closet.

"What made you suspect Anna was a man?"

"I knew spies often work in pairs, and they pair a man with a woman whenever possible. Despite their efforts to make us think an outsider was behind the crimes, I felt all along it had to be someone in the house."

They went next to the room occupied by the disguised Hemlich.

"What if after you struck her you had found you were wrong?" Joan asked.

"That would have been a mess," Charlie admitted. "But I saw his eyes when I told of finding your husband, and if ever eyes had murder in them, his did."

After demolishing another room without success, they went into the bath.

"At breakfast you said you knew why George wasn't killed?"

"That was a compliment to his ability as an inventor. They kept him alive to take back to Europe where he would be forced to continue his work. So, you see, he simply had to be kept alive."

"Wouldn't it have been easier to just do away with me and keep him in the house?" Joan asked.

"That puzzled me, at first. But you were important, too. They could use you to make him obey. Letting you leave in the plane was their first mistake. You went so unexpectedly. I think it was Kirta who opened the fuel tanks while you were preparing to leave. She probably took the shot at you, too, as soon as she could lay her hands on a gun."

"Just one question more" she said. "Why didn't Kirta and Hemlich just take us away in the plane?"

"It lacks the range for a non-stop flight across the Atlantic. With war imminent, any plane that put down anywhere for fuel would likely be checked."

Joan's face turned into a mask of determination. "If more spies come, I'll kill George first, and then I'll kill myself, too."

"I might even help you," Charlie replied frankly. "But it won't be necessary if we can find what we're looking for."

Charlie stood on the seat to look in the toilet's elevated tank. Two bundles lay on the bottom. "Found it," he told Joan.

One waterproof bundle contained an electric condenser. The larger held Malverson's engineering notebook.

"This makes me so happy," Joan cried, and Charlie felt quite a bit better himself. Their discovery had a different effect upon the prisoners. Kirta said furiously to Hemlich, "I wanted to throw that stuff in the sea. But you wouldn't let me."

Anna spoke as Hemlich for the first time. "They will not get away," he said, and his cool assurance chilled Charlie.

He gave the condenser to Lew and said, "Put this back on the engine and replace the stuff you took. Do it as fast as you can. Go with him, Mrs. Malverson. When he's done, start the engines. I can carry your husband, and I'll bring him as soon as I hear motors running."

Lew had already left, but Joan came over to say, "The plane only holds three people with full tanks. I'll have Lew dump some gas so it will carry all four of us."

"Don't," Charlie said. "You have to get clear away to safety. Besides, it won't be necessary. Lew and I are both staying."

"But you'll be killed!" she cried.

"We can take care of ourselves. But I'm depending on you to land at the first airport and send men back to help us."

"I could take one of you without dumping gas," she suggested.

Charlie shook his head. "That would only start a dandy argument about who had to go, and we've no time for that."

Before leaving Charlie examined the knotted ropes on the prisoners. All were tight. He went back to the doorway and stood watch, rifle in hand. He wasn't taking any chances.

He figured it would take Joan about four and a half hours to reach settled country. She could get in touch with the right authorities by wire. Planes filled with Canadian police or army could reach White Goose Bay sometime in the night. He told himself he must not forget to build a beacon fire on the beach, to guide them in.

He looked at his watch. It was only 10 a.m.

The engines should have been going by now, he thought and walked out on the porch to listen. Joan was down there, for he heard her voice. Then he heard hammer blows on metal. That worried him.

He hoped Lew wouldn't break something in his nervous impatience. His own nervousness grew as each precious minute passed.

He knew the two of them couldn't defend the big house. The safest place for them would be back in the timber.

A blasting roar came from the hangar. Charlie breathed a sigh of relief and started into the front bedroom for Malverson. The man was still unconscious. Then the roar of the engines ceased. He heard them idling again, only slowly. He didn't like that. He ran out to check, carrying an armful of bedding for George on the plane floor. Joan was in the plane but Lew stood in the dinghy winding a rope about the flywheel of the outboard motor. Charlie remembered now the plane had been towed headfirst into the hangar. It had to be towed out and turned around before it could take off across the bay.

"Better wait until I bring Mr. Malverson back," he told Lew. Then he ran back to the house and picked the man up. He pushed the porch door open with his foot, and glancing out in the bay he saw a ripple coming towards shore. As he crossed the yard he saw the ripple rapidly grow larger. Suddenly, something like a slender rod rose swiftly and then the water parted and a large rounded object emerged. Charlie recognized the conning tower of a submarine. It looked like the help Hemlich and Kirta expected had arrived from an unexpected place.

Charlie shouted a warning to Lew.

Instead of carrying Malverson back into the house, he ran down to the shop and laid the man on the ground a few yards from its door. That would be on the way of their retreat towards the timber.

The submarine had fully surfaced by then. It was a seagoing brute some 400 feet long. A hatch swung open, and two men stepped out on a small deck enclosed by a low iron railing. One held a flag, the other a machine gun. The one with the flag shook out its folds and began to signal towards shore.

Charlie stopped when he saw Joan come out and run to meet him. He motioned her to hurry. Unconsciously, he looked at his watch. The hands still read exactly 10:00.

It had stopped dead.

He had forgotten to wind it the night before.

Chapter 11 – Battle in the Bay

Charlie had believed the help Kirta and Hemlich expected would come in by air. Now, with a submarine parked out in front of the hangar, things didn't look good for escape in the plane. They were trapped, facing overwhelming odds. A submarine as large as this would carry at least 100 men, and they would be supplied with a complement of rifles, machine guns, torpedo tubes and a naval gun on the forward deck.

He knew there wasn't a chance of getting a plane off the water. It would be blown to bits before it made it 50 yards out of the hangar. Nor was there time to retreat back into the safety of the woods behind the buildings on White Goose Bay.

Lew was still inside the hangar, and Charlie wondered what he was doing. Suddenly, Charlie found out. A shot came from inside the building and he recognized the sharp report of Lew's magnum. Apparently, Lew had decided it was time to fight.

Men were boiling up out of the big cigar-shaped hull, moving swiftly with trained discipline. A team of four stripped the covers from the deck gun. A line of sailors formed to connect the open hatch with the gun and began passing shells up from the bowels of the ship. He thought the caliber was at least 3-inch.

Charlie started running towards the rear of the house. Joan followed, and he pushed her behind the corner of the log building. He leveled his own rifle on the sub. There might be a slim chance that Lew and he together could keep the crew from serving the gun with their combined rifle fire. Then he saw the armored shield that screened the gunners. No rifle could even put a dent in that kind of metal, and he took his gun down from his shoulder.

"It's all over now, isn't it?" Joan asked quietly.

Charlie knew she was thinking of her husband and the fate they both faced. Then in a hard, dry voice she demanded, "Remember what you promised to help me do if it looks like we'll be captured?"

She thrust a hand in Charlie's coat pocket where the 9mm automatic pistol lay. But he caught her wrist. She struggled furiously then backed away from him panting.

"Don't worry," Charlie said quietly. "I'll give you the gun when all else has failed. But we aren't there yet."

Lew ran out of the hangar's rear door, keeping the building as a screen between himself and the sub. Charlie looked out across the water and saw the naval gun belch bluish-gray smoke. Two shells screamed across the water in swift succession. One would have been enough. The building and the plane were blown into splinters.

Bits of debris showered down as Charlie glanced about with anxious eyes, searching for Lew. He noted now the air was becoming charged with a new odor. He sniffed, recognized the fumes of gasoline and remembered the 20 barrels that had been stored in the hangar. Charlie wondered why it had not ignited and decided the concussion of the explosions had blotted out the flame.

Then, a burning piece of wood tossed high into the air must have dropped into the spilled gasoline, for with a tremendous roar it blazed up into a wall of flame 30 feet high that ran swiftly out over the bay. Clouds of black smoke hid the submarine from view.

As soon as the fire hid him from the gunners, Lew got back on his feet and ran to them.

"We're going to run for the timber," Charlie explained. "It's our only chance. Malverson's by the shop. We'll have to carry him."

"Give me half a minute," Lew said, and Charlie ran by himself to get Malverson, Joan doing her best to keep up. Charlie reached the drugged man and lifted him in his arms. He was thankful for the lightness of the wasted form.

Lew was nowhere in sight when Charlie started back towards the house, but Joan clutched his belt and literally pulled him back. "Don't," she cried. "We can't waste a second."

Charlie knew this was true. While he stood hesitating, a third shell hurtled over the water, plunged through the wall of flame and smoke and struck the front of the house. Fragments of shattered logs belched up, and stones from the blasted fireplace and foundation filled the air. Yelling for Joan to follow, Charlie plunged inside the machine shop with Malverson in his arms. They reached the shelter of its sturdy roof just as a deadly hail came raining down. A few of the bigger rocks smashed through the split log roof.

A sudden fear smote him. "I wonder if Lew was in there?"

Then a figure came running out through the smoke and dust. It was Lew, limping slightly. He had lost his hat. But his eyes were dancing with excitement. His grin, although a bit crooked, was confident. He carried his rifle in one hand and had something bulky pressed against his chest under his coat with the other.

"Where have you been?" Charlie demanded. "I told you we needed to run to the timber."

"We'd never make it," Lew replied. "It's a mile away. But maybe now you won't have to run so far."

Lew ran inside the shop. Charlie took two steps after him, stopped and turned around. Joan again was pulling him, pleading with him to hurry. He obeyed reluctantly, shifting Malverson's weight in his arms so the man balanced more easily.

The confident grin fell from Lew's face the second he entered the shop. He had committed himself to a desperate venture, and unless he won, he and his companions were doomed.

Lew limped up to the bench supporting Malverson's anti-tank gun. He opened his coat and eased four shells down beside the cannon. He flung open the window and spun the turntable wheel until the long, slender barrel pointed out across the bay.

Lew snapped the breech open, pushed in a shell and closed the block. He wiped the blood, sweat and grime from his face with one sleeve, waiting for the smoke to clear and give him a glimpse of the enemy. It was too bad, he thought, Malverson couldn't witness a real test of his compound powder charge.

A second shell struck the house. He saw about two-thirds of what remained disintegrate before the blast hit and shattered every window in the shop. One more shot, Lew thought, would demolish the house. Then the gun crew would aim for the shop.

Lew waited, his head thrust forward, one hand on the aiming control of the cannon. His eyes bored into the curtain of flame and smoke concealing his target.

Another roar shook the shop. Clay chinking burst out from cracks between the wall logs and filled the air more thickly with dust. More fragments from the house hammered down on the roof. Lew thrust his head out the window, and so far as he could see, nothing of the house remained save blackened heaps of rubbish and stone.

"Good Lord," Lew muttered. "Hemlich and Kirta were in there. I had forgotten them."

Still another shell hit amid the ruins of the house. Lew wondered if the gun crew could see some bit of remaining wall or if they were merely making sure of an efficient job.

A fresh breeze came from the land behind, and Lew caught a glimpse of the big ship before the smoke rolled back to blot it out. That glimpse was enough for him to register the sub's position. He turned the muzzle of the cannon and aimed it a little lower.

He examined the sights on the gun again. They stood up 10 inches above the barrel. The front sight had a little ring at the top, and Lew knew he must center his target inside that. He breathed a short prayer that when his chance came he wouldn't miss.

The breeze freshened; he caught a second glimpse of the enemy sub and made a slight correction in his aim. His fingers went to the firing lever. The air cleared again, he checked his aim, made a swift change in elevation and pulled smartly on the trigger.

Wham! The little two-inch shell screamed out over the water like a banshee. Simultaneously, or so it seemed to Lew, the sub's gun and crew disappeared from the deck. The shell had made a center hit on the armored steel shield, smashing the gun loose from its moorings and sweeping everything into the sea.

"What a load," Lew breathed. He dropped a second shell into the breech, which had snapped open automatically. He saw it trip the bolt with its weight, saw the action close, and the gun was ready to fire again. But where? The conning tower was so streamlined he feared a shell would glance off without penetrating the armor plate. He decided to shoot at the bow, pointed almost straight towards him.

Men came pouring up from the conning tower and out of a second hatch farther back along the deck. Balancing themselves on the rocking craft, they lined up at what was left of the steel railing. Some carried rifles; others were armed with short machine guns. They opened fire, and bullets thudded into the thick log walls of the shop.

Lew knew he had to hurry, but he forced his fingers to move deliberately as he screwed the muzzle of the gun down until it bore upon the sub's bow. He checked the sights twice. They seemed perfectly aligned, and he jerked the trip. There was only a click. The shell had misfired. He choked down nausea, remembering the shells were an experimental combination of powder and projectile and there wasn't any assurance any of them would be as effective as the first.

Then he opened the breech and reloaded.

By then literally thousands of bullets were pounding the front of his shelter, eating their way through. He heard two zing past his head. His fingers moved a little faster, but never did they fumble. He pulled the lever, and this time the cannon boomed.

Flames shot into the air, and some 50 feet of the front end of the submarine disappeared in a terrible blast.

Lew knew the 2-inch shell hadn't made that much havoc by itself. It must have penetrated a powder magazine, or, more likely, struck a torpedo inside one of the bow tubes.

"That was real shooting," said a voice in Lew's ear.

Charlie stood behind him. He placed one hand briefly on Lew's shoulder. It was as near as either ever came to showing the deep affection they felt for each other. Lew knew those four words would be his companion's only thanks for saving both of their lives.

The sub sank slowly because of the many bulkheads. Men were crowding the slanted deck, sliding off into the bay. Charlie nodded at the dark heads bobbing in the water.

"They are going to be as dangerous as the sub itself. Put another shell in the gun. Swing the muzzle down so you can cover the beach. When those fellows swim ashore we'll be in a tough spot. I'm going to try and line them up as fast as they come in. If I can make them dump the pistols I'm sure they are carrying in their clothing, we might be able to keep them under control."

Charlie had stopped running for the timber when he heard Lew's first shot. He knew Lew had recovered shells for the cannon out of the house. Now he picked up Lew's rifle—it had more range than his .30-30—and taking shells for it from Lew's pocket, walked out through the smoke and dust towards the beach.

His eyes were grave. Lew already had accomplished the impossible. But the desperate men who were jumping from the deck of the doomed ship were still deadly. He had to figure out some way to keep them cowed, and that job was going to be tough.

Chapter 12 – Four in a Boat

Lew had won the first round of what had seemed a hopelessly one-sided battle. Now it was up to Charlie to win the second. The crew swimming to shore, eager for revenge, was the problem. Somehow he had to disarm them as their feet hit the sand. True, Lew was waiting back in the machine shop with the cannon trained on the swimming men. But he had only one shell left.

The nearest of the swimming men was about 400 feet out when Charlie saw several sailors hoist a rubber raft up out of the sinking sub and fling it into the sea. Six crowded into the inflated boat and began to paddle ashore. Then a second group staggered up out of the hold with another, larger raft. They laid it down on the deck and worked swiftly. Charlie saw sides appear, and a minute later it was a fair-sized boat with decked ends, thwarts and seats. Three men slid the craft off into the water and steadied it while others climbed aboard.

There were seven in the boat, and Charlie thought they were the officers because the others had been catering to them. That is, all but one, who appeared to be an ordinary seaman standing in the stem. The seaman bent over, started a small outboard motor, and the craft started for shore at a fair speed.

"Here is a real break," Charlie muttered. The rubber raft with its load was still ahead of the folding boat, and one of the paddlers pulled a pistol and fired. Charlie ducked instinctively, although he knew it was too late as the ball had already whizzed past his face. He lifted his rifle to make an example of the assailant, but before he could shoot, Lew went into action with the cannon.

The shell struck the raft amidships. Craft and crew simply disappeared in the blast. It left Charlie shaken and a bit sick. But he knew Lew had acted in the only way this crew would respect. Ruthless force was their way, and Lew had simply struck first.

All of the men in the sea ceased swimming and started treading water. Some cried out in hoarse, frightened voices. The men in the motor launch lifted their hands in the air, and the motor went dead.

Charlie stepped closer to the edge of the water and waved the boat in. The motor started again, and the helmsman ran it cautiously up until the prow wedged fast in the sand. Some of the swimmers had started in at the same time, but Charlie threatened them back with his rifle. The shot had been Lew's last shell. The cannon was useless now.

"Anyone speak English?" Charlie demanded.

"I do," a short, heavily built man with a close-cut black beard replied in a correct Oxford accent. "I am Commander Schwartz."

"All right. Tell the rest to come on shore one at a time. Drop your guns on the ground as you step out. My men have the cannon trained on you. Make one wrong move, and it will blow you to bits."

The commander stepped carefully out on the beach, took an automatic pistol from a pocket and let it fall. The others followed suit, each dropping a similar handgun. When all had landed he said, "Tell your men in the water to stay off. If they come closer, they'll be killed." The commander barked orders. The swimmers who had been edging closer stopped and either floated or kicked water to stay up.

"Now, a hundred feet down the beach," Charlie continued. "Keep close ranks. If you break apart, my gunner will blast you."

The officers obeyed, shuffling along the edge of the sea. He wondered how long he could control them all this way. He yelled, "All right, Lew. You and Joan bring her husband. Tell Jim to keep these fellows covered with the cannon."

He was sure additional guns were concealed in their clothing, and only the threat of the cannon was keeping them in check. He glanced around again. His back was still clear. The helmsman sat quietly in the stem of the folding craft. Give them just three minutes more, Charlie thought, and they would clear.

Lew came up carrying Malverson in his arms. Joan walked behind him, and a low murmur arose from the group of officers when they saw her. Lew put the unconscious man on the bottom of the boat, helped Joan in and followed.

"Have the fellow start the motor," Charlie ordered without turning his head. When he heard the engine running, he shoved the boat clear of land and scrambled aboard. Lew was covering the group with his own rifle. Charlie grabbed the steering lever away from the sailor, swept the craft around in a wide curve to dodge the thickest of the swimmers, and headed for the open sea.

Lew jabbed the end of his rifle barrel into the sailor's ribs. "Jump," he said. The fellow did and then started swimming for shore.

"Looks like we're going to make it," Lew said.

Charlie's legs felt shaky, and he sat down on the thwart beside the motor. He couldn't remember when he had felt this way before, and he wondered if he might be getting old. He opened the throttle a little more. The outboard was a very accurate copy of a popular three-horse model made in the U.S.A. The tank looked like it held 4 gallons of gasoline, and he hoped it was full.

The group of officers on the beach had broken up. One ran along the beach with pistol in hand. Where the land curved out he got closer to the boat. He halted, leveled his gun and fired. The bullet struck the water four feet away. Lew shot out one of the man's legs.

Some of the swimmers that had landed grouped about the officers for a few seconds and then the entire gang came running along the shoreline. The little boat was out of pistol range, and Charlie had just told his companions that fact when a hail of bullets splashed all around them. One of the enemy had somehow carried a submachine gun to land, assembled it and was rapidly getting their range.

It took Lew a second or so to locate the gunner standing behind two other sailors, firing between them. Joan cried out as a bullet pierced the fleshy part of her upper arm. The cry didn't hurry Lew any. He aimed the .300 magnum deliberately. Then he shot three times. The gunner and his two shields crumpled to the beach.

"That should put a stop to the sniping," Lew announced.

Joan held her arm out over the side of the boat so the drops of blood that seeped between her fingers would drop into the sea. Lew put his gun down, got out his knife and cut the sleeve of her jacket away. The wound was a clean hole of small caliber, and the bullet had missed the bone. He bound the arm enough to stop the bleeding, but not tightly enough to stop circulation, wedging a small pellet of cloth into each opening in her flesh.

"See if you can find any more fuel aboard," Charlie suggested. There was a canvas-enclosed bulkhead at each end of the boat and one under two of the seats. In one he found a 2-gallon tin of gas; in another rubber raincoats and hats. Lew wrapped a coat about Joan to shelter her trembling body. Under a seat they found a short-handled axe, a five-gallon tin of water and several coils of small rope.

Another locker held a good-sized tarpaulin and four packages of emergency food. Lew opened the latter and found each package contained a dozen smaller units, each apparently sufficient for a one-man meal. The food looked just as good to him as the tarp and the gasoline. He was getting hungry again.

"Where are we going, anyway?" Lew asked

Charlie laughed. "I haven't figured that out yet."

"We have to go somewhere," Lew insisted.

Charlie was winding his watch. "What time you got?"

"Eleven fifty-six," Lew replied. "No wonder I'm starving. It's almost time for lunch."

"We'll try some of those rations in a few minutes," Charlie said. "But we don't dare stop yet. Those men know how much fuel is in this boat. They can figure out how many miles it will take us. This boat is slow enough they can follow along the shore and be ready to attack when we have to come in and land.

"You're right," Lew agreed. "They won't give up. But I suppose if the gas holds out and we keep on around the bay and then out to sea, it can't be more than five or six hundred miles back home."

"We'll get there, alright," Charlie replied quietly, slowing the motor a little to get the absolute maximum mileage from the fuel. "We'll have to keep close in, follow the shoreline. We haven't much food or ammunition, no tent, clothes or blankets. But we'll make it."

They cruised in silence for a quarter-hour. Then Lew opened three packages of rations. When he took his turn at the tiller, Charlie folded up the tarpaulin to make a pad on the bottom of the boat. He laid Malverson on it and covered him with three rubber coats.

"How's the arm?" he asked Joan.

"It hurts, but not bad," she replied. Charlie's eyes remained grave. They had a wounded woman and a badly emaciated, drugged man aboard. Only a smoky film high up in the sky marked the place where they had left danger and death behind.

Lew kept them about three hundred yards offshore. After a while, Joan lay down beside her husband and went to sleep, too. Charlie dozed a little, and then he took a turn at the helm while Lew stretched out to ease his cramps. A heavy bank of clouds hid the sun at four in the afternoon. Charlie awoke Lew and Joan for another meal. It started to rain a few minutes after they finished eating. They wrapped themselves in the raincoats, donned the rubber hats and spread the tarpaulin over Malverson and Joan.

The little outboard motor sputtered then went dead. Charlie broke out the extra can of fuel and poured it carefully into the tank. He started the engine again, let it run until daylight failed and he could not see to steer. Then he shut it off.

"We'll take turns sitting up to see the boat doesn't drift ashore," he told Lew. "You can't doze off a minute. If you hear surf, start the motor and head directly away from the sound."

The wind turned colder, and a fine drizzle of rain started freezing as soon as it struck the boat. Charlie, trying to rest on the forward thwart, got so chilled he finally crawled down beside Joan and her husband and pulled two of the raincoats over him. After awhile he slept.

He awoke with dazzling light in his eyes. He looked around amazed that morning could have come with such brilliance Lew had not aroused him once to take a turn at the watch.

Then Charlie realized it was not the sun in his eyes, for the light swept away and went searching out across the expanse of water. Charlie stumbled up to the stem. Lew was slumped forward, head hanging on his chest, sound asleep.

Charlie shook him. Lew straightened with a gasp. "Good Lord," he said. "I went to sleep. I tried to fight it, and the last thing I remember I had made up my mind to call you. What's that?"

The light came sweeping back again.

"A ship's searchlight," Charlie told him. "They're searching the bay, probably for us. Now that they've found us, they will keep us in the beam."

Lew's mouth tightened. "More of the enemy?"

"Another sub, I suppose," Charlie said. "Who else would be up here in this desolate water."

"Can we run for land?"

"No chance. They're too close. I can hear the engines."

Lew nodded. "How about jumping overboard and swimming?"

"You go," Charlie replied. "I'll stay with the ship and the folks."

"Me, too," Lew said. He leaned back against the gunwale, head turned away from the brilliance of the light.

The other ship was bearing down on them. Suddenly a voice hailed over the water. "Ahoy there. Identify yourself."

"No ship name," Charlie replied in a clear, loud voice. "We're adrift. Who is there?"

"Dominion Sub Chaser D-57," the voice replied. "Come aboard and explain yourselves."

"We're coming!" Lew yelled back. He almost jerked the flywheel off the outboard starting it. Then he swung the boat around in a tight circle and headed for the gray shape in the mist. They eased alongside, and Charlie made fast to lines that dropped down.

Joan was still asleep when Charlie lifted her, and she cried out.

"It's all right," he soothed. "Everything's finally all right. This is a Canadian naval boat. They'll have a doctor who can sew you up and bring your husband out of his stupor."

"Pass more lines down," Lew said. "We have an unconscious man and a wounded lady." Joan climbed the rope ladder with a little help from above, but George had to be hoisted bodily.

On the deck an officer saluted smartly.

"Captain Hardcourt," he announced. "We had news of an enemy submarine in these waters. Have you seen her?"

"Too much of her," Lew replied. Then he managed a poor imitation of his usual grin. "It is now partly sunk in shallow water, about forty miles behind us. And there are a hundred sailors off her scouring the beach, looking for a chance to cut our throats."

"We need a doctor," Charlie spoke quickly. "The lady took a bullet hole through the arm and her husband has been in a drugged stupor for days. They need attention at once."

Twenty minutes later, Charlie and Lew were drinking coffee in the captain's quarters.

"That," concluded Charlie, "is our story. After you put landing parties ashore and round up the enemy sailors, do you suppose you could get a plane up here to haul us back home? We've a lot of business we simply have to attend to as soon as we can."

"I'll radio at once," Capt. Hardcourt replied. "We'll need air support to spot the enemy on land. One will take you wherever you want to go." He looked at them with quiet admiration in his eyes. "You have done wonderful service. I will recommend you for medals."

"The only thing I want now is sleep," Lew broke in. "But I'll bet you can arrange for that, too."

"Immediately," the captain promised with a smile.

"And," Lew went on, "if you can arrange it, load me in that plane without waking me. I want to sleep until I get back to Shadow Lake."

The End